SORROW'S ECHO

A DARK CROSSROADS ENCOUNTER

JEFFERY A. MOULTON

HINDSIGHT studios

For Jim and Connie

PRELUDE

THE HELICOPTER CARRYING THE SURVIVORS ROSE TOWARD THE
stars. Its flashing signal lights briefly came into view in the sliver of
night sky visible from the bottom of the canyon, then it was gone.
The broken, dying man on the canyon floor raised a feeble, blood-
streaked arm to signal them, but there was no way they could see
him, no way for them to know he was still alive, and no way for
them to reach him in time. He dropped his arm and continued to
watch, hoping for another glimpse of the aircraft.

The glimpse never came.

A gust of wind blew over the top of the canyon, sending a
deep, penetrating moan echoing down the sandstone walls. The
man shuddered, suddenly cold in the desert night. He groaned.

A faint scrape and clatter of rocks echoed from somewhere up
the canyon. The man froze, his heart thudding painfully as he
strained to hear over the wind. For an interminable moment, he
heard nothing out of place, but then, far up the canyon, there came
the soft chittering of insect-like clicks.

Ice shot through him, and he trembled. It had found him. He

drew a sharp, trembling breath, every fiber of his being screaming for him to run.

Desperate, the man reached for the canyon wall with his good arm. The tips of his fingers caught hold of a crack in the sandstone, and he pulled. Hot agony lanced through him, but he still strained.

He moved an inch then another. Hope blossomed in his chest. His fingers slipped, scraping against the stone, and he collapsed back to the earth, slamming his head against the hard ground. He screamed.

The clicking came again, louder and closer than before. He flinched, trying to push himself against the cliff, as if he could vanish into it. He whimpered as his eyes scanned the shadows that encased the far end of the chamber-like space where he had fallen in the canyon. There was nothing but darkness.

Still trembling, he thought of the helicopter. He wondered how many had survived. *One? Two? What about Liz?*

The wind moaned again. The deep, sorrowful sound filled the chamber-like space. He shuddered again.

Another scrape against the rocks, closer this time, brought him back to the moment. He closed his eyes and furrowed his brow, struggling to think of something he could do to escape, hide, or warn others, but there was nothing. Nothing!

Or perhaps... The whisper of an idea formed in his mind. It was a long shot—a million to one—but he didn't have anything to lose.

He reached down and fumbled at the pocket of his shorts. Spots flashed at the edge of his vision as he found his phone and slid it out. Panting from the effort, he lifted it and peered at the small screen.

A spiderweb of cracks crisscrossed the glass face. Shaking, he pressed the power button. The screen sprang to life, its glare painful in the darkness.

He didn't bother to check for a signal. There would be none. He hadn't planned on making a call anyway.

Another moan of the wind. Another clatter of rocks. Another series of clicks.

Hurry! Fumbling with the tiny icons, he managed to open the camera app and set it to selfie-video mode. He pressed record. The timing indicator ticked upward.

For a moment, he just stared at the shattered image of himself displayed on the screen. The whole left side of his face was bruised and swollen, his eye unable to open. Blood was smeared across his forehead and dripped from a gash on his temple into his unkempt six-day stubble.

He drew a breath and spoke, his dry throat unable to muster more than a broken whisper.

"My name is... is Paul Lambert. My wife... Liz... and I were part of a group. We... were attacked. Something..." He paused and closed his eye against the memories of the horror that had struck at them from the shadows. When he opened it again, his eye stung with tears.

"The rest are dead. I... don't know how many survived."

Clattering rocks echoed down the canyon. He shuddered, his heart beating even faster.

"I won't survive," he whispered to the camera. "If you see this message, get out of here. It isn't safe."

He paused, his mind swimming with confused words and phrases. They slipped from his grasp, but one remained.

"Liz," he whispered, "I love you. You have always been the best part of my life. Don't blame yourself. It's not your... not your..."

Blackness formed at the edge of his vision, and a tremor of pain shot through him. He flinched, losing his grip on the phone. It tumbled from his fingers and clattered onto the rocks, its pale glow lighting the canyon.

Rocks scraped just over his head. Panting, the man looked up. In the phone's dim light, a shadow moved.

"You found me, you son of a bitch," the man whispered.

In time to the rising howl of the wind, the shadow rushed forward. Its angry, insect-like chatter filled the air as it reached for him.

The man's screams filled the night.

ONE

THE DRY WIND BLEW ACROSS THE DESERT, PLAYING A mournful requiem on the instruments of rock and sand. The melody rose and fell as it moved over the landscape, lamenting the dead and those who would soon join them. It moaned through canyons and stone arches and trilled around spires and shadowy mesas before rising in a crescendo to the top of the cliff, where it sang warnings to those preparing to jump off.

Helene closed her eyes and drew in a deep breath, inhaling the warm Arizona air as it blew past. It tugged at the wide-brimmed hat cinched tightly under her chin and rippled through her T-shirt and khaki hiking shorts, its whistle drowning out the bustle going on behind her. For a moment, she was the only person in the world. She was free.

And then her husband ruined it.

"Hey, Helene," Sven called from beside the two vans parked a handful of yards behind her, "could you help Tybet unload the packs?"

At hearing his voice, familiar anger flashed through her. She gritted her teeth and drew a sharp breath through her nose, feeding the fury building in her. Her anger wasn't fair or warranted, but it was her lifeline. It was the only thing that kept the shadows at bay.

The desert below her stretched out to the horizon, godforsaken, sun bleached, and inhospitable. The thought of spending ten days out there with anyone, least of all with Sven and his misfit engineering team, churned the acid in her stomach. It was, she lamented, almost as bad as the thought of losing her husband altogether.

Just like they lost Kyle.

The shadows pressed in as a lump formed in her throat, and her chest constricted at the thought of their son. An onslaught of memories and images surged through her. In that moment, she both cradled Kyle as an infant and nervously let go of his hand as he stepped into kindergarten on his first day of school. She cheered as he made the winning goal at a high school soccer game and beamed as he graduated and moved on to college. His whole life spread before her, the images, bright and filled with pain, flashing through her consciousness. They resolved, as they always did, into her memory of the last photo she had of Kyle, the one in the car with Emily. In the photo, the new ring sparkled on Emily's finger and both her and Kyle beamed, their life together stretching out ahead of them, all fifteen minutes of it.

Trembling, Helene closed her eyes. Following the advice of the grief counselor Sven had insisted they visit shortly after the accident a year earlier, she drew a long, deep breath and let it out slowly, willing the memories and heartache to go with it. The trick didn't work. It had never worked.

Helene opened her eyes and stared into the valley again without seeing it, feeling the darkness and the grief close in. Her hand lingered near the pocket of her shorts. She could feel her phone nestled there, could feel it calling to her, could feel the need for what it could deliver building inside her. Her fingers twitched in anticipation, and her heart thundered in her chest.

"Helene?" Sven called again.

Her fading anger burned again, brighter and hotter than before. Helene grasped onto it, feeding it, forcing the darkness back with its painful light. Slowly, the trembling subsided as the need retreated to the shadows.

Gritting her teeth, she spun and walked toward the second of the two dust-covered vans. She pointedly ignored Sven, who was talking with Ryan, the pimply-faced technician who had driven the first van, and concentrated instead on the McTiernan Group logo stenciled on the side of the vehicle. She was vaguely aware of Tybet, the linebacker-sized security chief who'd come along as the second driver and was currently unloading and sorting equipment. In spite of herself, Helene stole a glance toward the large white trailer parked behind the van. She stifled her curiosity about the thing inside being prepped by Marcos and Pato, the two nerds who'd dreamed up the whole trip. Her eyes lingered for a moment on Stacee, the gorgeous mechanic who had busied herself with the tools near the trailer, then Helene moved on to Vivek, the Indian guide who was carrying rappelling equipment toward the cliff. Except for Sven, none of the others so much as glanced in her direction.

Without a word, Helene threw herself into her job with single-minded focus: sorting the packs and supplies then checking and double-checking the equipment. All the while, she kept the fire of her anger burning. As long as she was angry with Sven, she didn't have to face the real truth: Kyle's death was her fault.

———

Sven sighed as he watched Helene work. Even from this distance, he could feel the familiar burn of her fury. He wondered again why he had agreed to bring her along.

Shaking his head, he turned back toward Ryan, the acne-prone young man who would be monitoring their progress from the lab back in Phoenix. He hesitated when he realized that the young man's attention was directed elsewhere.

Sven turned and followed Ryan's gaze straight to Stacee's ass. The mechanic, who was too good-looking for her own good as far as this trip was concerned, was bent over a toolbox, checking items off a list. Her denim shorts rose all the way up, hugging her backside.

Sven sighed with frustration. If they ever got moving with her around, it would be a wonder. He could only hope Stacee was as good a mechanic as Marcos swore she was. He turned back to Ryan and snapped his fingers inches from the young man's nose.

"Pay attention."

Ryan blinked with surprise, as if he had just come out of a trance.

"What?" he asked, a little defensively, his thick glasses flashing in the sunlight as they reluctantly turned toward Sven.

"Do you have everything ready?"

"Yeah, sure." His eyes drifted back toward the girl.

With a growl, Sven stepped in front of him. "We're counting on you," Sven reminded him. "You have the maps? The supply drop schedules? The monitoring equipment? Is there anything you need from Marcos or Pato before we head out?"

"You worry too much," Ryan said, giving Sven what he probably thought was a reassuring smile. "We're all good."

The words did very little to comfort Sven. He stared at the young man for a long moment, scrutinizing him. Ryan wilted under his gaze and shifted nervously from foot to foot.

"Okay," Sven said at last. "As soon as we're down the cliff, lower the supply net and head out. It's about seven hours to Phoenix, and we need you there as soon as possible."

"Right-ee-oh." Ryan gave him a thumbs-up.

Sven began to say something else but was cut off by an excited shout from Marcos.

"Hey, everyone," the engineer called from the back of the trailer, "we're bringing her out. You don't want to miss this."

Ryan whooped and quickly pushed past Sven as Marcos disappeared back into the trailer.

Sven hesitated. He stood for a moment, watching Helene and Tybet approach the trailer, the latter more eager than the former. Ryan got there at the same time and chattered excitedly at the security chief, who responded with noncommittal grunts. Stacee seemed to appear out of nowhere and bounced excitedly next to them, staring fixedly into the trailer. Helene, of course, kept her distance, crossing her arms, and setting her jaw to ward off any who would attempt conversation.

Sven raised his eyes toward the pristine Arizona sky, wondering if Kyle was watching. "Keep an eye on us, okay?" he whispered to his son's ghost. "We're going to need it."

As if in answer, the wind gusted by. Sven grabbed for his hat, saving it just before it was tossed from his head. With a sigh, he turned to join the others, ready to jump off the cliff.

TWO

Marcos rocked back and forth on his heels as the others gathered at the bottom of the trailer's ramp. His grin was so wide and so persistent, his cheeks hurt.

He caught Stacee's eyes. She beamed at him, looking just as gorgeous as she had when they'd first met at the gym all those months ago. His insides—and other parts—tingled when he thought about it.

Sven was last to join the group. The project leader's eyes lingered on Helene as he took his place behind Stacee. His wife stood apart from the rest, scowling.

Marcos shuddered. He and Pato didn't call Helene the Ice Queen for nothing. He just hoped that she would keep her side of the bargain they'd made before the trip. If she did, she wouldn't be a problem.

Pato dropped down from the trailer, landing next to him. His ever-present tablet was gripped in one hand. "I think we're a go," he said. "She's as ready as she'll ever be."

Marcos's grin grew even wider. This was the moment he'd

dreamed about since he and Pato had first thought up the whole crazy project over five years ago. He wagged his eyebrows at Stacee. She rolled her eyes but still smiled.

"Patricio, my good man," Marcos said, gesturing to his friend, "would you do the honors?"

Pato tapped out a command on his tablet, and both joined the others in staring into the dark recesses of the trailer.

"I never get tired of this," Ryan whispered, perfectly expressing Marcos's feeling. Marcos wished he had popcorn.

Stacee giggled.

For ten interminable seconds, nothing happened. Then something within the trailer whirred. The sound rose to a whine and was soon joined by a series of sharp, metallic clicks. The shadows inside the gloom shifted.

Even though he had seen it dozens of times, watching the shadowy angles bend and stretch as his creation woke up still sent chills down Marcos's spine. The machine clicked and whirred as it unfolded spindly spider-like legs, stretching them to their full length before bringing them down onto the trailer bed with a scrape of metal on metal. Slowly, meticulously, the shadow rose.

Stacee squeaked, the sound bursting from her as if she couldn't contain it. Marcos laughed. In the trailer, one of the metallic legs rose into the air. It hung for a second as sensors calibrated and servos adjusted then came down on the steel floor with a resounding clang. It was followed by another and another. The machine moved forward.

"Ladies and gentlemen," Marcos said softly, "I give you the Burro."

With a flash of chrome and a clatter of steel claws, the robot emerged into the sunlight. It was seven feet long and ant shaped, with six chrome-plated, insect-like legs extending from its torso. Its head was round and covered in spiny antennae and sensors, with screens on either side like big, glowing eyes. It was awe-inspiring. It was monstrous. It was beautiful.

The three who hadn't seen the robot day-in and day-out for the past several years reacted. Stacee hopped up and down and squealed with excitement. Vivek gasped. Helene only grunted.

The machine stepped cautiously toward the ramp, testing the sturdiness of the ground. Its sensors clicked and whirred as they collected and processed data. Satisfied, the robot rushed forward, moving down the ramp with a speed and agility that belied its size and bulk.

The group stepped back, giving it room. It came to a stop a respectful distance from the humans. The look of relief on Vivek's face caused Marcos's grin to sour just a little. Pato had been right, some people wouldn't think the Burro was quite as amazing as they did. Some might even be scared of it. *Ten bucks down the drain,* he thought, glancing toward his friend.

Pato smirked back and wagged his eyebrows. Marcos rolled his eyes.

Turning back to the moment, Marcos watched as the robot settled at the bottom of the ramp. Pushing past Pato, he rushed to it. He patted its head and whispered to it in a sing-song voice. "That's it. Who's a good girl? You are. Yes, you are."

With the exception of Helene, who continued to glare from her place a full step beyond the rest, the others surrounded the machine, oohing and aahing. Stacee was practically shaking with excitement.

Marcos sidled up next to her, thinking through what he could say to make her even more impressed, but Sven thwarted his attempt.

"How's she doing?" Sven asked.

"The Burro?" Marcos responded. "She's fine. We had to calibrate the sensors a bit for the wind, but she's good to go."

"You're sure?" the project leader pressed. "You remember what happened to Dave?"

"Dave was stupid," Marcos scoffed. He rolled his eyes at the idiocy of their former mechanic. As far as Marcos was concerned, he deserved his broken leg. Besides, it had opened the door for Stacee. Seeing Sven's impatient, give-me-more-details look, he added, "We upped the sensor sensitivity. She won't be any trouble."

"All right." Sven nodded, checking a paper on the clipboard Pato and Marcos had been trying to get him to replace with a tablet since forever. "Then let's get going. We're already behind schedule."

With his trademark grin, Marcos turned back to the robot, but his grin faltered when he saw Stacee standing far too close to his friend a few feet away. Their heads were close together as a flushed and blushing Pato explained something to the gorgeous mechanic. A flash of jealousy shot through Marcos. He hoped Pato would notice his glare as he stepped around the machine toward them.

"Why don't you call her the Ant?" Stacee was asking.

"Uh..." Pato stumbled for the words. "The... uh... Burro. She's a robotic pack mule. So, when we—Marcos and I—dreamed her up, we called her the Burro. It means 'mule' in Spanish. She was originally only going to have four legs, but we realized middle legs would be more useful, especially scaling cliffs and things, so we shifted the design to be more insectile. But the name stuck. Her real name is 'the Epona Project.'"

He shrugged and tried to grin at her, but it came out as a grimace.

"Epona?" Stacee asked, leaning closer to him, obviously teasing.

Inside, Marcos seethed.

Pato cleared his throat and tried to back away but hit the ramp behind him. "Uh..." he stammered. "Epona was the goddess of horses and mules. Steve McTiernan has a thing for gods and goddesses." His attempt at grinning had more success the second time.

Stacee smiled back.

In that moment, Marcos hated him. He raised his hand to say something witty, but Stacee didn't see him.

"Is she really going to Mars someday?" she asked.

"That's the plan," Pato replied with a shrug. "At least if Steve gets his way. He also has a thing for Mars." His third grin was lopsided, and his cheeks burned red, but even to the very hetero Marcos, the look was cute and endearing. He suddenly wished his best friend would fall off a cliff.

With a giddy laugh, Stacee turned back to the machine. She ran her hand along the nearest leg, caressing it.

"Well, it's beautiful," she said, giving Pato the same smile that turned Marcos's insides into Jell-O.

Marcos felt his face grow hot as jealousy consumed him, but before he could react, Sven interrupted.

"All right, people," the project leader called, "showtime is over. I want everyone at the cliff, ready to go, in thirty minutes. Let's get moving."

The group broke up, scattering to their individual jobs. Looking relieved, Pato turned away from Stacee and bolted up the ramp into the trailer to secure the equipment before it headed back to Phoenix. Helene went back to sorting supplies. Sven and Ryan returned to the first van, and Vivek went to the cliff to secure the rappelling anchors. Tybet did whatever his job was. In a moment, just Marcos and Stacee stood beside the Burro.

She didn't notice him at first. She just ran her hand over the robot's outer casing, her face alive with delight and interest.

"Told you it was amazing," Marcos said, causing her to jump.

Getting over her shock, she grinned back at him. Marcos was disappointed that it wasn't the same smile she'd given Pato, but he shook the thought away, just happy to be this close to her.

"And just wait until you see what comes next," he added, casting a glance toward the valley stretching into the hazy horizon. "It's going to be epic."

THREE

PATO SHIFTED NERVOUSLY AS HE STARED DOWN THE FOUR-hundred-foot drop to the rocky bottom of the cliff. Beneath him, the Burro purred and clicked, the metal warm under his legs. The harness that held him in place astride the robot dug into his thighs.

How, he wondered, *did I let myself get talked into this?* In answer, he glared at Marcos. His friend stood a couple yards from the Burro, leaning back over the cliff in his own harness—a standard rappelling one. Marcos saw him looking and gave him his patented jackass smile and a big thumbs-up. Pato turned away, feeling sick.

"Vivek? How's it going?" Sven called into his radio. It crackled with static before the guide's voice came back.

"The cable is secure," Vivek said over the radio. "Send them down."

"Roger," Sven replied. He lowered the radio and stepped close to Pato. With a comforting smile, the project leader reached out and patted his shoulder. "You okay?"

"Yeah, sure," Pato said, hearing the squeak in his voice and hoping Stacee didn't notice. "Yes," he repeated, sounding a little less like he was about to wet his pants.

"You look great, Pato," Stacee called.

He glanced at her. She was standing next to Helene a few yards away, her dark, curly hair dancing in the wind. He tried to grin at her, but his facial muscles didn't cooperate. The result was a confusing twisting of the lips and cheeks that probably did more to frighten the girl than anything. Feeling the blush rise in his cheeks, he looked back down the cliff. Falling didn't seem so bad all of the sudden.

"Marcos, you ready?" Sven called past Pato.

"Ready and waiting," Marcos shouted back.

In his peripheral vision, Pato could see his friend doing some kind of funky dance along the rim. Even without looking at him and seeing the drop to the bottom, it made his toes curl.

"All right," Sven said, stepping back. "Take it nice and slow. Remember, this is just a test, and we have a long way to go." He waved dramatically at the cliff and the world beyond. "Whenever you're ready."

Pato swallowed and stole a final glance at Stacee. She smiled and waved, causing his stomach to flip. He looked back at the bottom of the cliff, set his jaw, and triggered the sequence to move forward.

The Burro responded immediately, whining and clicking as gears and servos engaged. Moving slowly at first, it inched toward the cliff. It paused at the edge, sensors and electronics registering and testing the empty space. Pato tightened his grip. In one swift movement that jerked Pato back in his harness, the robot went over the edge and started to climb down the sheer rock.

The ride was not as bad as Pato had feared. The Burro's movements were smooth and graceful as it walked down the cliff, carefully picking its way around outcrops and over cracks. Pato swayed gently in his harness as they went, listening to the whir of the winch that attached the robot's rear to the anchor planted at the top of the precipice as it spooled out more security line with each step.

Marcos flanked them, steadily rappelling backward down the cliff, matching their pace. Every once in a while, he would whoop his excitement to the wind. Otherwise, they walked in silence.

"You're about a quarter of the way," Sven's voice came over the Burro's shortwave radio. "How is it going?"

"Uh, everything is under control. Situation normal," Marcos replied in his horrible Han Solo impression. "We... uh... had a slight weapons malfunction, but everything's perfectly all right now. We're fine. We're all fine here, now. Thank you. How are you?"

"Just stay focused." Sven sounded annoyed.

Both Marcos and Pato laughed.

They continued walking, carefully making their way down the cliff. Three minutes passed, then five, then ten. They were halfway to the bottom.

"You know what would be fun?" Marcos said suddenly.

A chill went through Pato. He glanced at his friend in time to see a very dangerous grin spread across his face. "Whatever you're thinking, the answer is no," he said, trying to sound firm.

Marcos put his hand on his heart and feigned offense. "All I was going to say is that we should really test her." Marcos pointed at the Burro. "Open her up. See what she can do."

"Says the one not strapped on top of her."

"I was just thinking..."

"No," Pato snapped. "We're doing this by the book."

"Fine." Marcos stepped away, looking sullen.

The silence lasted about five seconds.

"I was just thinking," Marcos said, "that with Stacee watching and all..." He trailed off, letting his words linger in the air.

Another chill shot through Pato. He swallowed and tried to glance behind him, though the harness made that impossible. Even still, he could picture the beautiful mechanic leaning over the cliff, following them with binoculars. He shivered in the heat.

"I don't think it's a good idea," Pato said, feeling himself give in.

"You're probably right," Marcos agreed in that way he had of agreeing and disagreeing at the same time. "Besides, Sven would have a cow." He paused then added dramatically, "But Stacee would love it."

Pato swallowed again as the memory of her standing so close to him that he could smell her perfume flashed into his mind. Every word she spoke, every gesture and blink, were captured in the memory. Even more was the electric moment when she had touched his arm while asking a question about the Burro and how it worked.

Stacee would love it.

"Let's make a bet," Marcos said. Somehow, he'd moved closer without Pato noticing. "First one to the bottom wins first shot at her."

Pato hesitated.

With a whoop, Marcos was gone, racing down the cliff as fast as he could go.

For an eternal second, Pato watched him. Conflicting thoughts raced through his mind, meshing and overlapping, trying to out-yell one another.

Stacee would love it.

"Sven is going to kill me." Pato leaned over the controls, tapping out the new commands.

He tightened his grip and braced himself. The whine from the Burro's rotors grew louder, and then the robot shot forward.

Pato screamed.

FOUR

"Marcos! Pato! What are you doing?" Sven's voice crackled over the radio. He sounded pissed.

Pato ignored the project leader as he gritted his teeth and tightened his grip on the metal handles just behind the Burro's head. Beneath him, the robot lunged over a foot-wide outcrop and lurched around a wide crack in the cliff. The harness dug into Pato's legs as the robot jerked this way and that, rushing toward the valley floor at breakneck speed. The winch sang as it unspooled line behind them, barely able to keep up.

"Stop! Slow down, you idiots!" Sven was getting angrier.

Ahead, Pato could see Marcos scrambling as fast as his legs and rappelling harness allowed. He grinned. The Burro was catching up.

Pato waved as he and the robot blew past his friend as if he were standing still. He heard Marcos whoop as they whizzed by him.

Pato laughed. This was everything they had hoped for since

they were two poor kids with a dream back at the barrio. He leaned into the wind and smiled.

No. It's better.

The Burro abruptly skidded to the left, dodging a sharp rock protruding from the side of the cliff. Pato's heart plummeted as he was thrown against the harness. His fingers slipped from the handgrips.

"Shit!" He flailed for the grips that bounced and jostled just beyond his reach.

The robot jerked again to the left, narrowly missing a large crack. Pato yelled as he was thrown to the side. The harness cut into his legs as his head neared the machine's churning legs. He scrambled for the handgrips. At last, his fingers closed around one and, with a heave, he pulled himself up. Panting, he leaned forward on the Burro and tightened his grip. His knuckles turned white.

Unaware of its rider's close call, the robot continued to charge down the cliff. Pato held on, watching the ground come at them with alarming speed. His eyes watered, and his heart thundered.

"Going to suggest some modifications when we get home," he muttered through clenched teeth. Evil thoughts about the friend who had gotten him into the situation flashed through his mind.

The Burro lurched to the right as it dodged another outcrop. Pato tightened his grip and blurted a quick Hail Mary. He hadn't prayed since attending midnight Mass with his mother at Christmas, so he was only sort of confident in the words. He hoped God would understand.

Behind him, Marcos whooped again. Over the radio, Sven yelled. Both were lost in the wind and Pato's panting breath.

Suddenly, the ground in front of the Burro disappeared.

A massive arch that cut into the side of the cliff seemed to materialize out of nowhere. There was no time to stop or go around. Pato yelled as the Burro skittered right to the edge and leapt.

They soared into the air. Pato's stomach plummeted as the cliff fell away under them. The wind whipped his face, and tears formed at the corners of his eyes. His heart pounded against his ribcage. The winch whined.

It was the most terrifying feeling in the world.

It was the most incredible feeling in the world.

And then, with a screech of metal, everything stopped.

Sharp pain lanced through Pato as the Burro slammed to a halt in midair. He was thrown forward in the harness, smashing his chin on the back of the robot's head. A spiderweb of pain exploded from his jaw and through the rest of his body. Stars swam before his eyes. His ears rang. His legs burned where the harness had cut into them.

Gasping for breath, he struggled to right himself, but the world tilted around him. Dimly, he felt the Burro arc back toward the wall, swinging like a pendulum at the end of the cable attached to the winch. A moment later, they crashed into the side of the cliff, the impact jolting both machine and rider.

Darkness began to crowd the edges of Pato's vision. Beneath him, he could feel the robot's clawed feet as they scrambled for purchase on the sandstone wall. Gears and servos whined and clicked frantically as they scraped against solid rock, but they failed to establish a grip.

Pato's stomach lurched as the Burro spun back into open air. He closed his eyes and wrapped his arms around the robot.

"Hail Mary, full of grace," he prayed, his words breathless and rapid, "the Lord is with thee."

The Burro reach the end of its swinging arc. For a second, man and robot hovered motionless over the deadly drop.

"Blessed art thou amongst women, and blessed is the fruit of thy womb, Jesus."

The robot fell back toward the cliff. Pato tightened his grip. "Holy Mary, Mother of God, pray for us sinners now and at the hour of our death. Amen."

The Burro slammed into the cliff with the screech of metal against stone. Pato felt the machine's legs bend under him and heard something snap, but somehow, one of the clawed feet found a hold. The spinning world came to a sudden halt.

Pato remained still for a long time, his head pounding and his heart thundering. His legs had gone numb, and his chin stung, but to his surprise, he was still alive. Behind him, the sounds coming to him as if through a fog, he could hear Marcos scrambling down the cliff, yelling his name. Over the radio, Sven screamed incoherently.

Pato closed his eyes. The world fell into darkness.

FIVE

Stacee hid her smile as she watched Sven yell at Marcos and Pato. The project leader's face turned a deeper shade of red with every word he spat. He was already the color of a tomato.

"It was the most irresponsible thing I have ever seen," he shouted for probably the fifth time. The engineers, who had flinched the first few times, barely reacted. "You should both be dead."

That was, in Stacee's opinion, a bit of an exaggeration. Racing the Burro down the cliff had been undeniably stupid and incredibly irresponsible. It had also been amazing and impressive in ways she couldn't articulate. She felt an unexpected warmth spread through her cheeks as she glanced at Pato. He was holding an icepack to his forehead, his eyes on the ground, not daring to look up at Sven. It was adorable.

After the accident, the two engineers had spent a full hour repairing the robot enough that it could limp the rest of the way to the valley floor. Apparently, the trouble had been caused by some issue with the winch. Sven had paced atop the cliff the entire time, alternately ranting and muttering about "those two irresponsible jackasses."

Once they had gotten the Burro to the ground, it had finally been time for the rest of the group to rappel down, a drop that was amazing but too quick for Stacee's taste. That had been nearly twenty minutes ago. Sven was still yelling.

Stacee sighed and fanned herself with her hand. She glanced around, admiring the sandstone cliffs, boulders, and the vast expanse of desert behind them. She really hoped that Marcos and Pato's stunt didn't cause them to turn around and head back. She still hadn't gotten a good enough look at what made the Burro tick.

Surreptitiously, she looked at the robot. It sat a few yards from the group, humming as if with anticipation. One leg had been shattered in the accident, and the rest of the machine's chrome plating sported new dents and scratches. The defects didn't matter, though.

It.

Was.

Beautiful.

The Burro was, in fact, the most gorgeous thing Stacee had seen since the '67 candy-apple red Ford Mustang convertible she'd restored with her father back in high school. Everything about the robot entranced her. She itched to open it up.

"It was immature and thoughtless," Sven yelled, pulling Stacee back to the show. Veins stood out on his forehead. She worried he might have a heart attack, which would definitely end the trip.

Marcos caught her watching and winked.

She rolled her eyes. *As if!*

Sven's tirade crescendoed, echoing off the cliffs and carrying on the wind.

Pato flinched and bowed his head even lower, his cheeks

flushed. Shame was kind of cute on him. Stacee smiled, thinking of the way the software engineer had nearly stumbled over himself when she'd been talking to him earlier.

Shaking away the thought, she stretched and yawned. Leaning forward, she flipped her hair over her head and ran her fingers through the black curls. With all the dust and wind, she was going to have to tie it back soon.

Not far from her, Helene moved about the pile of food, packs, and other supplies Tybet and Ryan had lowered in a big net ten minutes after they had touched down. Helene's lithe figure moved quickly from one item to the next, sorting through them with focus and efficiency.

Stacee sighed. She'd been happy to hear there was at least one other female on the trip, but Helene's cold abrasiveness had quickly dispelled any illusions of bonding. It left Stacee feeling alone among strangers.

Vivek's shadow passed over her as the guide paced nearby. He was on the satellite phone, talking with Ryan, the perv who had been gaping at her all morning.

"Everyone is fine," the older guide was saying in his adorable Indian accent. "We are just behind schedule. We will let you know when we get going again. We will call in a couple hours to check in. Do not forget the drop schedules... Okay. Sure, sure, sure. Bye."

The guide lowered the phone and sighed. He saw her watching and stiffened.

"We're not heading home, right?" Stacee asked then gave him her most disarming smile.

The guide stared at her for a moment, his dark face inscrutable. At last, muttering in Hindi, he turned and wandered toward his pack.

Stacee furrowed her brow but didn't dwell on the slight.

Instead, she stretched again and took a drink of water. She stole another glance at the Burro, a thrill going through her. If the boys would just let her get close enough to see how the machine worked, it would make having to put up with Marcos's leering, Helene's coldness, and Vivek's disdain worth it.

Sven's voice was growing hoarse, so he fixed the engineers with a withering glare. It looked like he was finally winding down. "Well?"

"I'm sorry," Pato muttered, his face beet red. Yes, shame was indeed very cute on him.

"Sure thing, hombre," Marcos said, grinning like a jackass.

Sven glared at Marcos for a full thirty seconds. The idiot grinned back.

"Good," Sven forced through clenched teeth. He glanced toward the robot, his face twisting into a grimace. "How soon can you have her working again?"

"We need to run some diagnostics," Pato said, looking relieved to be on more comfortable ground.

"And replace the leg," Marcos added.

"How long?"

The two nerds exchanged a look and shrugged.

"Thirty minutes, give or take," Marcos said.

"Maybe forty-five," Pato amended.

Sven's expression grew even more sour, and he shot a meaningful look at Vivek. "Fine. Get to work." He stomped off, muttering.

The young men watched him go.

"That wasn't so bad." Marcos slapped Pato on the shoulder.

Pato winced and adjusted the icepack without looking at his friend.

"Right?" Marcos persisted.

Pato grunted and, without a word, walked toward the Burro.

Marcos followed. "By the way," he said, reaching into his pocket, "I thought you should have this." He pulled out a shiny black stone about two inches wide, with sharp faceted sides that flashed in the sunlight.

Pato stopped and stared at it. "What is it?"

"That, my friend, is what all the fuss is about. Got stuck in the winch gears, jammed it up. You should thank it for the bruise on your chin."

Pato rolled his eyes and looked away.

"You're going to hurt its feelings," Marcos called, holding up the rock. "Come on, give it a kiss—ouch!" He flinched and dropped the rock.

"What?" Pato asked, pausing to look back at his friend.

"I cut myself." Marcos sucked on his finger.

Pato rolled his eyes again and turned back toward the robot. He hesitated when he saw Stacee sitting just a few feet away, his cheeks growing an even cuter shade of red.

Marcos caught up to him, still sucking on his finger. He looked down at Stacee and grinned lecherously. She wanted to knee him in the balls.

"How can I help?" Stacee asked, flashing them her most winning smile.

"Uh..." Pato said uncertainly, his lost expression making him even more adorable.

"We can use all the help we can get," Marcos said, gesturing toward the Burro.

Stacee almost squealed as she leapt to her feet and led the way.

"Sweetheart, this could be the beginning of a beautiful friend-ship," Marcos said, doing the worst Humphrey Bogart impression she'd ever heard.

She laughed anyway and added a bit more shake to her ass, just to keep them interested.

SIX

JONATHAN TYBET WATCHED THE OTHER VAN DISAPPEAR DOWN the dirt road in a cloud of dust, starting the long trip back to Phoenix. He imagined Ryan in the driver's seat, singing the wrong words to the loudest playlist he could find and chugging a monster-sized cup of Dr Pepper. He doubted the young man would even think to look in his rearview mirror for miles, but Tybet still waited until the van had completely disappeared from view.

Glancing around out of habit, he reached for the satellite phone resting on the passenger seat. He quickly dialed and waited.

It was picked up on the second ring.

"This is Tybet," he said, his deep voice filling the cab. "They're off."

"And?" the voice on the other end asked. The speaker sounded nervous.

"I'm not sure. I didn't find any evidence up here, but I will be keeping an eye on them."

"So, you still think the other group was an encounter?"

Tybet hesitated before answering, remembering what he'd

discovered about the other group that had suffered a tragic accident in this same desert only seven months earlier. All the evidence he had read had pointed to a freak landslide, but something nagged at him. Perhaps it was the fact that the sole survivor, a woman named Elizabeth, still couldn't remember what had happened, even after months of therapy, before she completely vanished. Perhaps it was the location. Perhaps it was intuition.

Then again, perhaps he was just jumping at shadows.

"It's possible," he said. "There are too many unanswered questions."

"Do you think it's safe to let them go ahead with the trip?"

Again, Tybet hesitated. He did not think the trip was a good idea, but he also hadn't come up with a good way to stop it. When Marcos and Pato had raced the Burro down the cliff, he'd been hopeful that their recklessness would be enough to call the whole thing off, but Sven had argued that too much time and money had been spent to give up so quickly. Without another reason, the project leader was set on seeing it through.

"I think we should keep a close eye on them," Tybet said at last.

"What about Sven?" the speaker asked. "How much do you think he knows?"

"I don't know. He could know nothing. I'm going to see what I can find out while he's gone."

"And what about the girl?"

Tybet winced. He'd anticipated this question, but the answer wasn't going to make anyone happy. "She's off-grid. I have feelers out, but nothing yet."

"We need to find her," the other speaker insisted. "She could ruin everything."

"I'll find her. I promise."

"Good."

The two sat in silence for a long moment, each processing what had been said and what hadn't. At last, the speaker added, "Keep me informed. I want to know the moment you find her or anything happens with Sven and the team."

"Right," Tybet replied.

Without another word, the other man hung up.

Tybet remained still for several seconds, staring at the phone. He made a mental list of everything that needed to be done in the next ten days. He was going to be very busy.

At last, the large man turned and looked toward the valley beyond the cliff. He wondered how the group was doing after their rocky start. His eyes drifted farther, wandering through the ravines and towers and over hills and valleys. He drew a deep breath and let it out in a rush.

"Good luck, guys," he muttered. "I hope you don't need it."

Turning away from the valley and struggling to ignore the nervous flutter in his chest, Tybet started the van, shifted into drive, and pulled away, leaving behind a cloud of dust that drifted in the wind.

SEVEN

HELENE WATCHED STACEE AND THE TWO BOYS LAUGH AS they worked on the Burro. The girl's laugh felt a little false, and Helene wondered, yet again, what had brought her on the trip in the first place, but she shook away the thought.

Sven and Vivek were huddled over a map, discussing the lost time to their schedule and possible alternates if more delays should occur. They didn't even look in her direction. No one was looking at her.

After a nervous glance at the three huddled around the robot and a quick check that all the supplies and packs were sorted, she quickly walked into the desert. A minute later, she was standing atop a small rise almost fifty yards from the group, gazing into the distance.

The rise was really just a mound a few inches taller than an ambitious anthill, and the view was disappointing—just more desert. In spite of that, Helene stood for several minutes, staring into the endless expanse of red rock and sand.

Her hand twitched toward the pocket of her shorts, where her phone was hidden. She could feel the shape of the phone as it pressed into her thigh. It called to her, taunting her.

The need was building. She had to resist. She closed her eyes and held still, trying to focus on her breathing.

"Breathe in the good and out the bad," she muttered. Opening her eyes, Helene growled in frustration. She kicked at a fist-sized black rock at her feet. It skidded off, landing in the shadow of a prickly pear cactus a couple yards away.

It's not fair. None of it.

The wind picked up, gusting around her. It whistled and moaned as it tugged at the wide-brimmed hat cinched around her neck, the sound almost rhythmic in its ebb and flow. It blended in Helene's mind with a song Kyle had played nonstop that final week, one of the hits from Javen, that YouTube star who did all those crazy stunts in his music videos. Helene had hated that song, now the memory was like a knife through her heart.

Unconsciously, she began to hum along, the melody rising and falling with the wind. She closed her eyes again, feeling the world around her fade into the half-remembered lyrics. Her disappointment and frustration were swept away in the music that brought her close, once again, to her son. The need started to fade.

With a sigh, she reopened her eyes and took in the red-and-yellow world around her, the dark-green scrub, the spires, and the distant shadowy mesas. For that moment, it was enough.

Something moved at her feet. Her heart leapt, and she jumped back. She scanned the ground for whatever had startled her and found nothing but rock and sand. Helene inched backward, her mind conjuring up spiders, scorpions, and rats. She didn't know which would be worse.

Another movement, to her left. She snapped her head toward it, again searching the ground and again coming up empty. A creeping sensation inched across her neck and down her arms. She thought she could feel someone's eyes on her.

Turning, she looked back at the others, expecting to find one of them watching her. Marcos worked on the Burro while Pato pointed something out to Stacee, and Vivek and Sven were still hunched over the map. No one so much as glanced her way. Still, the feeling wouldn't leave her alone. She turned back to the desert, taking another instinctive step backward.

And then she heard it, carrying just over the wind: a soft insect-like chattering that came in short bursts then died away. Something about the sound unnerved her, and she shivered, her eyes darting from left to right. She found nothing but more desert.

"Pull yourself together," she muttered, her heart pounding.

Another movement to her right. She jumped and almost shouted before the jackrabbit moved again, its long ears twitching in the wind. Helene sighed and shook her head, feeling the pounding in her heart subside. She looked at the small rabbit's bony body and forced a laugh.

"What did you think it was?" she said, feeling the wind toss her words to and fro across the desert.

The clicking sound came again, closer than before. It startled the rabbit, which stood taller, ears alert. The sound repeated a third time, and the rabbit darted away, disappearing behind a thick sagebrush.

Helene swallowed, thinking that perhaps she should head back to the others.

A twig snapped behind her. She screamed and spun around, her heart leaping into her throat.

"Whoa," Sven said, raising his hands and taking a step back. His face filled with shock and wariness. "You okay?"

Helene's adrenaline faded into anger and resentment. "What

are you doing here?" she demanded, her voice filled with so much vitriol that he took another step backward.

He cleared his throat and dropped his eyes to the ground, refusing to meet hers. "I... uh..." he stumbled, seeming to lose his ability to speak in coherent sentences.

"Yes?"

"I... I just came to tell you we'll be going in about ten minutes." He glanced up at her but looked away at the unrestrained fury he must have seen on her face.

"Fine," Helene said, her teeth clicking together to bite the word short.

"Right." Sven shifted from foot to foot, avoiding her glare. "Well... I'd better get back to the others."

She watched him turn and walk away, feeling her anger die with each step that separated them. He didn't look back at her as he went. Helene didn't expect him to.

With a sigh, she turned back to the desert, her fear from moments ago forgotten in the confrontation with her husband. She stared into the distance for a long while, searching out the outline of the plateau that marked the end of their journey. It was so far away that it was little more than a shadow on the horizon. At last, she turned and walked back to the others.

EIGHT

VIVEK JUMPED AS THE ALARM BLASTED INTO THE HOT afternoon. Ahead of him, the Burro jerked to the left. It collided with Marcos, who had been walking alongside, knocking him to the ground. The engineer yelled and scrambled away from the robot's anxiously pawing feet. Thirty seconds later, the machine stopped moving, but the alarm still filled the air, blasting again and again into the wind.

"What the hell?" Marcos screamed, stripping off his pack and leaping to his feet. He kicked one of the Burro's legs, connecting with a clang that barely registered over the alarm.

"Ow!" he yelled, hopping back.

Stacee and Pato burst out laughing. Vivek sighed. Four days had passed since Marcos and Pato had nearly killed themselves racing down the cliff—four days filled with malfunctions, delays, and too many near-accidents to count. It seemed they couldn't go more than a half mile without something going wrong with the damned machine. The group was already way behind schedule, and the trail was only going to get harder.

Sven came forward. "What happened?"

"This piece of shit keeps malfunctioning." Marcos slumped onto a nearby rock and flexed his pained foot.

"Don't blame her," Pato said defensively, stepping close to the machine and tapping at his ever-present tablet.

"I'm not blaming her," Marcos snarled. "It's probably the software."

"No way in hell," Pato snapped back. "It's a hardware problem, and you know it."

"I'll show you a hardware problem!" Marcos lunged for his friend over the still-quivering robot.

Pato danced away, giving Marcos the finger.

"Hey, guys, cut it out," Sven shouted.

The two engineers ignored him, circling the machine, shouting over the alarm, and making crude suggestions about each other's parentage and anatomy.

Vivek sighed again, wishing he'd never taken this job. He had never been a huge fan of technology, and a hike through the middle of the desert was dangerous enough without the added complication of an overengineered robot, but the paycheck had been too big to pass up. There was Rajesh's college tuition to consider. He just wished he had asked for more.

"Guys," Sven yelled, his face turning red.

The engineers reluctantly turned and glowered at their project leader.

"Turn off the damn alarm." Sven jabbed a finger at the dust-covered machine.

Without a word, Pato raised his tablet and tapped the screen. The alarm fell silent. The last remnants of sound echoed down a slot canyon cut into the wall of nearby cliffs. The echo dissipated, leaving absolute silence in its wake.

The quiet closed in on them, as oppressive as the alarm had

been. A chill ran down Vivek's spine. He glanced around, searching for any sign of desert life amid the red cliffs and sage. There was none, not even a bird in the sky.

He furrowed his brow. The Burro's alarm would have frightened away any wildlife, but he hadn't seen much of anything since the trip began. He had hiked this desert many times, but it had never before seemed so barren.

"What is wrong with the Burro now?" Sven demanded of the two engineers, pulling Vivek back to the moment.

Marcos and Pato exchanged angry, bitter looks, daring each other to speak first. At last, Marcos threw his arms up and turned away, muttering under his breath.

"It's the sand," Pato said, turning back to Sven. "It's too fine and is screwing up the sensors."

"The software isn't compensating," Marcos snapped. "It's supposed to adapt to sand granularity, but it's buggy as hell."

"Bullshit!" Pato shouted back. "If the filtration system was doing its job, the software wouldn't have to compensate."

The two stepped toward each other, raising fists.

"What is it doing to the sensors?" Sven asked before it could come to blows.

The two engineers hesitated and turned toward him.

"She keeps seeing phantoms," Pato said, pointing at the Burro's head.

Vivek cocked another eyebrow, curious in spite of himself.

"Phantoms?" He reminded himself that he didn't believe in ghosts. Of course, he had heard too many crazy stories from Navajos who wouldn't walk the mesas at night to be completely immune to the idea.

"No," Marcos explained, rolling his eyes. "The Burro just keeps sensing things that aren't there."

"Like a minute ago," Pato said, pointing to his tablet, "it sensed seismic activity right over there, coming nearer."

"And it keeps detecting movement." Marcos pointed at the nearby cliffs. "Right now, it's saying there is something moving in that wall."

"In the wall?" Sven asked, turning to look at the cliff of solid stone.

The engineers both shrugged.

"So," Stacee asked, "all that is caused by sand getting into the system?"

They nodded.

"I might have an idea," she said, sounding more excited than Vivek thought the moment warranted. "I used to trick out dune buggies, and we found this way of keeping the sand out of the engine. It's simple and works like a charm. I bet we even have the stuff for it."

Vivek raised an eyebrow. Up to that point, the girl had been nothing more than a distraction for the two idiots, but maybe she would be useful after all.

"Couldn't hurt to try," Pato said, sharing a skeptical look with Marcos.

Stacee asked a question about valves and intake manifolds, and the engineers launched into a technical conversation that was far over Vivek's head. Sven leaned in, nodding occasionally, though Vivek didn't think the project leader understood any more than he did. Drawing a breath, the guide drifted away, glancing at his watch and growling in frustration at how far behind schedule they had gotten. At this rate, they weren't going to make it to the next supply drop before dark, much less the ultimate rendezvous. He was going to have to have another conversation with Ryan. The thought soured his stomach, and he turned away from the group, their conversation becoming little more than an annoying babble drifting on the wind.

His eyes caught on Helene. As usual, Sven's wife stood several feet away from the rest of them. She had dropped her pack on a large rock and stood staring at the nearby cliffs. Vivek followed her gaze, and an unexpected chill traveled the length of his spine as he saw the slot canyon he'd noticed earlier. The shadowy crack in the wall seemed more pronounced than before, a sharp slice of black against the bright-red sandstone, just wide enough to swallow a person whole. Marcos and Pato's words about phantoms and movement in the walls sent a shiver through him, a dark foreboding flooding into him. His heart thundered and his chest constricted. He swallowed, wondering what was putting him so on edge.

Turning back to Helene, he was startled to discover her walking toward the canyon. He raised his hand and almost called out to stop her but hesitated. What would he say that wouldn't make him sound foolish? Helene, he had quickly learned, was irritable under the best of circumstances. She wouldn't react well to someone jumping at phantoms. Scolding himself, Vivek lowered his hand and looked back at the others. They were still deep in conversation. It looked like it would last a while.

He found a large rock and stripped off his pack. He pulled out a water bottle, took a sip of warm water, then sat, staring at the canyon. Helene had disappeared into its depths, and Vivek's uneasiness grew stronger.

A breeze picked up, whistling through the sagebrush. The sound startled him, and he stared down at the plants, watching them dance in the wind. He wondered again where all the wildlife had gone, suddenly feeling very alone in the vast desert. Unbidden, his eyes returned to the canyon, and another chill ran down his spine.

NINE

HELENE PAUSED JUST INSIDE THE ENTRANCE OF THE NARROW canyon, listening to the whistle of wind that resonated down the red sandstone walls and vanished into the shadows beyond. A nervous flutter twisted her stomach as she took a step forward, still trying to decide what had drawn her to the canyon in the first place.

She looked at the walls, thinking about what Marcos and Pato had said earlier about the Burro sensing phantoms and movement in the stone. Tentative, she reached out and touched the sheer wall. Its solid, rough surface was reassuring.

"Nothing but rock," Helene muttered, shaking her head.

She moved deeper into the canyon, taking slow, measured steps. Absently, she reached out as she walked, running the tips of her fingers along the walls, feeling their rough surfaces lined with tiny, glass-like black veins that almost made them look organic. The trail curved around a bend then another. Helene continued moving forward, trying to ignore the nervous feeling that grew stronger with every step.

The memory of a hike she and Sven had taken with Kyle when he was seven years old sprang into her mind. Helene paused, trying to catch her breath, as the memories caught up to her. She remembered their exuberant son running ahead, discovering colorful rocks and chasing striped lizards. Her heart twisted at the memories.

Closing her eyes, she concentrated on her breathing.

In. Out. In. Out.

She let the images and memories slide through her, ending, as they always did, with that single image of Kyle and Emily in the car on that worst of all days. Her fingers itched to hold her phone, but she had given it to Marcos to charge. Helene shuddered and opened her eyes. She breathed long, slow breaths, feeling the darkness subside. At last, she straightened and kept moving forward.

A few minutes later, the canyon split into two. Helene paused and looked down both paths.

"Two roads diverged in a yellow wood," she quoted. It didn't help. With a grunt, she chose the path on the left.

After a quick bend, the trail narrowed to a tight corridor. She had to turn sideways to fit. Claustrophobia pressed in on her, turning her nervous flutter into near panic. Breathing heavily, she pushed through the last few feet to the wider chamber beyond.

She paused, struggling to catch her breath. When she looked up again, she gasped.

The chamber was round and bowl shaped. The multicolored sandstone walls curved down from a narrow opening nearly twenty feet above. The base was at least twelve feet across and fifteen feet long. The other side narrowed back into another shadowy passage that stretched into the darkness. But the most striking feature, the one that took Helene's breath away, was the altar-like mound.

The mound stood in the center of the space. It was lit by

filtered rays of sunlight, making it glow against the dim light of the canyon. The rocks that formed it were striped red, yellow, and brown, but it was the thick vegetation—the grass and brightly colored flowers—that drew her eye.

The grass was so green and bright, it almost looked neon. It grew all the way up the pile of stone, seeming to sprout directly from the rock. It also surrounded the base, stretching almost a foot into the world around it, where it abruptly stopped as if hitting an invisible barrier. The flowers were red, yellow, and orange with distinctive black stripes on the petals and spiky-looking leaves sprouting from their narrow stems.

Helene stared, her mind spinning as she struggled to think of a logical explanation for what she was seeing. She found none.

She swallowed and took a step forward then another, moving with slow reverence, the crunch of her shoes on the pebble-strewn earth blaspheming the sacred stillness of the chamber. Helene reached the mound and paused at the edge of the grass, feeling the thick air close around her. The moan of wind faded into the background. She hunched down, examining the green strands where they came to a sudden halt. There was no indication that it had ever been cut or cultivated. The rocky soil under it was just as inhospitable as the ground under her feet.

Her eyes moved to the mound, her brow furrowing as she made out more details. The pile of stones was oblong. It was nearly seven feet in length and three feet high. The rocks that composed it were piled on top of each other in an ordered yet haphazard way, reminding Helene of the misshapen LEGO creations Kyle had made as a child. *What kind of natural force would position rocks that way?*

Uncertain, she reached out and touched the grass. It was soft and cool under her fingers. She reached for a flower but hesitated, noting the tiny prickly thorns along the stem and leaves. Maybe it was best to leave them where they were.

Standing, she took a step forward. The grass cushioned her boot, feeling strange and comforting after four days of nothing but rock and sand underfoot. She took another step. Something crunched under her, the sound echoing through the chamber like a gunshot. Startled, she jumped back, her heart thudding.

Drawing deep breaths, she knelt and probed the flattened blades of grass with her fingers. Underneath, she found rock and sand. At last, she found what she was looking for—a sharp, rectangular corner sticking partially out from under the pebbles sprouting the strange grass. She tugged at the corner. The ground resisted. She pulled harder. It came free, the pebbles clattering together as they shifted to fill the empty space it left behind.

Standing, Helene stared down at the blank screen of a smartphone, a spiderweb of cracks breaking its once-smooth surface. It was covered in dirt and fragments of grass, its casing chipped and scratched well beyond any warranty coverage. Obviously, it had been in the cavern for some time.

Curious, Helene thumbed the power button. Nothing happened. She grunted.

Flipping it over, she brushed away the dirt, uncovering the back casing. She froze, her breath catching in her throat and ice shooting through her veins. Covering the lower half of the case was a reddish-brown handprint.

Blood!

Helene's heart pounded in her ears as she lifted the phone to the light, trying to get a better look. Her hand trembled, and her stomach twisted.

The memory of a conversation she'd overheard between Sven and Tybet floated through her mind. It had been just before the group had gone over the cliff on that first day. They had been discussing another group that hiked through this same area months before. Helene hadn't heard all the details, but from what she'd been able to make out, most of the group hadn't returned. *Could the phone have belonged to one of them?*

Helene looked at the mound again, the size and shape taking on a new, chilling possibility. She took an involuntary step backward then another. Her breaths came in quick, shallow gasps, and she swallowed against her suddenly dry throat. Her fingers tightened on the phone, the edges cutting into her palm.

A sharp wind blew across the top of the canyon, sending a deep, penetrating moan down the walls. Helene shuddered.

A clatter of rocks echoed from the opposite end of the chamber. Helene jumped and stared down the far passage, squinting to make out the details in the dark shadows. For moment, she saw nothing, but then, deep within the gloom, something moved.

TEN

HELENE'S HEART LEAPT INTO HER THROAT. HER HANDS trembled as she stared into the shadows, probing the darkness.

Whatever it was moved again, just a twitch, but Helene saw it. Holding her breath, she leaned forward, trying to make out more than a black silhouette against the darkness.

Bit by bit, her eyes adjusted. Angles and lines that blended with the jagged rocks around it emerged from the black. Slowly, Helene could make out two points that looked like ears and the rough triangular shape of a body that stood about a foot high. The outline almost looked like a rabbit or a young coyote standing on alert, sensing danger, but it was off somehow.

The silhouette twitched again. It chattered at her with sharp, insect-like clicks, the sound muffled in the strange chamber. Helene released her breath and swallowed, a chill running down her spine.

Clearing her throat, she took a cautious step forward then another. The creature didn't move. It just watched her, its eyes lost in the darkness. Helene took another step. Gravel crunched under her foot.

The animal jerked upright, rising another six inches in height. Helene froze. For a series of heartbeats, neither moved. They just stood, staring at each other across the mound and the space that separated them.

Helene felt her heart beat. Sweat trickled down her forehead, stinging the corners of her eyes. She breathed in slow, shallow breaths as she squinted to see what the animal would do. Around them, the wind moaned.

Suddenly, moving in a series of quick jerks, the creature vanished into the shadows of the passage. Helene continued to hold still, staring after it for a long time. At last, her heart began to slow, and the knot eased from her throat.

"It was just a coyote," she whispered, knowing it was a lie. She looked down at the phone in her hand again. A shudder passed through her.

"Helene?"

She jumped as the voice echoed through the chamber. Spinning around, she found Sven standing just behind her, his face filled with confusion and unexpected concern.

"Sven?" she gasped in surprise. Instinctively, she shoved the phone into her pocket. She didn't think her husband would react well to it.

"What are you doing here?" he asked, stepping forward.

"I..." Helene glanced around the chamber, searching for a ready excuse. "I was just exploring."

"Oh." He seemed to lose whatever he was going to tell her in that single, disappointed word.

For a long moment, they stared at each other in awkward silence. Her heart beat as the blue eyes that had first drawn Helene to him all those years ago searched her face, as if he were still looking for the woman he loved, in spite of all that had happened, in spite of what she had become. She almost flinched away but somehow managed to stand strong, feeling the anger stir inside her again.

With a sigh, Sven looked away, seeming to become aware of their surroundings for the first time. She watched his eyes comb the multicolored walls of the chamber then widen as they landed on the mound.

"What the...?" He stepped past her, his brow furrowed.

Irrational panic surged through Helene as she watched him kneel next to the mound and reach toward the grass waving in the wind. She turned, forcing her breathing to calm and ignoring the twist in her stomach as he touched the greenery, running his hands through it.

"What did you need?" Helene asked, her voice coming out sharper and more strained than she'd planned.

Sven hesitated, his hand still on the grass, his brow furrowed. Slowly, he turned and looked up at her, his face filled with the same sadness he'd worn for the last year. He didn't answer her at first. He just stared. Steeling herself, Helene glared back.

"Well?" she demanded, letting her anger burn a little more.

He sighed. "They've almost finished with the Burro," he said, rising to his feet, refusing to meet her eyes. "We should probably head back."

"Fine." Helene stepped back, letting him go first.

He started back toward the chamber entrance but paused as he passed her. He turned and looked into her face one more time. Their bodies were so close, Helene could feel the heat coming off him and smell his sweat and breath. She swallowed, the need for him struggling against the fury that burned through her. She wanted to reach out to him. She wanted to slap him.

She just stared.

For a moment, it looked like Sven was going to say something. His lips twitched as the words began to form, but then he shook his head and looked away. "We'd better hurry. Vivek might leave without us."

The next moment, he was gone, vanishing into the crack in the cliff leading back the way they had come.

Helene stared after him, feeling her heart pound and her spirit splinter. The anger ebbed. She looked down at the ground, her eyes burning, though she knew from long experience that no tears would come.

For a brief moment, she turned back to the chamber. She could feel the phone in her pocket, filling her mind with questions. Her eyes lit on the strange mound and then moved beyond to the far passage. In spite of the heat, she shuddered.

With a shake of the head, she turned and followed her husband.

ELEVEN

MARCOS GRUNTED AND TOSSED THE INEDIBLE INSTANT GOO that claimed to be stroganoff onto the rock next to him. The others, seated on their own rocks in a loose ring around the electric lantern, glanced his way before returning to their respective instant concoctions in silence. The heat and exhaustion of the day had burned away all their desire for communication.

Getting the Burro running again had taken nearly two hours. Two long, hard hours working in the blazing afternoon heat and constant wind. Two hours trying to coax a stubborn robot to accept lower sensitivity thresholds for its sensor array and an improvised —though, Marcos had to admit, genius—filtration system. They'd walked for only a couple of hours after getting it running, but by sunset, they'd all been ready to call it quits for the day. So they sat around the lantern, eating soggy instant meals and feeling the aches in their muscles slowly ebb into the silent darkness around them.

"You should have heard it," Helene whispered, continuing a conversation she'd started several minutes earlier that had already died away twice only to be reborn each time a few minutes later. "The sound it made was so odd, almost machinelike."

"I'm telling you," Marcos said, leaning forward, feeling grateful for any distraction. "It was an alien."

Stacee snorted incredulously.

"You don't believe in aliens?" Marcos asked, appreciating the way the lantern made her face glow.

"You mean Roswell, Area 51, and all that? No, I don't."

"Okay, maybe some of those were fake, but there are tons of unexplained incidents all over the world. Hell, even out here." He gestured toward the dark shadows of nearby cliffs. "Explain that."

"Okay, wiseass," Stacee retorted. "Name one legitimate sighting that didn't involve a drunk hick out in a cornfield."

"The Phoenix Lights," Marcos said excitedly, leaping at a chance to discuss one of his favorite topics.

Stacee looked confused.

"Flares," Pato muttered, not bothering to look up from his tablet, where he was scanning the Burro's code for bugs.

"Flares?"

"The Phoenix Lights were flares." Pato glanced up. His eyes met Stacee's over the lantern, and his cheeks flushed. He returned to his tablet.

"Flares that burn long enough to cross an entire city?" Marcos shot back at his friend as a streak of jealousy flashed through him. *I was the one to invite Stacee, for Christ's sake.* "You forget, I saw them."

"You were, like, seven," Pato countered without looking up.

Marcos growled and ground his teeth.

"What about Travis Walton?" Vivek asked.

In unison, everyone turned to stare at the guide, who had scooted to the edge of his seat and was leaning forward with interest.

"Travis Walton?" Stacee asked.

"He was taken in front of his friends," Vivek explained, "by Snowflake. They made a movie about it. *Fire in the Sky.*"

The movie, Marcos understood, had been less than accurate, but he let it pass. If the old dude wanted to help him win the argument, so much the better. "Right. There's tons of unexplained things. What about the Williams Event?"

Helene's horrified gasp turned Marcos's insides to ice. He froze, the knowledge and meaning of what he'd said slamming into him. Without looking at her, he knew that she was glaring into his soul with a mix of shock and revulsion.

The stroganoff turned in his stomach. He tasted bile. "Helene..." he tried, turning toward her but wilting before her gaze, "I... I'm sorry... I..."

Without a word, Helene stood and retreated into the night, her thin frame disappearing into the moonless darkness. The others watched her go in terrible silence.

"What's stuck up her butt?" Stacee asked.

"Um... Stacee..." Pato started, but his voice trailed off.

"What?" she asked. "What's going on?"

No one replied.

Marcos glanced up at Sven. The project leader was sitting rigid, his face white and drawn. His hands clenched and unclenched rhythmically as he stared vacantly into the night, pointedly not looking toward his wife.

"I'm sorry, Sven," Marcos whispered, guilt twisting his insides. "I didn't mean... I didn't think..."

Sven met his eyes, causing Marcos to shudder. He looked toward the ground, his cheeks burning. The knot in his throat made it hard to breathe.

"What is going on?" Stacee demanded.

"Sven and Helene lost their son," Pato whispered.

Stacee drew a sharp breath. She glanced at Sven then into the darkness after Helene. "How?"

"It was an accident," Sven said, his voice strained, "almost a year ago, now. Kyle was twenty-four. He and Emily..." The words caught in his throat, and he looked at the ground, shaking his head.

"Emily?" Stacee asked.

"Kyle's girlfriend," Pato explained.

"His fiancée," Marcos corrected, his throat dry and choked.

Stacee mouthed, "Oh."

They sat in silence, lost in the somber revelation. Marcos thought back to the dozens of times Kyle and Emily had visited the lab. Kyle had been on his way to becoming a terrific engineer—some of the Burro's features had even started as his ideas—and Emily had been both beautiful and amazing. The day the team had learned about the accident had been hard on all of them. Sven had never fully recovered.

"Emily loved space," the project leader whispered, pulling all eyes toward him. He was looking at the night sky with the most sorrowful expression Marcos had ever seen. "She wanted to be an astronomer. Kyle was going to be an engineer. One day, they were going to travel the stars."

"Have you ever heard of the Williams Event?" Pato asked.

Stacee shrugged noncommittally.

"You mean the alien encounter near Flagstaff?" Vivek asked.

Everyone turned to stare at the guide again, but the only response was Pato's nod.

"Emily was obsessed with it," Pato explained. "She did all this research and everything. Anyway, Williams had a big star-gazing event on the fifth anniversary. Kyle and Emily went, and on the way back..." He shook his head, unable to continue.

"Kyle proposed while they were there," Sven whispered, still staring at the stars. "He'd been planning it for weeks. I'd helped him get the ring. They were coming home that morning." He lowered his eyes and stared into the lantern. "They were going to take Helene and I out for breakfast and tell us the good news. And then..." A shudder cut off his words, and he lowered his eyes to the ground.

"It wasn't anyone's fault," Pato continued. "Kyle just lost control. They both died instantly."

Stacee sighed and leaned forward, resting a comforting hand on Sven's arm.

"It's been hard," Sven whispered. "And Helene... I thought... I hoped..." The words failed him, and he dropped his head once again.

The five of them sat in silence for a long time, feeling Helene's absence as the darkness closed in around them.

Guilt settled in Marcos's chest. Sometimes, he really hated being the way he was.

TWELVE

PATO STRETCHED AS HE WATCHED MARCOS PACE BACK AND forth at the edge of the lantern light, giving Ryan the nightly report by satellite phone. As usual, they were two hours late reporting in.

"No, we didn't disable the seismic sensor," Marcos explained. "We just reduced the movement sensitivity. The seismic readings are all over the board and annoying, but they aren't hurting anything."

Pato turned back to his tablet, looking at the screen without really seeing it. Almost an hour had passed since the awkward conversation prompted by Marcos's idiotic comment about the Williams Event. Helene still hadn't returned. The others had gone to bed thirty minutes ago, leaving Marcos and Pato behind.

Usually, the two friends would have joked and laughed until Sven told them to shut up, but after the earlier scene, Pato didn't really want to speak to his friend.

And then there was Stacee. A smile twitched at the corners of Pato's mouth as the image of her face flashed through his mind. He turned and looked toward the sleeping bags laid out a handful of yards away. It was impossible to make her out in the shadows, but a thrill went through him just knowing she was there. She was the most amazing girl he'd ever met—funny, gorgeous, and one hell of a mechanic.

Of course, he didn't stand a chance with her, and there was the problem of Marcos, but he couldn't help dreaming.

"Yeah," Marcos said to Ryan, cutting into Pato's thoughts, "we're doing the canyon test tomorrow. It's going to be epic."

At the mention of the canyon, Pato frowned. It was the most critical test of the whole trip. It was also the most dangerous. With the Burro acting up, he thought that maybe they should skip it. Unfortunately, he was certain Marcos would never agree to that.

Looking back at his tablet, Pato scanned the curly braces, cryptic variable names, and logical operators. There was a bug in there somewhere. He just couldn't find it.

He heard Marcos end the conversation. A few seconds later he flopped down onto the rock next to him, stowing the satellite phone in his pocket. "Ryan's all set. We'll call again after the test tomorrow."

Pato nodded without looking up.

"Don't everyone thank me at once," Marcos muttered, not even bothering to use his Han Solo voice.

Pato ignored him, focusing on the code. His friend leaned back and hummed a few bars from a Javen song. And then Helene was standing in front of them.

Pato jerked back in surprise as her shadow fell across him. He peered up at her, still able to make out her disapproving frown in the darkness. Beside him, Marcos stiffened. Pato thought his friend might even be trembling.

No one spoke for a full thirty seconds. Helene's eyes burned with so much heat they were almost visible in the darkness.

Marcos cleared his throat. "Helene... I... I'm sorry... I..."

She fixed an even more intense glare on him. He wilted.

"Do you need something?" Pato tried.

Without speaking, Helene reached into her pocket and pulled out a phone. She held it out to them.

For a moment, Pato thought she wanted them to charge her phone again, a service they'd been providing as part of an arrangement Marcos had made with her before the trip, in spite of the fact that they hadn't seen a signal for days. But then he remembered her phone was already attached to the Burro. She was holding a different one. Furrowing his brow, he peered down at the phone in her hand, making out a shattered glass face.

"Where did you find that?" Marcos asked.

"In the canyon," Helene said, her words clipped and angry. "Look." She turned it over and raised it to the light, revealing a dark handprint across the back.

"Is that mud?" Pato asked, somehow knowing it was something much worse. A chill went through him.

"Do you think you could get it working?" Helene asked.

Pato exchanged a dubious look with Marcos.

"I don't know," he said, reaching for the phone and looking it over. Besides the shattered glass, the ports were caked with dirt and grime. The likelihood of it accepting a charge was—

"We can try," Marcos said, jumping to his feet with uncharacteristic enthusiasm. Anything, Pato supposed, to get back into Helene's good graces.

With a shrug, he stood, and together, the three of them walked to the Burro a few yards away. Pato blew into the phone's ports, clearing as much dirt as possible, and Marcos swapped it for Helene's on the charging cable. They waited, staring at each other in awkward silence.

After a full minute, Pato thumbed the power button. Nothing.

"Give it a few more minutes," Marcos suggested hopefully.

Pato shrugged and returned to waiting.

The seconds ticked by. Marcos fidgeted. Helene glared. Pato stared at the stars, wishing he were somewhere else.

At last, he tried the power again. Still nothing. "I think it's too damaged."

The phone lit up with a *bing*. It was so unexpected that Pato let out a yelp and almost dropped the phone.

"No way," Marcos whispered.

They all leaned in, watching the phone go through its boot cycle. Only half of the damaged screen was working, but it still shone with shocking brightness in the gloom. At last, they were looking down at the image of a good-looking, dark-haired woman standing next to someone cut off by the broken side of the screen.

Pato swiped across the glass, revealing a series of icons.

"Try contacts," Helene suggested.

The contacts app wasn't readily visible. Pato tried swiping right and left. No luck.

"Check the camera." Marcos pointed.

Pato tapped the app, and they were looking at a half-complete, cracked image of themselves.

"Selfie mode," Marcos observed.

"What was their last picture?" Helene asked.

Pato tapped the icon at the bottom, and they looked down on a black screen with a gray play button in the center. Suddenly nervous, he pressed the button.

The video that played had been shot at night, but Pato could still make out half of a man's bruised and bloodied face.

"What in the world?" Marcos whispered, perfectly expressing Pato's thoughts and probably Helene's as well.

"My name is... is Paul Lambert," the man whispered, his voice tense and quavering. "My wife... Liz... and I were part of a group.

We... were attacked. Something... The rest are dead. I... don't know how many survived."

A chill went through Pato, and he tightened his grip on the phone. He glanced at the darkness around them, suddenly feeling the strange and oppressive silence as if it were closing in on them. Not for the first time, he wondered where all the wildlife had gone. He shuddered.

"I won't survive," the man continued. "If you see this message, get out of here. It isn't safe."

He paused. The image shook and steadied again.

"Liz," the man whispered, "I love you. You have always been the best part of my life. Don't blame yourself. It's not your... not your..." His voice drifted, and the image shook again. A confused, pixelated flash of shadows crossed the screen then resolved into a sliver of night sky bisecting the darkness.

"That's the top of the canyon where I found it," Helene whispered, causing another chill to run down Pato's spine.

The man on the video was moaning. The sound was cut off by a chattering of insect-like clicks.

Helene inhaled sharply, and Pato's throat went dry as he remembered what she had told them about the strange creature she'd seen earlier. He'd only been half listening, but hearing the sound brought it all back.

On the phone, the clicking grew louder. The man whispered something lost in the chatter. A shadow with sharp angles surged forward. The man screamed.

THIRTEEN

Sᴠᴇɴ sᴛᴏᴏᴅ ᴀᴛ ᴛʜᴇ ᴇᴅɢᴇ ᴏꜰ ᴛʜᴇ ᴄᴀɴʏᴏɴ ᴀɴᴅ ᴘᴇᴇʀᴇᴅ ɪɴᴛᴏ the abyss. The group had passed several canyons over the past five days, but this one was larger and deeper than the rest. The far side, over two hundred feet away, was hazy in the desert heat, and the bottom was lost in shadow. A cool draft wafted up from the floor, making him shiver in spite of the heat.

To his right, Marcos, Pato, and Stacee talked excitedly as they prepared the Burro for crossing. Sven's stomach twisted.

When Marcos had first proposed the trip, Sven had been excited. It was going to be the opportunity to do all the crazy things he had talked about with Kyle but never done. But he hadn't really thought the canyon test through. Faced with the reality of it, he wished he'd called the whole thing off.

He turned and looked at Helene. She was apart from the rest, organizing the packs and laying out the harnesses. She worked with the single-minded efficiency and focus that he had once found endearing, but it had become part of the shield she used to keep him and others at bay. Today, that shield seemed even more solid than usual. She barely glanced at the others, and more than once, Sven had caught her looking nervously back the way they had come.

For that matter, Marcos and Pato hadn't been acting like themselves. They'd talked a little too loudly, laughed a little too much, and moved a little too quickly. They'd also looked over their own shoulders a few times, as well. Sven wondered what had gotten into all of them.

"Do you really think this is a good idea?" Vivek asked, stepping up next to him.

Ignoring the twist in his stomach, Sven shrugged. "I don't think we have much choice at this point. It will take too long to go around, and we've lost too much time already."

The guide grunted but didn't say anything.

The two of them stared into the canyon, studying the yellow and red layers of rock that formed the walls. Over the abyss, a raven bobbed up and down, riding the updrafts.

Sven stared at the bird. It was the first animal life he'd seen for at least three days. Even the nights had been devoid of the normal desert sounds. The silence had started to get to him. Seeing the bird should have been reassuring, but it presented too much contrast with the silent, lifeless world around him. He shuddered.

"We're ready," Marcos called excitedly, ushering everyone to join them.

They gathered around the Burro, which stood about ten feet from the canyon's edge. A metal tube about two inches in diameter and three feet long rose from its back, looking for all the world like a World War II grenade launcher. That, Sven thought, wasn't far from the truth.

"Watch this," Marcos said to Stacee as he motioned everyone back a few feet.

Pato tapped at his tablet and looked up expectantly.

Sven swallowed and cleared his throat, his stomach churning.

The Burro began to beep out a steady, rhythmic countdown. *Beep. Beep. Beep. Beep.*

A motor whined to life. *Beep. Beep. Beep.*

The readouts on the Burro's head scrolled through dozens of lines of diagnostics and calculations. *Beep. Beep.*

The whine reached fever pitch. *Beep.*

With a loud crack, a three-foot-long metal spike shot out of the tube and arced over the canyon, a thin cable trailing behind it. A moment later, it slammed into the other side with a resounding *thunk.*

Stacee gasped.

Before anyone could react further, the robot was moving, reeling in the slack in the cable as the tube rotated, aiming at the stone ground at the Burro's feet. Another crack split the morning, and a new metal spike protruded from the rock. Two more cracks. Two more spikes embedded in the solid rock.

Using its middle legs as arms, the Burro connected the cables from the three spikes to the first, securing it so that the line hung suspended almost two feet over the ground. Its work complete, the robot stepped back and fell silent.

"Look at this," Marcos said, rushing to the edge of the canyon and pointing down.

They followed, with Stacee rushing ahead of the rest.

Sven's toes curled as he neared the edge. He swallowed and forced himself to look down the canyon wall to the ledge about five feet below them.

"We jump off that," Marcos said, sounding far too excited at the idea of leaping out over nothing.

Stacee giggled again, matching his excitement.

"I said this would be epic." Marcos told her, grinning wider than Sven had ever seen.

"You're joking, right?" Helene protested, her voice sharp and angry. She pointed at the thin cable stretched over the canyon. "We're trusting our lives to that?"

"It's safe," Marcos replied. "Here, I'll show you." He reached for the cable.

"No one is going near that cable until it is fully secured," Vivek snapped.

Marcos stepped away, raising his arms in surrender. He turned toward Pato and nodded.

The software engineer tapped furiously on his tablet, and the Burro whirred to life, bustling toward them. They moved out of its way as it reached the edge. It hesitated, the front legs testing the empty space over the canyon. Satisfied, the Burro bent over and scaled the sheer rock to the ledge below. It positioned itself directly under the cable, and its middle legs reached up, gripping the thin line with its clawed feet. The right foreleg joined them, followed by the left rear leg, and then the left front. Seconds later, the last leg left the ground, and the robot dangled from the metal wire. The line creaked and bobbed with the weight, but it did not give. Moving like a spider on a web, the Burro started across the canyon.

Sven held his breath as he watched, a thrill going through him even as his fingers and toes curled from watching the robot bob over the impossible height. His stomach churned even more.

It took fifteen nerve-wracking minutes for the Burro to reach the other side. When it finally touched down on the opposite ledge, everyone cheered.

"See. It's safe," Marcos sniped at Vivek, who didn't reply.

While the Burro set about securing additional anchors to the other side, the group turned to the harnesses Helene had laid out, pulling them on and fastening them in place.

"Who goes first?" Stacee asked, rocking on her heels with excitement.

"Pato," Marcos said, punching his friend in the arm.

"Hey!" Pato rubbed the point of impact. "I'm going to need that."

Marcos laughed.

"Pato has to go first in case the Burro or the line needs any tweaking," Sven said, reassuring Stacee, who looked ready to pout. "After him, we'll all go, except Vivek. He will send the supplies over and then cross himself."

Stacee considered that and nodded.

"Okay," she said, as if they needed her permission.

Pato and Marcos were already on the ledge beneath them, the latter helping his friend connect his harness and backup line to the metal brake box resting on the cable. Pato's face was tight and nervous, but a glance at Stacee seemed to firm his resolve.

"Just make sure to brake before hitting the wall," Marcos said, handing him the line attached to the box. "Otherwise, squish, just like grape."

Pato glared.

Marcos kissed the air at him.

Stealing another glance at Stacee, who grinned at him and waved, Pato drew a deep breath. He hesitated then launched himself over the canyon. His yell echoed through the abyss as he shot away from the ledge.

Everyone cheered.

Sven's stomach churned.

FOURTEEN

Stacee held her breath the full two minutes it took Pato to cross the canyon. When he reached the other side and waved back, she cheered.

For weeks, Marcos had followed her around the gym where they'd met, dangling the desert trip before her, hoping to get her interest. At first, she had ignored him. When he didn't take the hint, she'd started nodding and saying "uh-huh," "wow," and "no way" at random intervals to seem like she was paying attention. But slowly, as he'd prattled on and on about his super-secret project and the über-awesome trip they had planned, she began to listen.

She didn't relish the idea of being out in the desert with these nerds and the Ice Queen, but the idea of working on a machine like the Burro excited her, especially given how things had developed at work. In fact, the whole trip sounded amazing, and the fact that her overbearing mother disapproved was just icing on the cake. An adjustment of her sports bra and a sultry "wow, I'd love to go on a trip like that," and the invite was hers.

The one thing she could never get Marcos to spill was the details to the test he called "most epic." This was it—and he was right.

"How was it?" Sven asked Pato through the radio.

"Awesome!" his voice crackled back. "That was amazing."

Stacee giggled in spite of herself.

The motorized brake box came back along the cable, and Marcos grabbed it. Stacee leaned forward to call dibs.

"I'm next," Helene said, cutting her off and dropping to the ledge next to Marcos before anyone could contradict her.

Marcos glanced up at Sven, who shrugged. With a sigh, Marcos snapped Helene's harness to the box and cable.

Moments later, Sven's wife leapt from the ledge and flew across the canyon. She didn't yell, scream, or whoop. She just rode, looking stiff and awkward as she clung to her shoulder straps and the brake line. No one cheered when she reached the other side.

An interminable ten minutes later, the brake returned. Stacee squealed and climbed down to the ledge, her heart pounding.

Marcos strapped her in. To her relief and surprise, he was all business. His hands didn't even brush her on accident.

"Here's the brake," Marcos said, holding out a thin nylon rope to her. "The box has a timer that will alert you when it's time to use it. When it goes off, pull for all you're worth. If you pull too late—"

"Squish, just like grape," Stacee repeated.

Marcos grinned and nodded. "You'll be fine. Just listen for the alert." He reached out, hesitated, patted her shoulder, and stepped back.

Stacee's heart pounded in her ears as she inched to the edge. Her toes curled as the darkness stretched out beneath her. She swallowed and drew a deep breath, then another. The picture of her mother's disapproving frown flashed into her mind. She grinned.

"Watch this, Mom," she said, and launched herself into space. Wind whipped past her. The brake box sang as she soared across the canyon. A scream bubbled up, and she let it out, yelling with everything she had.

It was the most amazing feeling. Ever. Too soon, the brake buzzed, warning her it was time to stop. With a disappointed frown, she tightened her grip on the line and pulled. Nothing happened.

Stacee pulled again, harder this time. Still nothing. The wall was speeding toward her. Pato was there, waving. He was yelling, but she couldn't make it out over her own scream.

She yanked at the brake again, throwing all her weight into it. For a terrible, breathless moment, nothing changed. The wall still came at her. Pato still yelled incomprehensibly. She still screamed her throat raw. Then something in the brake clicked. Its whistle changed to a shriek. Stacee's whole body jerked with sudden deceleration. Her head snapped forward, sending pain shooting across her neck.

Her hands slipped on the brake line. She tightened her grip, pulling with all her might. The wall was still coming. It was too fast. She was going to hit it.

She closed her eyes, feeling the tears streaking her dust-covered face. Hands grabbed her around the waist, clinging to her and dragging her down. She slowed and jerked to a sudden stop.

Panting, still clutching the brake line, Stacee opened her eyes. The wall was six inches from her nose.

She whimpered and closed her eyes again, whispering, "Squish, just like grape."

Eventually, she opened her eyes again and looked down. Pato was still there, clinging to her waist and staring up at her. His eyes were wide and filled with panic. Behind him, she could see gouges in the dirt where she had dragged him across the ledge, which was thankfully wider than the one on the other side.

"You okay?" he asked after a moment, his words coming out between gasps.

"I... I think so," Stacee managed, feeling her racing heart slow to only five times its normal speed. "You?"

He nodded but continued holding onto her as if she had saved him and not the other way around. The radio crackled with Sven's voice, urgently asking to know what happened. They both ignored him.

"Um, Pato..." she said at last, glancing down at his arms.

Realization dawned across his face, and he leapt back, scrambling away. "Sorry! I didn't mean... I... I'm sorry."

"It's okay."

His adorable blush was back.

"Um... can you help me get out of this thing?" Her hands were shaking too much to remove her harness herself.

"Huh? Oh! Right."

He rushed forward and reached up, unhooking her harness and backup line. The tension around her thighs and waist went slack as the ground settled beneath her feet.

"What happened?" he asked as he undid the last buckle. His hands were shaking almost as much as hers.

"I'm not sure. The brake didn't work."

He looked up at the brake box, muttering something incoherent, as she wriggled free of the harness. "I'll let the others know you're okay and send back the brake. Marcos'll check it before anyone else comes over."

Stacee nodded, and Pato turned to walk away. On an impulse, she grabbed his hand. He jumped with surprise and spun back to her. Without thinking, without analysis or debate or second-guesses, she leapt forward, throwing her arms around him, and kissed him, hard.

Pato went stiff, his arms locking to his sides and his breath catching in his throat. Stacee focused all her energy and gratitude into the kiss. Tears sprang from her eyes. She tasted salt as they trickled down her cheeks to their joined lips.

"Thank you," she said, pulling away and peering into his eyes. The brown irises were so light, they were almost green. "Just, thank you."

"No... problem..." Pato said, breathless. His whole face looked like it was on fire.

Stacee smiled and brushed the tears from her cheeks, suddenly embarrassed. She nodded to him.

He nodded back.

Noting how the color of his eyes contrasted perfectly with the red in his cheeks, Stacee spun and headed up the cliff to find Helene and the Burro. As she climbed, she could feel Pato behind her, watching.

She didn't think he looked at her ass at all.

FIFTEEN

STACEE REACHED THE TOP OF THE CLIFF, ADRENALINE STILL racing through her. The Burro was parked next to a large boulder a few yards from the canyon rim, but Helene was nowhere in sight.

"Figures," Stacee muttered. She looked toward the others on the other side of the canyon, but it was too far to see anything, and she was too wired to wait. She spun around and went looking for Helene.

Nearby, the ground sloped away into a small valley. Stacee found Helene at the bottom, hunched over something, cradling it in her hands. Not caring about the woman's privacy, Stacee marched toward her.

"What are you doing?" she asked as she got close.

Helene leapt to her feet and spun around in surprise. She pocketed whatever she'd been holding before Stacee could get a good look. *Was it a phone?*

"Nothing," Helene said, her voice panicked, as if she were a child who'd been caught stealing a cookie.

Stacee decided to let it slide. There was too much on her mind.

"You should have seen it," she blurted, the words rushing out in a jumble. "Pato... He grabbed me and... and the wall. And... and..." She threw up her hands as words for what happened failed her.

Helene narrowed her eyes.

"Pato grabbed you?" She asked.

"Yes," Stacee said. Then, realizing how it sounded, she back-tracked. "No! Not like that. I was coming in too fast. He—"

A sudden gust of wind cut her off. Dust flew into her eyes, and Helene's large hat was jerked from her head, catching on the cord around her neck. Both women raised their hands, shielding their faces. Behind them, the canyon moaned. A moment later, the wind died as quickly as it had begun, returning to a light breeze.

Stacee and Helene lowered their hands and stared at each other. Before either could comment, a sharp chattering of insect-like clicks came from the top of a ridge twenty yards away. They spun toward it.

Helene's face went white, and the muscles in her neck tensed. She looked like she was ready to bolt at the slightest movement.

"What is it?" Stacee asked.

Helene didn't answer.

A nervous lump rose in Stacee's throat. She took an instinctive step back.

The sound came again.

Helene flinched.

As they stared at the ridge, the wind stirred again, the whistle over the canyon rising to a howl. The women raised their hands and closed their eyes against the buffeting sand. From beyond the ridge came an explosion of clicking chatter. The sound was deafening.

Stacee put her hands over her ears to ward it off and shouted to Helene, "What is it?"

The older woman shook her head.

A piercing wail joined the cacophony: the Burro's seismic alarm.

Stacee's blood turned to ice. Before she could turn back toward the canyon, the ground bucked, tossing her and Helene into the air. They crashed back to the earth, falling to their knees and grunting in shock as they landed on the hard ground. Stacee's hands and knees scraped against the rocky terrain. Pain shot through her.

The ground lurched again, flattening her and Helene to the earth. Stacee's head hit the rocky soil with a crack. Stars swirled across her vision. She tried to push herself up, but the world swam around her. Her arms refused to move. It was hard to breathe.

Helene was yelling something, but it was lost in the wind, the constant clicking chatter, and the continued wail of the alarm. Stacee squeezed her eyes shut, feeling the world swim around her. She sensed the older woman draw close and felt her arms wrap around her, holding her tight.

Again, the wind ceased as quickly as it had begun. The clicking died with it, and the world went still. Helene and Stacee lay in the dust for several heartbeats. Stacee's head throbbed. Helene still held on to her. The pressure of the older woman's arms was suffocating in the deafening quiet.

Stacee squirmed, but Helene tightened her grip.

"Hold still," the older woman hissed. "You hit your head and might have a—"

A new sound cut her off. Someone was screaming.

"That's Sven," Helene whispered, her voice filled with unmistakable terror.

Moving faster than Stacee thought possible, the older woman

sprang to her feet and raced toward the canyon. Sven was still screaming.

———

HELENE REACHED THE CANYON, AND HER EYES FOUND THE cable. Where it had been taut, it now hung slack. Her husband dangled over the center of the canyon, his body twisted into a painful-looking pose, the harness cutting into him. He had gone quiet, his scream dying in the canyon below.

Sven!

Frantic, Helene scrambled down to the ledge below. "Sven!" she yelled, rushing to the canyon's edge.

He didn't respond.

She spun around. The two engineers were there, straining at the cable. Their faces were pinched in concentration. Their muscles and veins bulged from effort.

"The primary and secondary anchors broke," Pato grunted, answering her unasked question. "The last anchor is barely holding."

"Sven?"

They didn't answer.

"Sven?" she demanded again, her voice rising.

Still no answer.

Her throat constricted as she turned back to the canyon. Sven still wasn't moving. "Sven!"

Nothing.

She fell to her knees, too weak to stand. Tears blurred her vision. "Sven!"

Darkness closed in on her, oppressive, suffocating. She gasped for breath. Her tears dripped onto the red dirt.

Just like Kyle.

Behind her, Stacee joined the others. Their hurried conversation blurred around her.

"The cable?"

"Not secure."

"The Burro?"

"Inoperative."

"Shit."

"Tools?"

"Back compartment."

"Hold on."

Someone scrambled back up the cliff. Helene didn't turn to look; she just stared at her husband's lifeless body.

He moved. It was just a twitch of a hand, but it was enough.

"He's alive," Helene shouted, leaping to her feet. She called to him, her voice echoing through the canyon.

His hand twitched again.

"We have to help him," she yelled, spinning back to the others.

"We're trying," Marcos growled back.

"Stacee, where are those tools?" Pato shouted.

Helene spun back to the canyon. A breeze had caught the cable, and it swayed, creaking and groaning. The engineers grunted. Helene screamed, the panic bubbling out of her.

I can't lose him. I won't. She grabbed the cable. It hummed in her hand but felt stronger than she'd expected.

Behind her, Marcos and Pato groaned, but beyond them, one anchor still held.

Helene's mouth went dry and her head pounded as she looked at the discarded harnesses at her feet. A part of her screamed in warning. She ignored it and reached for a harness.

Marcos and Pato didn't notice as she pulled it on and stepped to the cliff's edge. They only saw what she was doing when she reached up and snapped the harness to the cable.

"What are you doing?" Marcos shouted.

"It won't hold," Pato yelled.

One of them lunged for her, but the cable groaned, and he leapt back into place.

"You're going to kill him," one of them shouted.

"Sven needs me," Helene whispered, gripping the line with her hands and kicking up with both legs, wrapping them around the cable.

She bobbed and swayed. The ground brushed her back. She could feel Marcos and Pato throwing even more strength and panic into their efforts. One of them yelled for Stacee.

The world faded away. There was nothing but her, the cable, and Sven.

"It will hold," she whispered and began to move hand over hand along the cable, pulling herself closer to her husband.

SIXTEEN

THE WORLD FELL AWAY UNDER HELENE. COOL AIR ROSE from the canyon depths, tickling the back of her neck and sending chills down her spine. She kept moving, matching her rhythmic hand movements with her heartbeat. *Right. Left. Right.*

Sweat dripped down her face. Her muscles trembled, and her legs cramped. The cable bobbed and swayed. She kept moving forward.

She lost track of time. *Have I been on the cable one minute? Ten? An hour?* She wanted to crane her head back toward Sven to check how close she had gotten, but she was terrified of what she might see. Instead, she focused on her hands. She would get there soon enough.

The cable dropped. Helene screamed as she plummeted toward the canyon floor. The emptiness reached up for her.

She jerked to a sudden stop, pain shooting through her legs, the cable cutting into them. Her gloved fingers slipped, and she tumbled back, dangling head first over the void.

She squeezed her eyes shut, feeling the world bob and sway around her. Her heart pounded, and her fingers trembled.

"You can do this," she told herself. "You. Can. Do. This."

She opened her eyes and saw Sven hanging just a few yards away. She was so close. Drawing all her strength, she grabbed for the line. She missed on the first try but caught it on the second. Barely pausing to breathe, she continued moving.

Right. Left. Right. Left.

A moment later, she arrived at her husband.

"Sven?" she called to him, reaching over her head and gripping his harness. He moaned. The soft, pitiful sound both destroyed her and filled her with hope.

He's still alive!

Steadying herself, she glanced up at him. She saw his scraped and dented helmet, his twisted arm and bloodstained shirt. Her chest constricted.

"Sven?" she asked again, feeling panic surge within her.

He moaned again, more loudly.

"Sven!" She shook him as she would have shaken Kyle when he was late for school. "Wake up. We have to get moving."

His eyes fluttered open. "Helene? Wha... what are you doing?"

A laugh burst from her in a rush. She wanted to cheer, but the look of pain on his face reminded her where they were. "Can you move?"

"I don't... I don't know. It hurts."

"What hurts?"

"Everything."

Before she could react, the cable plunged again. Helene screamed as her body became weightless for the full second of free fall. The plunge stopped just as abruptly as the first, slamming her into the harness.

Sven grunted, his head lolling forward.

"Sven?" she asked, desperate to hear his voice. "Sven?"

"H... Here..." he croaked.

"I have to turn around. Hang on."

"Nothing... better... to do." He coughed. It sounded wet and sticky.

She let go of him and grabbed the cable, trying not to see the blood that stained her glove. Sven's blood. Tightening her grip, she unwrapped her legs and let them drop. The cable shook and rocked, but her harness held. She twisted around and found herself staring at her husband. Her throat and chest constricted at the sight.

Sven hung in a tangle of harness and wire. A deep cut ran across his face. Blood streamed down his cheek and dripped into the darkness below. His right eye was swollen shut, a deep bruise already forming around it. His left arm was caught in the harness and snapped back into an impossible angle. Blood dripped from another gash down his right leg. His shoe was missing.

"Hello," he gasped, somehow managing a smile. His teeth were stained red.

Something stirred in Helene, something that hadn't stirred in longer than she could remember. In that moment, they were meeting again for the first time. She was the quiet pharmacy student, and he was the charming information management major. For one second, everything was perfect again. They were together. That was enough.

Helene reached for her husband, running gloved fingers across his cheek, feeling the face she loved under the five-day beard. His deep, compassionate hazel eyes met hers. He smiled again.

But then, with a shudder of cable and a gust of the wind, the world rushed back on them, carrying with it the pain, despair, and anger of the last year. Helene gasped, yanking her hand back as if it had been burned.

She chanced a look toward the ledge. Stacee stood there, waving her arms for them to hurry.

"We have to get out of here," she said, turning back to her husband. Without waiting for a response, she grabbed his shirt and pulled. He didn't move.

Helene looked up at the brake box. Straps from his harness were wrapped around it and the cable, jamming the wheels and preventing motion in any direction. To move him, she would have to cut him free and rely on his backup to hold him. It was risky but theoretically safe. The only problem was that the backup line was on the other side of the brake.

"I have to move your backup line," she said, meeting Sven's eyes.

He trembled but nodded.

She pulled herself forward, closing all the space between them. The touch of his skin and the warmth of his body almost overwhelmed her. Beneath the coppery scent of blood, his smell was awash with decades of memories and longings. Pushing them aside, she grabbed his shoulder. He gasped, and Helene wanted to flinch back, but she held on. If he was going to have any chance of survival, it had to be done.

Using her husband as leverage, she pushed herself up and reached over him for the backup line. He screamed as her weight bore down on him, tightening the harness about his body, cutting into his flesh.

Tears welled in her eyes, but she somehow kept her focus. The line danced away from her once then twice. She snagged it on the third try. A second later, it was free of the cable.

She pushed off her husband. He screamed again, but there was less agony in it. Her heart thundering in her chest and blood rushing through her ears, Helene reattached the backup line to the cable on the near side of the brake.

"That... wasn't... so bad," Sven gasped, failing at a smile.

She met his eyes, her own welling with tears. She wiped angrily at them. She didn't have time to break down.

"I'm sorry," she said, the words spilling out of her, filled with meaning beyond that moment.

Sven looked into her face and nodded. "Me too."

"I can't... I can't..." she stuttered, knowing the words but unable to say them. "Not you too."

He closed his eyes.

"I'm here," he whispered, his voice weak and strained but close, present, and alive. Trembling, he reached out his free hand toward hers. Their fingers met in the space between them, an electric surge traveling down Helene's arm and into her heart.

"I'm here," Sven repeated.

Unspoken words hung between them. Words of sorrow. Words of forgiveness. Words of regret. Words of love. Helene wanted to say them, was desperate to say them, but she couldn't. Not now. Perhaps never. But there, suspended over the void, the unspoken words filled the silence, and she knew that Sven understood.

The cable shook again, and the moment was gone.

SEVENTEEN

Helene refocused on the nylon straps wrapped around her husband. They were so tight, there was no way she would be able to untangle them, especially dangling over the canyon on an uncertain cable.

"I'm going to cut your primary line," she told him, inwardly shuddering at the thought.

Their eyes met again. His were filled with terror, but he nodded.

Moving as quickly as she dared, Helene reached for the small knife in the pocket of her shorts, nestled next to her phone. Her fingers fumbled for the knife, but she couldn't grasp it with her glove on.

Grunting with frustration, she yanked off the glove with her teeth. It tumbled away into the darkness below. She grasped the knife and pulled it free.

The knife was small and old. It had been her father-in-law's idea of a wedding gift. She'd laughed about it at the time, but over the years, it had been more useful than she could have imagined.

In this moment, it was the most precious things she owned. Using her thumb, she managed to get the blade open. It was dull but still flashed in the sunlight.

She glanced at Sven. His eyes were closed, and his face was ashen behind the drying blood that streaked his cheeks.

"Stay with me," she whispered.

"Still... here," he gasped.

Helene drew a deep breath, set her jaw, and sawed at the thick nylon strap binding her husband to the brake. The nylon slowly gave way to the dull blade. The cable twanged and groaned with each snapped fiber.

Behind her, Helene could hear Stacee yelling for them to hurry. She cut faster. Sven's line broke in a sudden jerk that sent him plummeting several inches into the canyon before his backup line caught him with a snap. Helene jerked back with a shout of surprise. The knife tumbled from her fingers, flashing in the sunlight as it fell into the void.

Sven groaned.

"Sven!" Helene shouted at him. "Sven!"

He groaned again but did not open his eyes.

No!

She stole a glance toward the ledge behind her. Vaguely, she could make out Stacee's shape, waving for her to hurry.

Turning back to Sven, Helene grabbed his backup line and, summoning all her strength, yanked him forward. He moved a few inches. She backed herself along the line and pulled again. A few more inches. Soon she had hit a rhythm.

Him. Me. Him. Me. The cadence in her head matched her sharp breaths as they inched back toward the ledge.

Helene's arms ached, and her hands trembled. The cable bit into the fingers of her ungloved hand. Soon they were sticky with blood. She ignored the pain and kept going.

They were almost halfway there when she felt a breeze stir her hair and heard the wind whistle through the canyon. Without knowing why, she paused and listened.

The whistle grew slowly into a moan, rising toward a howl. A memory stirred at the edge of her exhaustion, tugging at her. She furrowed her brow, trying to concentrate.

Another voice—Stacee's or her own, she wasn't sure which— urged her to hurry, but the memory whispered of new danger, new terrors.

Wind... It has something to do with the wind.

She and Sven were swaying back and forth on the cable, the howl around them tugging them this way and that. It tore at the hat still tied around Helene's head as she tried to concentrate.

What was it about the wind?

A new sound blasted into the air, wailing over the howl around them. Helene's blood turned to ice as she recognized the Burro's seismic alarm. "Oh God."

Frantic, she began pulling Sven again. She could hear Marcos, Pato, and Stacee yelling, urging her to move faster.

The wind rose around her, pushing against her efforts. Deep bass notes sounded in the canyon below as arpeggios trilled above. She worked faster and faster.

Him. Me. Him. Me.

The ledge inched closer. It was thirty feet away. Twenty. Fifteen.

The wind hammered into them. The cable creaked and groaned as they rocked back and forth. The others on the ledge screamed louder. Helene pushed as hard as she could.

Ten feet.

With a mighty pull, she yanked herself forward, dragging Sven behind her.

Seven.

They were going to make it!

Suddenly, the canyon wall seemed to buckle, cracking and shaking as a tremor struck it. Helene's eyes widened as she watched waves ripple up through the sheer rock, aiming straight for the ledge.

The cable jerked violently, tossing Helene and Sven toward the sky. The wind rushed past them with a roar. The canyon's maw opened wide to swallow them, the darkness grasping for them.

They came down with a painful snap that knocked the breath from Helene, but somehow, the cable and their harnesses held. From the corner of her eye, she saw Stacee race to the edge of the cliff, holding out her hands to catch them. Helene reached for her, but the girl was too far away.

The cable jerked through Helene's hands, slicing through her gloves and into her fingers. Blood dripped down her arms as she tried again to reach Stacee.

Just a few more inches.

The tips of their fingers met.

Just a bit more.

With a sudden lunge, their hands closed around each other.

"I got you," Stacee yelled over the wind and the alarm, pulling Helene onto the ledge.

The girl unsnapped Helene's harness from the cable. They stumbled into each other and fell to the earth, landing hard on the rocky ledge.

In the tumble, Helene lost her grip on Sven's harness and screamed, but Stacee was there, lying on the ledge, grabbing for it. Helene joined her, grasping Sven's harness and pulling him toward them.

The ground bucked again, throwing the three of them into the air. Helene slammed back down on the unforgiving rock. Stacee landed on top of her, knocking the wind from her and causing the world to flash red. Stacee screamed as Helene tried to catch her breath. The world around them convulsed.

Helene looked toward Sven. His harness had been torn from both their fingers. The shockwaves rippled down the cable, tossing him like a rag doll. He struck the line again and again. It cut into him, creating new gashes that splattered blood onto the rocks.

The tremor ended, and Sven came to a violent stop, hanging over the canyon five feet from the ledge. The cable groaned, and his harness creaked.

On intuition, she looked up at his backup line. It was badly damaged from the onslaught. More than one gash was fraying. It creaked as more nylon fibers broke.

Shoving Stacee away, Helene lunged for her husband. Her fingers closed around his harness just as his backup line snapped and he plummeted toward the darkness.

Her shoulders popped as they caught his full weight. She screamed as the pain hit her, but somehow, she held on. Sven's weight pulled her forward. She slipped toward the cliff's edge, the sand-covered rock ledge offering no purchase for her scrambling feet.

Then Stacee was there, her arms wrapped tight around Helene's ankles, her feet planted, trying to hold her back. It wasn't enough. Sven's dead weight was too much for both of them.

Helene screamed.

Another gust of wind howled through the canyon like a deep-throated laugh that echoed into Helene's bones. She closed her eyes and tightened her grip on Sven as the ground convulsed yet again.

They were thrown back into the air. Something inside cracked as Helene reconnected with the earth. Pain lanced through her chest and arms.

Behind her, the cable snapped. She felt it whip past overhead, missing her by mere inches before vanishing into the void. Someone screamed. Sven's weight tore at her arms. She yelled as her fingers began to slip.

Then Pato was beside her. He lunged forward, grabbing Sven and hauling him onto the ledge. Her husband landed in a heap as the engineer lost his balance and staggered back. Stacee caught him before he tumbled into the void.

Freed from Sven's weight, the pain and terror of the last several moments crashed into Helene. She lay on the ground next to him, wrapped her shaking arms around him, and pulled him close.

"I can't," she whispered, her voice trembling as the adrenaline left her. "I can't. Not you too."

He didn't respond. He didn't move. But she could still feel his breath on her cheek.

Helene cried.

EIGHTEEN

PATO SAT ON A ROCK AND STARED NUMBLY AT THE GROUND. He was only vaguely aware of the others, of Helene sitting next to the still-unconscious Sven, of Stacee leaning against the broken Burro, and of Marcos pacing back and forth, muttering to himself.

"The whole communications array," Marcos whispered. "How does that even happen?"

Sighing, Pato kneaded his aching shoulder, still feeling the lingering pain of catching Sven and pulling him back onto the ledge, not to mention all the effort and strain of keeping the cable from snapping before Helene could save him.

Four hours had passed since the cable broke. Four hours for the afternoon to turn into dusk. Four hours to bind up their wounds, to get the Burro back on its feet, and to determine that all communications beyond shortwave radio had been destroyed by a boulder that had landed on the robot during the tremors. Four hours to take stock of their nonexistent supplies and lack of water. Four hours for despair to consume them.

Pato glanced at Sven, who was laid out on a large flat rock a handful of yards away. The project leader's body was broken beyond anything Pato had ever seen. Pato wasn't an expert on human anatomy, but it didn't take a doctor to know that Sven wouldn't last long if they didn't get him to help very soon.

Helene sat beside her husband, gripping his hand as if terrified to let him go. She had fought Pato and Marcos when they had pried her away from him so Stacee could patch his wounds from the Burro's first-aid kit. She hadn't left his side since.

"What about the satellite phone?" Stacee asked for the fourth time.

Pato looked at her. She was covered in a combination of dust, grease, and blood. Her eyes were vacant and filled with the same desperation that ached inside him.

"Can't we just call Ryan?" she persisted.

"Sven was carrying the satellite phone." Pato repeated the same words he had said before. "It's at the bottom of the canyon."

She met his eyes without really seeing him past her shock and terror.

Pato sighed. The memory of the kiss still burned in his mind. In spite of the pain and horror of the last few hours, he could still feel her lips on his. He knew it hadn't meant anything to her. She had just been thanking him.

It had meant everything to him.

"We'll be okay," he said, trying to smile. "Vivek is coming. He'll know what to do."

She nodded without really understanding and looked away, staring across the canyon as if she could see the guide coming to rescue them on the other side. Pato frowned, thinking about his broken conversation with Vivek over the shortwave minutes after the ground had stopped shaking. The guide had said to stay where they were. He would find a way across the canyon and be there by dawn with extra supplies. They would figure out their next step once he got there.

Pato looked toward the horizon. The sun had just set, leaving traces of red and purple in the western sky. Sunrise was still a long way off.

"Besides," he said, looking back at Stacee and doing his best to sound hopeful, "Ryan is expecting us to check in. When we don't, he'll come find us."

Marcos snorted but kept pacing. Stacee nodded and looked away, her fingers absently tracing along one of the Burro's dented legs.

It had taken a full hour to dig the robot out from under the boulder but only five minutes to determine that the entire communications system, including the Burro's built-in GPS, had been destroyed with almost surgical precision. Without it or the satellite phone, they couldn't call for help, and no one knew exactly where they were. They were on their own.

Even worse, one of the Burro's forelegs had been pulverized, along with a dozen sensors and the left monitor. They'd swapped the broken leg for a middle one, making the robot mobile again—if not fully steady—but they couldn't do much about the rest of the damage. With any luck, the rescuers would find them before they had to go anywhere.

Marcos stopped pacing and slumped onto a stone shelf as the last of the sunset faded into darkness. He rocked back and forth, still muttering to himself. Pato left him alone. It was how his friend coped with loss or frustration.

The warm breeze picked up around them, whistling through a nearby scrub. Besides Marcos's mumbling, it was the only sound around them. The quiet was eerie. It reminded Pato of horror movies where animals fell silent in the presence of an alpha predator. That led him back to the video on the broken phone.

He and Helene had argued with Marcos about what to do about the video. Pato and Helene had wanted to tell Vivek and get the hell out of there. Marcos had pushed to hold off until after the canyon test.

"The best extraction point is just a mile from the canyon," he'd argued. "We'll be there tomorrow. We'll stick together and watch our back. What's the worst that could happen?"

The argument had been a lousy one, but eventually both he and Helene had given in. Now Pato regretted it.

In the distance, something chattered, filling the night with a series of insect-like clicks that sent a chill of recognition down Pato's spine. He leapt to his feet and peered in the direction of the sound. From the corner of his eye, he saw Marcos stiffen. He was certain his friend also recalled hearing that same sound on the video the night before.

Stacee turned to look with them. "What is it?"

"It was probably nothing," Pato said, swallowing the knot in his throat.

He lowered himself to the rock and reached down to pick up a two-foot section from the Burro's wrecked leg. Its weight felt reassuring in his hands.

Slowly, the tension ebbed as the sound faded into the past, and they returned to their prior state of shock, pain, and exhaustion.

"What about the quake?" Stacee asked minutes—or hours—later. "You all felt it. That wasn't normal."

The programmer side of Pato, the side that loved numbers, equations, and logic, wanted to disagree, but the rest shuddered with the certainty that she was right. The quakes, tremors, or whatever they were had not been natural. Somehow, they had been targeted and personal. He had no idea how that was true, but it was. He also had no idea what they could do if the tremors started again.

"It was the wind," Helene cut in, her voice strained and distant.

Pato looked up at her, surprised to find the older woman looking back at them, her thin face gaunt and haunted in the darkness. She hadn't said so much as a single word since they'd finally gotten her and Sven off the ledge and onto what they hoped was firmer ground.

"The wind caused the quake," she said again, holding Sven's hand a little closer. "Didn't you feel it?"

Pato thought back, remembering the sudden, violent gusts of wind just before everything had gone to hell.

"How does wind cause an earthquake?" Marcos asked. The question sounded insane, but Pato knew it was sincere.

As if it were mocking them, the breeze picked up again, whistling around them. It was followed almost immediately by another chattering of clicks from the darkness. They all turned toward the sound, staring into the night, searching for the source, finding nothing.

"I'm sick of this," Stacee said, pushing away from the Burro and looking down at Pato. "I'm going to find out what it is. You coming with me?"

Pato looked from her to the darkness, a chill going through him. The last thing he wanted to do was to go looking for whatever it was, especially in the dark. That was how people in horror movies got themselves killed. But from the look on her face, there was no way to stop her.

With a hard swallow, he nodded and stood.

"Stay and look after them," Stacee said to Marcos, nodding toward Sven and Helene.

Marcos pursed his lips to a thin line and nodded. Pato could feel his friend's burning jealousy. He knew it would come back to bite him in the future, but for now, Marcos let it pass.

"Fine." Pato's friend turned toward the robot. "I'm going to put the Burro in stretcher mode. The automation is shot to hell, so I'll have to do it manually."

His anger was almost palpable. Pato hesitated.

"Come on," Stacee said, already disappearing into the darkness.

"I'm coming," Pato called, running after her.

Ahead of them, the clicking sound came again, calling to them to join it.

NINETEEN

PATO AND STACEE WALKED AWAY FROM THE OTHERS AT A measured pace. She turned on a small flashlight she pulled from her pocket, but the tiny beam did almost nothing to dispel the darkness.

They were walking so closely their shoulders brushed together. The physical contact sent chills through Pato. His heart beat a little faster with every step.

As they reached the bottom of a small valley a dozen yards from their makeshift camp and started to climb the ridge on the opposite side, Stacee reached out and grabbed his free hand, her fingers twining around his. Pato stiffened, momentarily forgetting to breathe. He tried to convince himself she was just scared, but his mind fumbled the words.

His stomach fluttering, he glanced at her. She looked at him in that same moment, and their eyes met in the gloom. She smiled a crooked, shy smile he'd never seen before. He didn't think he would ever breathe again.

She looked away first, focusing on the climb that was steadily growing more difficult. The ridge was composed of red-and-purple clay broken by cracks from erosion that made footing treacherous. Still, she did not release his hand.

Pato kept pace, stumbling along beside her, hoping she didn't notice his sweaty palm. In his other hand, he felt his knuckles turn white as he tightened his grip around the broken robot leg. He didn't know if the panicked tremor in his chest was caused by Stacee or what he worried they might find beyond the top of the ridge. Both were equally terrifying.

About halfway up, the clicking chatter floated through the air again. It sounded like it was just a few yards ahead of them. They both paused and stared into the darkness until it passed. Pato's heart raced. Stacee squeezed his hand. They kept moving.

A half-moon peaked over the horizon behind them, bathing the landscape with pale blue light. The cracks in the ridge cast ominous shadows across their path.

They reached the top of the ridge and paused, panting for breath, still holding hands. At last, they turned and looked down into the small valley that stretched into the darkness before them.

"What the hell?" Stacee whispered.

Silently, Pato agreed with the sentiment.

The valley was filled with ordered piles of black rocks.

There were hundreds of them, each roughly shaped like a foot-high pyramid separated from the others by two to three feet of cleared ground on all sides. At first, their layout looked scattered and haphazard, but as Pato stared at them, a pattern emerged—concentric circles looping the valley, swirling together to a center that was lost in darkness.

"What the hell?" Pato echoed, stepping forward, drawn to the piles by almost-overwhelming curiosity.

Stacee came with him, tightening her grip on his hand, her

flashlight dancing over the piles of stone, causing their faceted sides to flash and sparkle.

"Why would anyone do this?" she wondered as they reached the one closest to them.

Pato shook his head, no likely answers coming to him.

Together, they bent down to study the pile. It was made of individual, crystalline black stones about the size of a fist with faceted sides cut at sharp angles that flashed in the light. The stones were similar to obsidian but more glass-like, as if they could shatter easily.

Already regretting what he was about to do, Pato let go of Stacee's hand and reached for the stone at the top of the pile.

"Careful," she hissed, causing him to hesitate and draw a deep breath before picking up the rock.

Trembling, he held it up for inspection. The stone was surprisingly warm to the touch and much heavier than it looked. Pato was certain the sharp edges would have no problems cutting through skin.

He shuddered at the thought, glancing nervously at the valley that, from the lower vantage point, looked like a nightmare landscape from Dr. Seuss. The whole thing was too weird, too surreal, too inhuman.

"That looks like the same kind of rock Marcos found in the winch," Stacee whispered, her voice hushed and uncertain.

Pato looked at the rock again, seeing the similarity to the stone Marcos had cut himself on that first day. For some reason, the thought made the hair on his neck stand on end.

Suddenly anxious to be rid of the thing, Pato tossed the rock back onto the pile and stood. The stone clattered as it hit the others and rolled down the side of the pyramid. The resulting clicking sound sent chills down Pato's spine.

"No way," Pato whispered as both he and Stacee returned to their knees and stared at the pile of stones.

Stacee grabbed his hand again, more tightly than before. With her other hand, she reached out and picked up one of the rocks. She held it aloft on the flat of her palm and tipped her hand, dropping the stone back onto the pile. It clattered against the others with a series of very familiar insect-like clicks.

Together, Pato and Stacee stood and backed away. She moved in close to him, clutching his hand with one of hers and gripping his arm with the other. Pato could feel her warmth as they stared into the strange valley.

Tearing his eyes away from the piles of rock, he looked down at her. She met his gaze, her face mirroring his confusion and fear. She was so close, he could feel her breath on his cheek. The smell of her almost overpowered him.

"I don't know..." she started but furrowed her brow in confusion. "Maybe..." She shook away whatever she was going to say and stared up at him in silence.

Pato could feel the tension in the inches that separated them. His body felt like it was on fire. She drew closer, nestling against him and lifting his arm around her. He felt her tremble beneath his touch. He stiffened, not daring to move or breathe.

She smiled and leaned forward, her lips reaching for his. He didn't know what to do or how to react. He just watched as she came closer, closer, closer.

They connected, her lips pressing into his. Electricity shot through him, burning to every extremity. Stacee pulled him closer, breathing him in. Her lips were soft and warm. Every inch of him called out for her. His heart pounded. It was painful. It was glorious. He wanted to run. He never wanted it to end.

A sudden wind gusted through the valley. Dust hammered

into them, forcing Pato to flinch back and raise his hand against it. He felt the loss of connection with her and regretted it.

Stacee buried her head in his shoulder, her long hair whipping around them. He pulled her close and closed his eyes, waiting for the wind to pass. Then he heard the clicks. Just a few at first, but then dozens, hundreds, thousands of them.

They both stiffened.

Pato opened his eyes and squinted into the wind, trying to find the source. He saw nothing but piles of rock. Then a shadow moved at the edge of the darkness.

"Did you see that?" He turned toward the movement, his hand tightening on the all-but-forgotten robot leg.

"What?" Stacee pulled away from him, scanning the valley.

"Something's out there." A chill went through him as her warmth departed.

The clicks multiplied and grew louder. Memories of the video flashed through Pato's mind. He hefted the metal leg and whispered the Lord's Prayer.

"I see it," Stacee shouted, pointing to the right.

"There's two of them," Pato hissed, spotting another movement in the opposite direction. He took a step back. Stacee joined him.

"Three," she said, pointing to yet another part of the valley. She gripped his arm, her fingers digging into his skin.

The wind grew stronger, and the whistle dropped to a moan that filled the air around them. The valley began to move.

TWENTY

"Shit!" Marcos swore as he shifted his tiny flashlight, trying to better see the Burro's inner workings. He could barely make out what he was doing through the jumble of wires and circuitry. Worse, rocks and dust had gummed up half the gears, and he didn't have a good way to clear them.

That wasn't what was really bothering him, though. He turned and squinted into the darkness, trying to make out where Pato and Stacee had gone. His stomach twisted at the thought of them out there together. Alone.

With a growl, he fumbled again with the screwdriver, working at a gear to dislodge another of those damned black rocks. When the cable had broken, it had slashed through the palms of his hands, leaving deep gashes and burns. They ached beneath their makeshift bandages, and while he was grateful he hadn't lost any of his fingers, he still wanted to scream.

The screwdriver jerked out of place and skidded across the gear with a painful scrape. It slammed into a circuit board with a crack.

Marcos leapt back. His leg caught on a rock, and he lost his balance. He crashed to the earth. Pain flashed through him.

Yelling with anger, he leapt to his feet and threw the screwdriver to the ground. He kicked the robot, shouting again as the resulting clang echoed into the night.

Slumping onto a rock, he buried his face in his hands. He gritted his teeth and growled, stoking the flames burning inside him. They were the best company he had.

He looked again in the direction Stacee and Pato had gone, remembering how they'd been as they'd worked together to patch up the others and repair the Burro after the earthquakes. Something in the way the two of them had interacted, the way they'd talked, and the way they'd looked at each other told him everything he needed to know.

It isn't fair.

He remembered the first time he'd seen Stacee at the gym, her ass perfectly accented by her yoga pants and her breasts lifted just right by her sports bra. She had smiled in his direction. It was the most beautiful sight in the world. He was in love.

For months, he'd gone to the gym every day, hoping to see her. He'd followed her around, ignoring the social codes prohibiting interaction between a girl like her and a nerd like him. Then, one amazing day, he'd finally built up the nerve to talk to her, and wonder of wonders—she'd answered. As he'd learned more about her, she became more amazing to him. The day she agreed to come on the trip to fill in when Dave, their idiotic mechanic, had broken his leg while they were out testing the Burro, had been one of the best days of his life.

But now...

Marcos looked at the darkened ridge, feeling his heart break. *It isn't fair,* he thought again.

The clicking sound drifted once again over the ridge, bringing with it vivid memories of the video on the broken phone. He shuddered.

"Good luck, hombre," he whispered to his friend while also wishing him bodily harm.

Sighing, he bent down and reached for the screwdriver. When he looked up, Helene's face was inches from his. He yelped and scooted back on the rock, his heart thudding.

Helene didn't blink or move. She just stared at him, her face a hollow mask revealing nothing but pain. Without speaking, she reached into her pocket and pulled out her phone. With a trembling hand, she held it out to him and whispered, "It's almost dead."

Marcos glanced nervously toward Sven, but the project leader hadn't moved since they'd laid him on the rock hours earlier. He swallowed.

"I'm not sure..." he started, but the fire in her eyes incinerated his words.

"Please," she begged. "Please."

"Sven..."

"I need it," she snapped suddenly, her voice filled with desperation and longing. "I. Need. It."

Marcos leaned back, swallowing at the lump in his throat.

He had seen addiction before. His older brother, Jorge, and his sister, Vanessa, had been in and out of rehab and jail too many times to count. Lots of kids from the old barrio were the same—seeking an escape from a world that didn't care and gave them nothing but heartache and pain.

That was part of why he and Pato did what they did. Engineering, robotics, and computers had been their drugs. Their addictions. Their escapes. From the moment a fifth-grade teacher had taken an interest in their budding talents, they had thrown themselves into that world to the exclusion of all else. The resulting awards, scholarships, and internships had given them their escape from the barrio. Marcos had never looked back. It had been years since he'd even visited.

Now here he was, years and miles away from home, staring once again into the face of addiction. A shudder ran through him. "Helene, I don't think—"

"I don't care what you think." She stepped even closer, shoving the phone into his chest. "You promised." Anger was etched into every line and seam of her face.

Marcos's heart pounded as fear surged in him. The memory of the terrible day when Jorge had accused him of taking his stash flashed into his mind. He clenched his right hand. His pinky had never fully recovered. He'd been eight years old.

Feeling guilty and defeated, he reached for the phone. Relief flooded Helene's face. Without a word, she spun around and returned to her husband's side.

Marcos watched her take Sven's hand and caress his cheek. He ached to have someone care about him as much as she cared about Sven.

Stacee...

With a sigh, he turned back to the Burro. Ignoring the still-open main access panel, he instead retrieved the charging cable. The old phone Helene had found the day before was still attached to it, but after playing the video the night before, it had been completely unresponsive.

Marcos unplugged the old phone and set it aside. He reached for the cable and hesitated.

What if, he wondered, *I just let the phone die and tell Helene the Burro's too damaged to charge it?*

He looked down at the glass face of her phone, knowing that not charging it violated the deal they'd made before the trip, but with everything like it was, he didn't think that mattered anymore.

He thumbed the phone's power button, and it sprang to life, glowing bright in the darkness. The battery only had ten percent left.

His heart pounding and his throat dry, Marcos slipped the phone into his pocket. He stole a furtive glance at Helene. She didn't even look his way.

With a guilty shudder, he forced the memory of his raging brother from his mind and turned back to the Burro. He managed to get the screwdriver into place and dislodge the rock on the first try. Five minutes later, he had the robot in stretcher mode, the straps ready to hold Sven if it came to that. He stowed the toolbox in its place beside the winch and closed the access panels.

Turning away from the machine, he looked again at the ridge. It had been a long time since Pato and Stacee had gone. Too long. A dry wind blew through his hair as he tried to decide what to do about it. It moaned in the canyon behind him.

Suddenly, the night exploded with a horrible clatter of clicks and snaps from the ridge. Chills shot down his spine. *Pato! Stacee!*

"What is that?" Helene shouted at him.

"I'm going after them," he yelled back. Without waiting for a reply, Marcos raced into the night.

TWENTY-ONE

THE RISING MOON'S GLOW LIT THE WAY AS MARCOS struggled up the ridge. With each step he took, the clicking grew more intense, like a thousand voices chattering in anger. He climbed faster.

"Don't be dead, Pato," he whispered again and again.

He crested the ridge and came to a sudden halt, his eyes growing wide. Pato and Stacee stood close together a few yards away, their hands intertwined in a way that lanced jealousy through him, but it was the valley that brought him to a standstill.

The valley was moving. It was a mass of blackness that rose and fell in waves like a dark sea. The waves flashed in the moonlight, and clicks filled the air in rhythm to the movements.

Without taking his eyes from the incredible sight, Marcos walked forward. Pato and Stacee did not see him until he was standing next to them. They startled apart as he approached. He barely noticed.

Standing closer to the valley, Marcos could see that the black mass was made up of countless fist-sized rocks. They twisted and undulated together, their sides splitting and blossoming like flowers or folding in on themselves to create movement. As they tumbled together, the night filled with their chatter.

"How?" Marcos wondered aloud.

Neither Pato nor Stacee answered him.

The memory of the video burned into his mind. In it, a shadow with sharp angles had made the same clicking sound that overwhelmed the man's screams. Marcos had thought it was some kind of creature.

Unconsciously, he took a step backward and shuddered. Around them, the wind moaned a deep melancholy lament. The rocks shifted with the sound, the waves swelling higher and dipping lower with the mournful melody. The clicks added percussion to the song.

The wind slowed, fading to a whistle. The moving rocks followed suit, their movements growing slower, as if in time to a song that was winding down. As the last gusts of wind blew across the valley, trilling over the ridge, the rocks separated into hundreds of pyramid-like piles that stretched away into the darkness. The wind ceased. The valley went still.

No one spoke. No one moved. The three people at the edge of the valley just stared in numbed silence.

"What... was... that?" Stacee asked, her voice breathless.

"The wind..." Pato looked at the rocks to the left and right and then the left again. His brow furrowed in confusion. He opened his mouth to say something, shook his head, and continued staring.

Curiosity raged through Marcos, battling his fear. Clearing his throat and ignoring the panic that rose in his chest, he took a step forward. Stacee inhaled sharply and reached for him but did not try to stop him as he knelt next to the nearest pile, studying it, searching for any explanation for what they had just seen.

Impulsively, he reached for one of the rocks. Behind him, Pato hissed in warning, and he hesitated. Shaking his doubts aside and ignoring his pounding heart, he gently lifted the stone from the top of the pile.

Nothing happened.

Breathing a sigh of relief, he stood and retreated to his friends. He pushed his way between them, feeling satisfaction at their awkward unwillingness to separate.

He raised the rock and peered at it, resting on the bandage across his palm. The others joined him. Stacee lifted her light, spotlighting it.

In the light, the black rock glowed with golden transparency. Inside, tiny cracks and fissures crisscrossed through the stone. They converged in a tangle near the center, like veins leading to a heart.

"How do they move?" Marcos asked.

"It's the wind, right?" Stacee asked. "Like Helene said?"

With a shrug, Marcos leaned over and blew on the rock. Pato and Stacee moved forward expectantly, their foreheads almost touching over his palm.

Nothing happened.

"Worth a try," he said, leaning back, feeling them push apart again.

The three of them stood for a long moment, staring at the stone in silence. Marcos tried to think, to find any explanation for how the rocks had moved, but was distracted by the obvious tension between the others. Rather than looking at the stone, they were staring at each other over his palm, their eyes filled with obvious longing. *Get a room*, he thought bitterly.

Suddenly Stacee gasped with realization, her eyes growing wide.

"What?" Pato asked.

Leaning forward, almost close enough to kiss the rock on Marcos's palm, she began to sing.

"Twinkle, twinkle, little star," she cooed. Her voice was soft, and her breath tickled Marcos's hand. Tension at the unexpected intimacy flooded through him, kept at bay by the intensity of the moment and the memory of how she had been looking at Pato just a moment earlier. "How I wonder what you are."

The rock began to move. The motion was barely noticeable at first, just a ripple along the stone's glassy surface.

"Up above the world so high..." Stacee continued.

The rock twitched, its sharp edges gliding and catching on the threads of the bandage as it spasmed across his hand, almost falling off the side. Stacee fell silent. The rock went still.

For a moment, the three of them exchanged a stunned, nervous look, but soon they were all leaning forward again.

Swallowing against his dry throat, Marcos began to sing. "Like a diamond in the sky."

The others joined in, their voices quavering with excitement and nerves.

"Twinkle, twinkle, little star. How I wonder what you are."

The rock began to move again, rippling and twisting to the notes, punctuating them with resounding clicks.

They repeated the song, their eyes widening as the stone danced across Marcos's palm to the simple rhythm. As the last notes faded, the rock stilled, and the three of them lapsed into silence. Behind them, a dozen other clicks faded into the darkness. Other rocks must have been dancing to the song, too.

An idea tickled at the back of Marcos's mind, slowly forming and dominating his thoughts. The tingle of excitement formed in his chest and spread through his body. The corners of his lips pulled back in a grin.

"Marcos?" Pato asked, sounding nervous. "Whatever you're thinking, don't."

A part of Marcos knew that Pato was probably right, he usually was, but that rarely stopped him. Smiling deviously at his friend, Marcos reached into his pocket and pulled out Helene's phone. It was locked with a four-digit PIN, but Marcos didn't hesitate before tapping the numbers that spelled out her son's name.

5-9-5-3.

The home screen greeted him. Addiction was so predictable.

"What are you doing?" Stacee asked.

Without answering, he shook his head and searched the phone for its music app. He found it and quickly scanned the list of albums. Most were classical symphonies and operas broken by the occasional Broadway musical, just what he'd expect from the Ice Queen. He almost chose a song at random, but then his eyes found something different and entirely unexpected: *Javen*.

The presence of the obscenity-heavy, obnoxious YouTube star who made his name by performing insane stunts in his music videos was so unexpected that it drew Marcos to it. *That's it*, he thought, his grin spreading even wider. He tapped the album eagerly and started the first song.

The phone began to play so quietly that the music barely carried over the breeze. Marcos thumbed the volume as high as it would go. It still sounded tiny in the open air, but it would have to be enough. With a triumphant look at the others, he spun around and lifted the phone over his head, the music echoing softly into the valley.

The rocks began to move, starting with those closest to Marcos, but then the motion rippled outward in a wave that vanished into the darkness. At first, the stones lurched and spasmed at random, but soon they caught the steady, pulsating beat, and their movements synchronized into a hypnotic dance.

Marcos held the phone higher, his eyes and grin widening as the hammering percussion and soaring guitar solos turned the valley into a rhythmic cacophony. The rock he had taken from the pile twisted and jerked in his hand, the sharp sides scraping along the bandage and his skin. Marcos laughed and tossed it into the valley. He whooped, the sound rippling through the mosh pit of dancing stone.

Stacee and Pato stepped to either side of him. They stared at the dancing rocks, transfixed, their faces a mixture of fascination and horror.

"This isn't right," Stacee whispered, her voice barely audible over the music and the incessant chattering clicks.

"I know," Marcos yelled back. "It's totally wicked." He began to dance himself, moving in his own series of random, spasmodic jerks. He whooped again.

The song died with a crash of percussion that echoed into the night. The rocks collapsed, lying in scattered, haphazard heaps across the valley floor.

Marcos paused the phone and leaned over to catch his breath. Looking up at the others, he said, "That was amazing."

Both Pato and Stacee stood ramrod straight, staring into the valley, their faces drawn with fear.

"What?" Marcos asked, annoyed that they didn't seem to be appreciating just how awesome that had been.

"I don't think you should have done that," Stacee whispered.

"Why not?"

Without answering, she took a step back and then another.

Marcos rolled his eyes.

The wind picked up again, starting as a low moan over the ridge but steadily rising in volume. A click echoed through the valley, then another. A dozen more joined them. Then a hundred.

Then thousands. The rocks began to move, waves traveling through the heaps as they seemed to swell together.

Stacee continued backing away, her eyes wide and her face filled with terror. Pato followed. The rocks were rising and falling, cresting and dipping to the incessant rhythm of the wind. A swell larger than the rest formed in the center, rising as the stones flowed toward it. Soon, it was a column of twisting, writhing stones rising into the night sky. It was two feet high, then three. Four. Five.

"Marcos," Pato called from the top of the ridge, Stacee by his side.

Marcos ignored them. The valley held him spellbound.

The column had reached eight feet and was still rising. Its sides twisted and coiled around it, like a million black snakes swirling together. Its furious clicks filled the darkness.

Marcos leaned forward, his mind swirling with random thoughts about harmonic frequencies and how much people would pay to see what he was witnessing. Behind him, he could feel his friends at the top of the ridge, their bodies tense and trembling as they stared in terror and wonder at what was happening before them.

The column stood ten feet straight into the air. On the ground around it, the stones swirled and danced, filling the air with dust. They flashed in the moonlight and filled the air with their insect-like chatter.

Marcos grinned.

Then the column collapsed, the rocks crashing to the earth and surging out in a massive black wave of clicking fury. The wave was headed straight for Marcos.

"Run!" Stacee shouted, disappearing over the top of the ridge, Pato on her heels.

Marcos turned and ran.

TWENTY-TWO

The scramble down the far side of the ridge was precarious. The hard clay gave way beneath Marcos, and his feet caught on the cracks left by erosion, turning every step into a near-stumble that threatened to toss him headlong down the slope. Somehow, he maintained his footing. The clatter of the oncoming wave of black rock behind him grew louder with every second, matching the fury of the wind that lashed the night.

Ahead, he could see the silhouettes of Pato and Stacee. They had already reached the bottom of the ridge and were sprinting up the other side of the small valley toward the canyon and their makeshift camp. Marcos urged himself to move faster.

His foot sank into a small fissure in the clay, pitching him forward. He hit the compact ground with a thud that knocked the breath from him and caused his injured hands to burn with pain. Stars swam before his eyes.

Shaking his head and ignoring his throbbing hands, he pushed himself up, gasping air into his lungs as he struggled to stand. He glanced back at the top of the ridge, his eyes widening in horror as the wave of rock crested it. The black mass streamed toward him, surging like the front of an unstoppable flash flood.

"*Padre Nuestro,*" Marcos whispered, pushing himself to his feet and stumbling down the slope. His ankle had twisted in the fall, slowing him. Each step was agony. He pushed harder.

He reached the bottom of the ridge and began climbing up the other side of the valley toward the others. The ground shook beneath him as the rocks thundered closer. In his head, the countless clicks turned into the shouts of an angry mob calling for his blood. They were gaining on him. He could feel them lashing out toward his heels.

A loud klaxon split the night, sounding again and again. *The Burro's seismic alarm.*

The sound blasted into the surging rocks, knocking them back. The wave shuddered and retreated as the alarm hit them over and over again. The edges of the sharp stone rippled in pain and fury.

Marcos whooped. Ahead of him, he heard Pato and Stacee cheer. But the rocks began to rally, piling together in the seconds between each blast from the alarm. A new column steadily rose halfway down the ridge, the twisting rocks fortifying each other against the sound that slammed again and again.

For a full ten seconds, the column twisted and writhed, the stones working themselves into a wild frenzy. Then it tipped forward and crashed to the earth, forming a river of black stone three feet wide that flowed down the ridge in a steady stream. The chattering of rocks overpowered the Burro's alarm and the howl of the wind.

Marcos yelped. He spun around and raced toward the others, already feeling the ground start to tremble under his feet. His ankle throbbed, turning each step into agony. Behind him, the front of the stone river lifted into a wave that reached for him, the crest flashing in the moonlight. Marcos knew he would never make it.

Suddenly, Pato was there, throwing himself at the river of stone, swinging the Burro's damaged leg like a club. The rocks shattered before it like glass, and black shards sparkled as they flew through the air and scattered across the ground. Pato screamed as he swung again and again. More stones shattered.

"Run," he yelled at Marcos. "Help Stacee."

Marcos hesitated, worry for his friend stabbing through him.

"Run!" Pato yelled again.

Marcos turned and raced up the slope. Stacee was frantically working on the Burro, trying to get it moving.

"We have to get Sven," she shouted at him over the robot's continuing alarm.

Marcos limped to help her, the pain in his ankle still sharp but lost in the terror of the moment.

"What is that?" Helene yelled. She was standing next to the still-unconscious Sven, pointing at the wave of rock battering at Pato, steadily pushing him back.

Stacee and Marcos didn't answer. There wasn't time.

Marcos leapt at the Burro's controls, his fingers shaking and fumbling as he tapped out commands. *Pato would have been better at this*, he thought. The seismic alarm echoed through his skull, making it hard to focus.

He glanced at Pato. Shards of black rock flew around his friend as he slammed the leg into them. It almost looked like a bullet-time sequence from *The Matrix*. Pato screamed in triumph every time a new assault shattered. His shouts rippled through the stones closest to him.

As Marcos watched, a tendril grew from the rocks, a spindly tentacle of twisting, writhing stone that hovered above the river of stone. Marcos shouted a warning just as it struck at Pato. His friend shouted in surprise and batted it away, shattering it into countless shards and slivers. Another tendril struck at him then another, coming in from all sides, pushing him back like a boxer maneuvering an opponent into the corner. Pato dodged and weaved, feinting left and right and striking the tendrils with the broken leg, but he was losing ground fast. He was almost to the edge of the cliff.

Suddenly, Marcos understood. "Pato!"

He moved to assist his friend, but Stacee grabbed him. "Help Sven, then we'll get Pato."

Marcos hesitated, but he knew she was right. Pato was buying them time. He had to take it.

Frantic, he turned back to the Burro, keying in the last commands and triggering the startup process. With the whine of rotors and the beep of systems coming online, the robot began to move.

"Hurry," Stacee yelled at him before sprinting toward Sven. Helene still stood next to her husband, staring in shock at the desperate battle between Pato and the rocks as they pushed him closer to the canyon's edge.

"Helene, help us," Marcos shouted as he limped past her, the Burro close on his heels.

She turned and looked at him, her face filled with fear and confusion. She would be no use.

"Grab his arms," Stacee yelled as Marcos undid the straps on the back of the robot. He rushed over and hefted Sven under his arms. Stacee grabbed his legs. Together, they lifted.

Sven moaned as they placed him on the back of the robot and tied the straps in place. Helene rushed to his side, getting in the way, slowing things down. Stacee snapped at her as she quickly did the straps.

Marcos spun toward Pato, yelling for him to run, but the words caught in his throat.

The rocks had pushed his friend to the cliff's edge. They swarmed at him, striking at him with tendrils on every side. The sharp ends of the tendrils tore through his clothes and sliced into skin whenever they met their mark. Blood coursed down Pato's hands and legs.

He desperately swung at the attacking tendrils, striking them down over and over, but more just took their place. Shards and slivers of rock flew through the air as the rocks shattered before him, but the stones just kept coming.

The inexorable tide of black pushed in at Pato on every side. A tendril sliced a deep gash in his cheek. The heel of his foot slipped over the edge, but he caught himself just in time.

"Pato," Marcos shouted, rushing forward. He screamed at the top of his lungs, words lost in the desperate need to help his friend.

The rocks hesitated, turning toward him, rippling as his scream passed through them. For a brief moment, there was hope, but then the rocks refocused, driving Pato back.

For an eternal, painful heartbeat, Pato and Marcos's eyes met over the flood of stone. The years passed between them: meeting at daycare, standing strong as bullies teased them in elementary school, building their first robot, winning the science award, scoring scholarships against all the odds, landing internships with the McTiernan Group, racing down the side of the cliff. The laughter, the shouts, the joys, and the pains of their accumulated lifetimes filled the impossible gap between them.

Then Pato was gone, tumbling over the cliff and disappearing into the darkness. The river of rock streamed over the edge after him, clicking in triumph.

Marcos screamed, anguish tearing the sound from his heart.

The remaining rocks flinched away. His scream went on and on, as though it would never stop.

Stacee grabbed his arm, pulling at him, urging him to run as the stones regrouped and charged toward them. Numb, he turned and followed. They raced away from the cliff as fast as they could move.

The wind ceased as they crested a distant ridge. As the last moan echoed over the landscape, Marcos glanced back. The remaining rocks stood at the edge of the cliff, reformed into small, silent pyramids, terrible sentinels that watched the night.

TWENTY-THREE

T HE BULLET PIERCED THE WARRIOR'S ARMOR. B LOOD splattered the earth around him. His life spent, he fell to the ground, dead.

"Dammit!" Ryan threw the game controller onto his desk as his monitor flashed "YOU'RE DEAD!" in big red letters. Growling, he reached forward and grabbed a handful of Cheddar and Sour Cream Ruffles. He stuffed them into his mouth and chased them down with a swig of Dr Pepper.

"Ryan, you suck," he muttered to himself, wiping the cheddary residue from his fingers onto his shirt. He picked up the controller to try the level again, mentally scolding himself for wasting too much time on the crappy game, but he still hit the option to restart the level.

"One more try," he said, taking another gulp of the soft drink.

As the game went through the level's opening cutscene—one he'd already seen about eight times that night—he idly looked at the three other monitors he'd set up at his workstation to monitor the Burro while Marcos, Pato, that sexy chick Ryan couldn't stop thinking about, and the others were traipsing through the desert.

His eyes wandered over the various readouts and feeds without seeing much of them. With all the damned malfunctions, Marcos and Pato had shut down most of the interesting sensors, and Sven had turned off the video feed two days ago when Sven had caught Ryan using it to watch the gorgeous, dark-skinned girl when he was supposed to be paying attention to other things. Even the GPS came and went with regularity. The whole thing made the "oh-so-important monitoring job" Ryan had agreed to a whole lot less interesting.

He glanced at the corner of the closest screen and sat up straight, a lance of fear shooting through him. The clock there read 7:42.

"Oh shit!" He was supposed to call the others more than an hour ago.

He threw the controller back onto the desk, barely noticing when his avatar died a quick and meaningless death seconds after it respawned. "YOU'RE DEAD!" flashed across the monitor again as he scrambled for the satellite phone under the mass of empty Dr Pepper cans and discarded fast-food containers that crowded his workstation. He found it under a McNuggets box.

Panting, he checked the screen. No missed calls.

Holding the phone to his chest, feeling his heartbeat return to normal, he slumped in the chair and breathed a sigh of relief. He might be late, but they hadn't called, either. That was good. Ryan didn't relish the thought of another chewing out from either Vivek or Sven.

"So, where are you guys?" he wondered, leaning forward to check the GPS screen.

The Burro's GPS indicator hadn't been working since earlier that day—yet one more stupid malfunction that he'd already added to the ever-growing list—but the satellite phone was still transmitting a signal. The indicator blinked from the center of the canyon the group had been crossing pretty much all day. Ryan furrowed his brow. The group should have been across the canyon hours earlier.

"What are you still doing there?" he asked the monitor, listening as his voice echoed through the massive warehouse lab. The screen didn't answer.

He glanced at the lab's sole window, a small thing almost twenty feet up on the far wall. It confirmed that it had already grown dark outside. Turning back to the monitor, he drew a speculative breath and blew it out in a rush. He wondered if there was an error in the GPS software putting them off by several feet. Of course, that would mean they were still at the canyon's edge when they should have been a couple miles away from it by nightfall, but it was better than being in the center of the canyon.

As he watched, the indicator blip moved, traveling a full inch up the screen, angling slightly to the left. Ryan grunted. "There's something alive down there."

Glancing at the clock again, he dialed the number of Sven's satellite phone and reclined in his chair as it began to ring. He grabbed another handful of potato chips then crammed them into his mouth before realizing they would make it difficult to talk when the others answered.

The phone rang. It rang again.

"Hi, Ryan," Marcos answered after the fifth ring.

"Hey, Marc—" Ryan started, but he was cut off.

"We're not able to take your call right now, because we've been kidnapped by aliens," Marcos's recorded voice continued. Behind him, Ryan could hear Pato snort. "Please leave a message, and we'll get back to you after our anal probes." Pato and Marcos burst into laughter before a beep cut them off.

Ryan rolled his eyes. "Hey, guys, it's more than an hour after check-in. Just wondering how you're doing." He hung up and tossed the phone back onto the desk.

Taking another swig of Dr Pepper, he looked back at the GPS indicator. It was moving again, to the right. *Someone must be carrying it. So why didn't they answer?*

Shrugging, Ryan reached for the game controller. "Time to finally beat this stupid level."

Before he could restart the cutscene, something clanged from deep in the warehouse lab. Ryan hesitated, his finger hovering in the air millimeters over his controller. Except for the soft music playing from his monitor, the lab was silent—as it should have been. He was the only one there.

Something clanged again, and Ryan's heart beat a little faster. Setting the controller back onto the desk, he stood and rose onto his tiptoes, trying to peer over the six-foot cubicle walls of the computer lab to the warehouse beyond. At five foot ten, he could make out only the tops of the machine and electrical shops on the other side of the lab and the climbing wall at the far end.

"Hello?" he called.

No response.

"Is anyone there?"

Still nothing.

He walked to the entrance of the computer lab and peered around the corner. His eyes traveled the length of the warehouse, past the utility shops to the simulated terrains used for testing the Burro at the back. Nothing stirred. Tools, carts, fake rocks, and trees were all in their places.

"Hello?" He called again. He was frozen by indecision and wondered if he should call Tybet.

He scanned the lab again. Still no sign of life. With a grunt, he turned back toward his desk then froze at a strange sound coming from above him, like someone shuffling along carpet. His heart pounding, Ryan raised his eyes to the admin office.

The office was a metal box with white walls and windows suspended fifteen feet above the computer lab. The only access was a narrow staircase leading up the wall. It was where Sven looked down on the workers below. Ryan had to take a full step back to see it well.

The office lights were off, and the windows were dark. Ryan squinted, trying to make out anything beyond the panes of glass. Nothing. But he was certain the sound had come from up there.

He briefly considered calling Tybet again, but he hesitated. The big man was pretty chill, but Ryan didn't want to find out what would happen if he was upset for having his time wasted on nothing. The guy wasn't chief of security for nothing.

Clearing his throat, Ryan looked around. He spied a large crescent wrench on a nearby workbench and picked it up, hefting it like a club. Swallowing back the knot in his throat, he started to climb.

The stairs were solid, but they still creaked and groaned under him, reminding Ryan why he didn't like going to the admin office. Halfway up, he paused to catch his breath and to switch the wrench from one sweaty palm to the other.

At last, he reached the door. He peered through the window at its center, taking in the room on the other side. A glowing monitor lit the small space, casting shadows from the conference table, filing cabinets, a water cooler, and a fake plant in the corner. Nothing stirred.

Ryan turned the doorknob, flinching as it squeaked. The sound was deafening in the silent lab. Swallowing, he pushed open the door and stepped into the office.

It took him a second to find the light switch. The fluorescent bulbs flickered to life, bathing the room in an artificial white light.

Ryan looked around. Across from him, Sven's computer lock screen glowed. Papers, notes, coffee cups, and picture frames were scattered across the two desks and the conference table. Maps and charts lined the walls. Filing cabinets kept silent vigils in the corner. Empty chairs sat motionless. An exit door leading directly from the office to the hot Phoenix night beyond the warehouse remained closed. Stenciled letters warned that an alarm would sound if it were opened. It all looked perfectly normal, but some detail—some little thing out of place—tugged at the back of Ryan's brain. He just didn't know what it was.

Pursing his lips, he walked to Sven's desk. The computer had gone to screensaver. A picture of Sven with his wife and their son, who had passed away before Ryan had joined the group, marched slowly across the screen. Ryan hummed tunelessly, tapping the wrench against his leg as he spun around slowly, trying unsuccessfully to identify what was bothering him.

With a shrug, he glanced once more at Sven's computer—now displaying a picture of younger versions of Marcos and Pato with his son. The project leader sure had a theme.

Shrugging again, Ryan turned back to the door and the stairs. Before he could take a step, he froze, his eyes growing wide. Swallowing, he spun back to the computer.

Why is Sven's computer on? It should have gone into power-save mode days ago. Also, screensaver mode was only displayed after a handful of minutes of disuse. *That has to mean...*

Ryan turned toward the door that led from the office to the world beyond. The notice about the alarm met him, warning him away. He bit his lower lip, considering. At last, mustering his courage, he reached for the crossbar and shoved the door open. Hot air wafted into the office, stirring the climate-controlled room. There was no alarm.

Ryan stepped back, panic rising in his chest. Someone had

been in the office. *But why?* He looked at Sven's computer again, watching as another picture—this one of Sven and Helene from happier times—marched across the screen. A chill went through him.

His hands shaking, Ryan pulled out his cell phone and dialed Tybet's number. It rang twice.

"Hello?" The security chief's deep voice resonated over the phone.

"Tybet?" Ryan said in a rush. "This is Ryan, at the lab. I... I think someone broke in."

There was a long silence before the larger man spoke. "Someone broke in?"

"I think so." Ryan proceeded to tell the security chief what he had found.

Tybet listened, calm and silent.

When Ryan finished, Tybet told him to wait and not touch anything. "I'll be right there."

The line went dead. Ryan put the phone back in his pocket and rocked back on his heels. He jumped at every sound in the silent space about him.

"Come on, Tybet, hurry," he muttered after a few minutes.

He looked through the windows of the office to the lab below. He could see the satellite phone resting on his desk. Just above it, his gaming monitor continued to flash the words "YOU'RE DEAD!" in big red letters.

TWENTY-FOUR

THE PILE OF LOOSE ROCKS UNDER HIS FEET COLLAPSED, AND Vivek slid forward. He cursed and grabbed for the canyon wall just in time to steady himself before crashing to the ground. His hand scraped the rough surface of the sandstone cliff, but at least he managed to keep his feet.

He held still for a long moment, leaning against the wall and gulping air to calm his nerves. His heart thudded with erratic, pounding beats. He hoped the more-than-directed caffeine pills he'd taken to stay awake wouldn't cause permanent damage.

At last, his heartbeat slowed to a rhythm approximating normal. He pushed away from the wall and continued down the winding canyon. His small flashlight did little to illuminate the path, and the moonlight didn't reach this deep, so he often had to feel his way. His progress was slow and agonizing. He felt the passing of every minute. The others waiting for him pressed him to keep moving forward.

His pack, filled with twenty extra pounds of food and water, grew heavier with every step. He wanted nothing more than to drop it to the canyon floor, but if he did, he knew he wouldn't have the will to pick it up again.

He kept moving.

He thought about Ryan and checked his watch. Sven should have reported in over three hours ago. Perhaps Ryan had already called for rescue. Perhaps they would reach the others first. Vivek could only hope.

His stomach churned. The protein bar he'd eaten a couple hours earlier had turned to acid that roiled inside him. He knew he should eat something else. He needed the energy, but the thought of more protein—the only food he had with him—turned his stomach. He decided he could hold out a little while longer. Instead, he paused by a large boulder, pulled out a water bottle. He took a long sip, followed by an equally long blink.

After the cable broke, it had taken Vivek nearly four hours to find a safe way into the canyon. Five more hours had passed since then—five hours of climbing over and around boulders and sliding through narrow passages, searching for a safe way up the other side. Most canyons had cracks and seams that made unaided ascent possible. This canyon had sheer walls with few handholds. Vivek didn't like the prospect of trying to scale those cliffs in the daylight, much less the dark, especially with the extra weight in his pack.

He had been in the canyon for so long he'd lost track of where he was in relation to the others. He was not sure if he had already passed the place where they had crossed or if it was just around the next bend.

His eyes drifted over the wall next to him. Noticing small, glass-like black veins that crisscrossed the sandstone. He leaned in for a closer look, running his fingers along one of the larger lines, feeling the smooth surface.

"Where did you come from?" he wondered aloud.

Vivek had trekked all over this desert, and he'd seen more than enough sandstone to steal any wonder he might have once felt at the sight of stacked red and yellow hues. To him, one rock looked much like another, but he was certain he had never before seen anything like these kinds of veins in sandstone.

Before life had turned his passion for the outdoors into a daily grind, Vivek had been a student of geology. He'd read everything he could find about the different kinds of stones in his new American home. Most of what he'd read had slipped away from him over the years, but he remembered enough to know that crystalline veins like the ones he was studying were almost always the result of volcanic activity. Sandstone, however, was simply formed of mud and centuries of pressure. A combination of the two should be impossible.

Vivek shook his head, running his fingers along another vein. The problem was that they weren't the only thing that should be impossible on this trip. The earthquakes that had caused so many of their problems, for example. *Where did they come from?*

Earthquakes and other seismic events were not unheard of in the Navajo Nation of northern Arizona, but they were rare. Localized quakes like the ones they'd experienced, however, were not just rare, they should have been impossible.

While the ground had trembled on his side of the canyon, it was nothing compared to what he had seen Pato and the others go through on the opposite side. More than that, a hundred yards from where the cable had connected, all traces of the quakes disappeared. The only possible conclusion was that the quakes had occurred in just that one area. Vivek would have bet money that they hadn't even shown up on the US Geological Survey monitoring equipment at Sunset Crater near Flagstaff. *How could that possibly happen?*

Pushing the thoughts away, Vivek drew a deep breath and

rolled his head from side to side, trying to ease the headache in the back of his skull. He blinked to clear the sand from his eyes. Neither action helped.

"One more hour," he muttered, pushing away from the boulder and stumbling back onto the path. "One more hour."

The canyon widened as he walked, the walls stretching farther and farther away from each other. He turned a corner and found himself in a wide moonlit area so large that the far end was lost in shadow. The ground changed too, as the boulders and constant pebbles eased, giving way to soft sand.

"Just to the far side," he told himself. "You can get that far."

The sand muffled his footfalls, which still sounded ominous in the silent, cavernous space. He wondered, not for the first time, about the lack of night sounds. *Where are the cicadas? The owls? The coyotes? The millions of other things that fill the desert night with life?* He had never heard so much silence out here before. It was one more impossible thing, and it disturbed him more than all the rest.

Something metal crunched underfoot. Vivek jumped back with a yelp. The heavy pack threw off his balance, and he barely avoided crashing to the ground.

Steadying himself, he flicked on his light and searched the canyon floor. Something half-buried in the sand glinted, and he turned toward it. Conscious of the unsteady weight on his back, he bent over and brushed away the dust, revealing a small silver-handled knife. Memory tugged at his tired mind. He knew that knife from somewhere, but he couldn't place it. Shaking his head, he picked it up and studied it.

The blade was still extended. He closed it, noticing how little dust was in the hinge. It hadn't been in the canyon for long.

There were no footprints around it. Vivek looked up, trying to figure out how the knife had gotten there. The walls were too far apart for it to have been thrown from either side. It was almost as if the knife had been dropped from straight above.

He stiffened as realization struck. He was standing directly below the place the others had crossed. The knife belonged to Helene. He had seen her use it while stitching up a tear in her pack a couple days earlier.

More alert, Vivek scanned the area around him. A few seconds later, he spied the broken cable hanging lifelessly on the canyon wall to his right. And there, a few feet away, something small and black protruded from the sand—the satellite phone.

Balancing his pack, he rushed to the small electronic device, praying that it still worked in spite of the fall. He squatted next to the phone and reached out trembling fingers. Hope soared as he made contact but disappeared just as quickly. He had found only the front cover.

He looked around, quickly discovering two dozen other pieces of the device scattered across the canyon floor. The phone seemed to have exploded on impact, but that didn't make sense with the soft sand.

Maybe it was torn apart.

A chill went through him. He stood and looked around, suddenly feeling eyes watching from the shadows. He took a step back then another.

Swallowing, he glanced down at Helene's knife still in his hands. It was a physical reminder of the others. He had to get to them, but first, he had to get out of the canyon. He pocketed the knife and continued hiking, leaving the shattered phone and the watching eyes in his wake.

TWENTY-FIVE

VIVEK WAS BREATHING HARD AS HE TURNED ANOTHER CORNER maybe twenty yards from where he had found the phone. The air had grown thick and dusty. He coughed and sneezed as he pushed forward, still feeling the mysterious eyes on him and the urgent need to reach the others. He held his shirt collar to his nose, breathing through it as the dust thickened.

He turned another corner and hesitated. Piled against the left wall of the canyon was a small hill of shiny glass-like black stones. The faceted sides flashed in the moonlight and the dim glow of his flashlight, looking hazy through the drifting clouds of dust.

Vivek wrinkled his forehead. He looked up at the canyon rim, trying to figure out where the stones might have come from. They'd obviously been dumped there. *But who would have done that and why?*

"What the hell?" he whispered to himself. A chill ran through him, sounding a faint warning. He almost kept moving, but his curiosity drew him to the stones.

"Five minutes," he told himself, stepping forward. "Just five minutes, and then I'm gone."

A few solo rocks lay scattered across the sand. Vivek bent to study the first without touching it. It looked like the same material that formed the veins he'd seen earlier. The warning buzzing at the back of his head grew more persistent.

Shaking his head, he stood and kicked the rock with the toe of his hiking boot. It sailed up and landed farther on the pile, clattering to a stop with a sound that rang with familiarity. He paused, his exhausted brain struggling to remember. The ghost of a conversation about clicking shadows floated through his mind, but the memory vanished before he could grasp it.

Coughing from the dust, he approached the pile. The warning grew louder with each step. He had almost reached the jumble of rocks when he came to a sudden halt, his eyes going wide at what lay exposed at their base.

A human hand stuck out from under the mass of black stone. It was cut in multiple places and covered in sticky blood. One of the fingers was missing, the stub grisly and ragged. The rest of the body beyond the wrist was lost beneath the rocks.

Bile rose into Vivek's throat, and he gagged. He stumbled to a nearby boulder, tearing his shirt from his nose. He vomited, heaving onto the sandy ground. Standing again and wiping his mouth, he looked back at the hand. His heart pounded. His stomach knotted. The warning buzzed so loudly in his head that it overrode all other sound.

A light breeze gusted through the canyon, moaning as it traveled along the walls. Up the canyon, some kind of insect chattered its response, the sound of life strange and unnerving after days of silence.

Vivek's mind spun with jumbled thoughts. He tried to think of what he should do next. At last, he decided that he had to find out who was buried under the pile. He had to know for certain.

His hands shaking, Vivek unbuckled his pack and lowered it to the ground. The momentary weightless sensation caused his head to spin. He steadied himself against the wall, panting and forcing himself to focus. It wasn't easy. At last, he stepped forward and crouched next to the hand. Hesitantly, he began to clear away the rocks.

The edges of the stones were sharp and sliced into his fingers as he dug. He knew he should retrieve his gloves from his pack, but he was afraid if he stopped, he wouldn't have the courage to start again. He proceeded with more caution, picking up the rocks one at a time and tossing each one aside.

Bit by bit, the wrist emerged, followed by a twisted, broken forearm sporting the same deep lacerations as the hand. Near the elbow, one of the rocks clung to the arm, refusing to be simply brushed away. Vivek gripped it and pulled. It separated from the flesh with a ripping sound, tearing away bits of skin, leaving a gaping wound behind.

Vivek heaved again but choked it back and kept working.

More rocks clung to the arm as he dug deeper. In the darkness, they looked like leeches. They came away from the skin with the same sucking sound as the first, leaving ragged wounds in their wake. Vivek gagged each time he pulled one away, but he kept digging.

Moments later, he had uncovered the ripped sleeve of a familiar blue shirt. He stopped, the lump in his throat and the dust making it hard to breathe. He coughed, staring at the fabric, his mind reeling. He knew that shirt. He'd seen it just that morning on the less annoying of the two nerds.

Trembling more than before but moving with a steady, deliberate cadence, Vivek resumed clearing away rocks. At last, he uncovered the young man's face. It was Pato.

The young man's entire head was cut and bruised. A gash ran from his forehead to chin, exposing bone and cartilage. Red bloody circles, where Vivek had pulled away rocks, covered the otherwise-unmarred patches of skin.

Vivek sat and stared for a long time, his mind spinning with thoughts and questions. *What happened? What should I do next?*

Another wind blew through the canyon. The breeze reached Vivek, tossing his hair and chilling his sweat-soaked skin. Something to his left moved.

Vivek jerked toward the movement and stared, trying to see through the darkness and the drifting clouds of dust. Something else shifted to his right, making a clicking sound that echoed through the canyon. He turned his flashlight toward it—and saw nothing but more stones.

The wind grew in intensity, its sound whistling around him. Then more clicking chatter joined it. Vivek flicked his light back and forth, searching for the source of the clicking, finding nothing but black rock.

His light landed back on Pato's face. One of the rocks was attached to his temple, its smooth sides catching the light. Vivek hesitated. He thought he'd removed all the rocks.

As he watched, the stone twitched.

"What the hell?" Vivek leaned forward, a chill shooting through him.

The rock twitched again, jerking to the left and then the right, clicking softly with each movement. Another rock next to Pato's head joined it, then another and another.

The guide stood and stepped back as the entire pile came to life. The rocks twisted and jerked, chattering like a flock of birds. Their movements steadily became more rhythmic and purposeful.

They crawled over Pato's body, moving in lines like writhing snakes. The pile swallowed the young man once again, burying him under a mass of moving rock.

Vivek shook his head, his exhausted mind unsuccessfully trying to follow the dancing, undulating stones and to make sense of them and their chaotic patterns. An outlier danced into his foot, connecting with his boot. Vivek kicked it away. Another moved toward his feet, followed by another. The guide backed away, alarm swelling inside him.

The pile of stone coalesced and swelled as the rocks came together into a three-foot column that rose before him. Its chatter echoed through the canyon. Tendrils grew from its side, weaving around the growing pillar like dancing serpents.

Vivek stared at the column, his mouth dry, the warning in his mind urging him to run, but the sight drew him in, inviting him closer. He leaned forward, his brow furrowed.

The tendrils struck at him so fast he didn't have time to react. One struck his cheek, its sharp end slicing a deep gash through the skin. Another struck his arm, slicing through his sleeve and into his skin.

He grabbed his arm and jerked back with a yelp that seemed to ripple through the stones. The column followed, moving toward him with surprising speed, the tendrils lashing out at him.

Leaving his backpack behind, Vivek turned and ran. Behind him, he could hear the column coming after him. Its chatter filled the air around him, and the ground trembled under his feet. He ran faster, adrenaline he thought he'd used up coursing through him, pushing him faster.

He rounded a corner and glanced back. The column had broken apart and scatted across the ground. In its place, the rocks had formed a wave that surged after him. The angry, clicking chatter became a roar. Tendrils of stone grew from the wave's crest, reaching for him.

Vivek ran as hard and as fast as he could. In the back of his mind, he thought of his abandoned pack and remembered the others waiting for him, desperate for those supplies, but all those thoughts were secondary to escape.

He prayed to the gods as he ran down the canyon. Behind him, he could feel death as it came closer.

Closer.

Closer.

TWENTY-SIX

"Marcos, slow down." The words were distant and muffled, but they penetrated the fog of Sven's unconsciousness, calling to him, bidding him to wake. Bit by bit, his awareness returned.

The constant, penetrating pain came first, followed by the thirst and the pounding, incessant heat. Last came the voices.

"Marcos! We can't keep up this pace."

"You want to stop? You want to slow down? What if those things catch us? You saw what they did."

"I know, Marcos. But we can't keep going like this. What about Sven?"

"Sven's as good as dead."

The words floated through Sven's mind, as intangible and uncatchable as smoke. He struggled to form images of the speakers, at last conjuring the hazy outline of an engineer and a dark-skinned girl with long, curly hair.

Slowly, painfully, he opened his eyes. Bright daylight seared into his brain. He snapped his eyes closed and groaned.

"Did you hear that?" A new voice. A new image. A beautiful woman with blond hair and penetrating ice-blue eyes.

"Helene?" his voice was raw and came out as a croak.

"Stop the Burro!" the woman yelled.

"Right here?" Marcos asked.

"Over there." Stacee this time.

The moving, shifting metal platform under Sven—the Burro, he realized—took another handful of jolting, uneven steps. The bright world beyond his closed eyes dimmed as the machine came to a shuddering halt. An echo of pain rippled through him. He groaned again. Someone grabbed his hand. Cool, familiar fingers caressed his.

"I'm here," Helene whispered. "I'm here."

Sven twitched his fingers around hers. That was the best he could manage, but it seemed like enough. He lay still, feeling the hum of the Burro's internal workings as they cooled. He tried to remember what had happened but managed only snatches of hazy images: a canyon, a cable, an earthquake, pain, and Helene's face.

"I can't," her memory whispered. "I can't... Not you, too."

"Helene?" Sven cracked his eyes open, just enough to see that they were under a stone arch cut into the side of a cliff. He raised his head a fraction of an inch, searching for his wife's face. An explosion of pain flashed through his brain. He groaned and lowered his head back to the Burro.

"I'm here," Helene whispered. "Don't move. Everything is going to be all right."

Even through the clouds of pain, Sven knew it was a lie. Helene tightened her fingers around his. She leaned over and peered down at him, the details of the face he loved coming into focus. Fear and terror filled her piercing blue eyes, and her cheeks were streaked with tears and blood. The bun that usually held her hair back was gone, and long blond strands hung down, tickling

Sven's cheeks. In all their years together, he had never seen her look so undone. So frantic. So helpless.

She had never been more beautiful.

"Hello," he whispered.

"Hello." She smiled back.

"I'm still here," he whispered.

She wiped at her eyes.

He didn't know how long they stayed like that, staring into each other's eyes. It was seconds. It was eternity. It was agony. It was heaven.

"What happened?" Sven asked at last. He lifted his head again, just enough to make out the others. Some were missing. "Where are Pato and Vivek?"

Speaking in turn, each relaying their own part, the other three told Sven what had happened. The words passed through him, conjuring the shadows of memories without substance. Sven's horror grew with each phrase more unbelievable than the last.

Minutes later, they were finished. The group fell into silence, the weight of their experience hanging over them.

Sven lay his head back and looked up at the rock ceiling above them, trying to make sense of what they had said. He closed his eyes, feeling tears trickle down his cheeks as images of Pato passed before him. In his mind, Pato looked like Kyle.

"So what do we do now?" Marcos asked, his voice filled with a bitter anger Sven recognized from his own loss.

No one spoke.

"No one knows where we are," Stacee added. "We don't have any food or water, and…"

Again, they lapsed into silence. Sven closed his eyes, feeling the call of unconsciousness. Helene tightened her grip on his hand, seemingly afraid he would slip away. Maybe he would.

"Still here," he managed, his voice growing weaker.

"Well," she addressed the others, her voice filled with authority, "what do we do?"

"Why are you looking at me?" Marcos snapped back.

"This whole trip was your idea. Now come up with something to get us out of this mess."

"You're blaming *me*? You think this is *my* fault?"

"We're not blaming anyone," Stacee cut in. "We just need a plan."

"What's the use?" Marcos growled. "We're already dead."

Sven heard a hard slap.

"Listen to me, you son of a bitch," Stacee hissed. "He was your best friend. He gave us a chance. You just want to throw that away?"

Sven could hear Marcos's heavy breathing. He could almost feel the engineer's spite-filled glare.

"Are all of the Burro's sensors and communications gone?" Helene broke the tension of that moment.

"Yeah," Marcos said, his voice tight, his anger simmering. "Pretty much."

"What *does* work?"

"Not much," the engineer replied. "The seismic sensor. A couple of other things."

"What about the radio?" Stacee asked. "Any way to get it working again?"

"I don't think so," Marcos replied. "It's gone. We just have the shortwave."

"Well, what about that?" Stacee asked. "Something is better than nothing, right?"

"We could turn it on, but it won't do much good. The range is shit."

"How far?"

"A mile. Maybe two, if we find the right place."

"What about boosting the signal?" Helene asked.

There was a pause. Sven could picture Marcos's furrowed brow and pinched lip as he considered. It was something he'd seen many times over the past few years when they'd encountered one impossible obstacle after another while building the Burro.

"Maybe..." the engineer said at last, his tone skeptical but burning with the creative passion that Sven recognized from the engineer's most brilliant moments. "Maybe if we cannibalize some of the sensor parts and reroute the auxiliary power and get the Burro high up—and I mean really high—maybe we could get ten miles out of it. Enough to maybe reach someone, especially if they're looking."

"Okay," Stacee said, sounding more hopeful. "So how high do we have to go?"

"See that spire?" Marcos asked.

Ignoring the pain, Sven turned his head and looked. A tower of red stone stood against the hazy horizon.

For a moment, they all stared at the spire. Sven tried to imagine the difficulties of reaching it and climbing to the top. It seemed impossible. *Is that our only hope?* he wondered. Helene tightened her grip on his hand.

"Will the Burro be able to make it to the top?" Stacee asked, her voice filled with the same thoughts and fears that plagued Sven.

"I think so," Marcos replied. He paused, then whispered, "I don't think we'll be able to get her back down, though."

The others fell silent, as if feeling Marcos's pain. The Burro had been his and Pato's whole lives for years. To abandon it like that, especially just after losing his best friend, must have been crushing.

"We can build her again," Sven whispered.

Marcos met his eyes and nodded.

"How can I help?" Stacee asked.

"We're going to have to take apart the sensor arrays and patch the radio," Marcos said. "I also need to look at the leg and the climbing gear."

"How long is this going to take?" Helene asked.

"Maybe an hour," Marcos said.

"Count on an hour and a half," Sven whispered with a smile, imagining the chagrined look on the engineer's face.

"Let's get to work," Stacee said.

Stacee and Marcos busied themselves around the Burro. Helene remained close, holding Sven's hand, the lines in her face growing more pronounced each time he groaned.

"Still here," he reassured her.

The minutes passed. He started to drift away again, lured by the comforting, painless darkness of unconsciousness.

Just before he fell into the void, he heard something that sent chills down his spine. The sound was soft and distant, and it could have been his imagination playing tricks on him. It was a chattering of insect-like clicks.

TWENTY-SEVEN

VIVEK'S ARMS TREMBLED AS HE STRAINED TO PULL HIMSELF onto the ledge. His feet scrambled against the cliff below him, searching for purchase. He groaned the last few inches.

He collapsed against the cliff wall, closing his eyes and panting. His chest rose and fell as the aches and pains of his flight the night before and his desperate climb that morning oozed into him. His every extremity throbbed.

The morning sun beat down on him, scorching him and parching his throat. He could feel his skin burning and blisters forming. He was past caring, though.

At last, he opened his eyes and peered down at the canyon floor. He had only made it halfway up the side of the cliff, but he felt lucky to have gotten that far. The rocks on the bottom couldn't reach him there.

Unbidden, his thoughts returned to the night before. He didn't know how long the rocks had chased him down the canyon, their angry chatter filling the night. He didn't know when or why they had given up. He still wasn't sure what they were to begin with.

Even after the tidal wave of rocks had fallen behind, Vivek had continued to run, getting as far away from them as possible. Eventually, his body had given up, and he had collapsed to the canyon floor. Even then, he had pushed forward, crawling on hands and knees until even that was too much. Then he had fallen to the ground, gasping for breath and wishing he were anywhere else.

Just before losing consciousness, Vivek had thought of his wife and son, Haritima and Rajesh, waiting for him back home. His heart ached with the thought that they might never know what had happened to him.

When he'd woken, the sun was high in the sky, its light filtering down to the bottom of the canyon. He had been surprised to still be alive. Uncertain which god to thank, he had thanked them all.

Ten minutes later, he'd begun to climb. The place of his ascent was not as safe as he would have wished, and he didn't have the proper equipment, but nothing could have kept him in the canyon with the rocks any longer.

Now, his strength spent, he didn't know if he would ever be able to make it to the top. He was almost certain he would die on the ledge.

He thought of the black stones, wondering what had happened to them. One moment, they had been right at his heels, so close that he could feel the ground shake as they pushed forward. The next moment, they had been gone. The wind had also vanished, leaving the canyon in eerie silence.

Why? What were they?

Sitting on the ledge, the sun beating down on him, Vivek found no answers.

"Have to keep moving," he muttered, his voice sounding harsh in the thick silence surrounding him. He tried to reach for a handhold to pull himself up, but his body didn't have the strength to obey. Letting out a deep sigh, he rested his head against the rough stone wall.

"Ten minutes," Vivek promised himself, closing his dry, burning eyes. "Just ten minutes."

He sighed and shifted, trying to find a more comfortable position against the rock. His body ached. He wondered idly if the rescuers would be able to find him there. *Maybe I should just stay put.*

He shuddered and swallowed. His throat burned. He regretted leaving his pack with its extra rations at the bottom of the canyon—as if he'd had a choice. Based on the condition of the satellite phone, Vivek imagined all the supplies had been torn apart and scattered by now. He was almost certain the rocks had done it to the phone. *They were cutting off our communications.*

Earlier, the thought would have lanced through him with sudden dread. Now, the physical and emotional exhaustion of the last twenty-four hours dulled his reaction.

He thought of Pato again, dwelling on the rocks that had clung to the young man's body, the ones that had come away with the wet, ripping sound, leaving bloody wounds behind. He wondered what the rocks had been doing. Perhaps they really were like leeches.

The thought made him gag, and he pushed it away, trying to force himself to think of Sven and the others. He had to concentrate on them. He had to reach them. They were his responsibility.

More than ten minutes had passed. Vivek drew a deep breath and tried to stand. His body protested, pain shooting through him. He collapsed back to the ledge, panting. He tried again with the same result. Leaning his head against the stone wall, he gave in. "Just ten more minutes."

He closed his eyes and adjusted his back on the rough stone. Something tickled in the back of his brain, a warning or a thought, but it refused to form into coherent understanding. He pushed it aside.

"Ten minutes," he whispered again. "Just ten." Even he didn't believe his lies anymore.

A moment later, he was drifting. Part of him struggled to stay awake, and part of him hissed dark warnings. The rest gave in. Sleep overtook him.

In his dreams, a massive wave of black rocks surged toward him, tendrils striking out. He raced away from it, but his body was sluggish. The rocks gained on him, inch by painful inch. Their hateful clicks filled the air.

One of the tendrils struck home, slicing deep into Vivek's back. He screamed and fell to the ground. Rocks swarmed over him, cutting into his body. They clung to him like leeches, draining him of life.

Vivek screamed as his world fell into darkness.

He gasped awake, his muddied mind taking in the canyon before him, barely aware that the sun had shifted. The wind had also picked up again, whistling softly through the canyon. Unbidden, his eyes closed again.

As he drifted, half asleep, he felt the wind pick up and heard it moan through the canyon. It rustled his hair and tugged at his clothing, the touch soft and gentle, reminding him of his wife's caresses. He smiled and allowed it to take him back into the world of dreams. The clicks from the wall behind him became the soft voices of his family, whispering him to sleep.

TWENTY-EIGHT

THE SUN BEAT DOWN ON MARCOS AND THE OTHERS AS THEY hiked across the desert. He wiped at his brow, trying to ignore his aching feet, pounding headache, and parched throat, trying not to think of the sun as the day changed from hot to broiling.

His guilt burned hotter than the sun ever could. No matter how much he tried, he couldn't banish the memory of standing at the edge of the valley, holding Helene's phone in the air while the rocks danced and gyrated to the beat. He had been so caught up in the moment, in the music and the mystery, that he hadn't considered the consequences. Now his friend was dead.

His fault.

All him.

He could sense Stacee and Helene walking beside the Burro behind him. With most of its automation shot or repurposed, he'd programmed the robot to simply follow. Once again unconscious, Sven still road on its back, groaning as the machine lurched because of its missing leg. That was Marcos's fault too.

A gust of wind blew past, rustling through nearby scrub.

Marcos froze, every muscle going taut, every molecule ready to flee. His breathing came in quick, nervous gasps as he searched their surroundings for movement. In his hand, he hefted a piece of metal plating he'd removed from the Burro before leaving the arch a few hours earlier. He doubted it would make much of a weapon, but it was comforting just to hold it.

The wind passed, and the desert returned to its eerie silence. Marcos swallowed, feeling the dryness of his throat. Without looking at the others, he continued moving, forcing his eyes and thoughts onto the spire as they drew closer to it.

"Helene?"

It had been so long since anyone had spoken that Stacee's whisper caused Marcos to flinch.

"Yes?"

"Sven told us about Kyle," Stacee whispered, halting through the words. "I'm... I'm sorry."

Marcos's chest constricted. He knew from painful, repeated experience that mentioning Kyle was a good way to bring down Helene's wrath. But Sven's wife said nothing.

"I'm sorry," Stacee repeated after a long moment. "I just... After Pato... I'm sorry."

Marcos felt his throat catch at the sound of his friend's name. His grip on his makeshift club trembled, and his heart thudded as the guilt burned hotter than ever.

For the first time, he felt as though he understood Helene and what she had become after Kyle and Emily's accident. He thought of her phone, secretly plugged into the Burro, recharging as they walked. He'd found it in his pocket that morning, with no memory of how it had returned there. Now it burned in his mind as a symbol of kinship with a woman he had avoided and mocked for almost a full year.

"You liked Pato, didn't you?" Helene asked.

Marcos's chest tightened at the memory of his jealousy the night before. It burned with the rest of his guilt. He gritted his teeth and continued moving forward.

"He was sweet and cute," Stacee whispered. "I don't know if anything could have happened, but yeah."

Helene didn't reply, and the group continued walking in silence. Another gust of wind drew them to a momentary halt. Muscles taut and heart pounding, Marcos listened for the telltale clicks. When none came, they kept moving.

"What are you doing on this trip, Stacee?" Helene asked unexpectedly.

The girl snorted a dry, mirthless laugh. "What? You don't think I belong out here?"

"No," Helene's response was curt and direct. "And I don't think Marcos and Pato are your usual type, either. So, what are you doing?"

Marcos felt his cheeks flush at Helene's harsh assessment, but deep down, he knew that she was right. He slowed and cocked his head so he could hear better.

"It was the Burro," Stacee said after a long pause. "Marcos told me about it at the gym. I just had to see it myself."

"That's it?" Helene asked.

"I'd never been able to work with anything like it," Stacee said. "I really wanted the chance."

"You seem to be pretty good with tools," Helene said, obviously prompting the girl for more details.

"Yeah," Stacee replied wistfully. "I love working on things. My dad taught me when I was young. We used to restore cars out in the garage. We had this '67 convertible Ford Mustang. It was gorgeous. Candy-apple red. All original parts. Ran like a dream."

Marcos could hear the smile in her voice as she related the memory, but it was tinged with sadness and regret.

"What happened?" Helene asked.

"My parents divorced. Dad got the cars. Mom got me. She didn't approve of me working on cars. It reminded her of him. So I had to do it in secret until I graduated and got a job at the shop." She snorted. "Mom actually believed that the grease stains from my auto-shop class were paint from art. Like I could paint!" She laughed for a few seconds before adding, "I've been on my own for almost four years now. Mom doesn't even speak to me."

"What about college?"

"Nope. I kinda blew off high school, so my grades are crap. Besides, who would take me seriously in an engineering or mechanics program?"

"I would," Marcos blurted before he could stop himself.

"That's sweet," Stacee said. "But would you three weeks ago?"

Marcos almost assured her that he would have, but he hesitated. The truth was, he hadn't really considered her skills as a mechanic until the trip had started. Up to that point, he'd mostly paid attention to her body. But she had proved herself again and again, often coming up with creative ideas that were even better than his.

Before he could complete the thought, another gust of wind whistled past. He stiffened, his eyes once again combing the desert around them. Nothing moved. Nothing clicked. A few moments later, they were walking again, a little tenser than before.

"I can't really afford college, anyway," Stacee said, picking up the earlier conversation where it had fallen off, "not on my salary. Besides, my credit score's shot to hell, and I'm not about to ask my mom for anything, and Dad is who knows where."

Marcos furrowed his brow as another thought struck him. He almost spoke but hesitated, mulling it over. Deciding it was worth a try, he turned and looked back at Stacee, bringing all of them to a halt.

"What?" she asked.

"The McTiernan Group has this really awesome internship program," he told her. "College tuition, housing stipend, the works, and the company hires something like ninety percent of their interns. That's how Pato and I got there."

Stacee cocked her head as she took in his words, as if uncertain how they would apply to her. He cleared his throat.

"You know," he added, hoping she understood what he was saying. "If you're interested."

"You think I could get a McTiernan internship?" Stacee looked incredulous. "Me?"

"Yeah," he told her honestly, feeling relieved that she at least seemed interested. "I've seen you work. I'd recommend you. Sven would, too, and he's on the selection board. You're a slam dunk."

"Besides," Helene added dryly, "after all this, the company owes you."

Stacee stared at the two of them, her eyes wide and her head cocked to one side, as if she were considering.

Marcos shifted under her gaze and cleared his throat without any idea how to read her expression. He was serious about her chances, though. Stacee had more raw talent than most interns the company hired, and the trip had proved her ability to improvise and think on her feet. She just lacked the resources. Hell, Marcos would take the matter straight to Steve McTiernan himself if he had to.

Without warning, Stacee rushed to him. Before he could react, she flung her arms around him, pinning his to his sides. She buried her face in his shoulder.

"That... sounds... amazing," she gasped. "Thank you." She laughed, the kind that shook her whole body, and the sound echoed into the desert around them. Then she pulled back and stared into his eyes. "Thank you."

"Yeah," he croaked, his voice having disappeared somewhere. "Sure."

Looking suddenly shy, she stepped back and resumed her place next to the Burro, but her wide smile remained.

Marcos held still, his whole body tingling from her touch as his internal systems reset themselves. Feeling like he was in a trance or having and out-of-body experience, he turned back toward the spire.

That was when he heard the helicopter.

TWENTY-NINE

"LISTEN," MARCOS HISSED.

Stacee stiffened, the excitement of Marcos's talk about an internship vanishing as she closed her eyes and listened to the world around her, uncertain what sound she was supposed to hear. Her mind conjured memories of the night before, the terrible chatter of the rocks as they charged down on them, and their triumphant glee the moment Pato tumbled over the cliff. She shuddered as those telltale clicks sent terror through her. What she heard was not what she'd expected, however.

At first, the sound was distant, barely audible above the desert's silence, but then she heard a soft rhythmic thrum drifting over the sand.

A helicopter!

She spun around, squinting into the sky, searching for the source of the sound. Her heart pounded as she desperately sought out the black speck on the horizon that would be their salvation.

"What is it?" Helene asked, looking into the air skeptically.

"Helicopter," Marcos replied.

Seconds passed as they peered into the cloudless blue. The thrumming grew louder.

"I can hear it," Helene hissed, joining in the search.

"There," Marcos pointed with an excited shout.

Stacee squinted into the distance where he was pointing. Her heart leapt as she found the dark speck against the sky.

Marcos whooped, and Helene laughed.

"Is it the rescuers?" Stacee asked. Her voice had become breathless, the muscles in her neck tight. She thought she might cry.

"It must be," Marcos replied. "Hey!" he shouted toward the speck, waving his arms. "We're over here."

"They're too far away," Helene said. "They can't see us."

Marcos apparently didn't care. He yelled again, "Over here!"

Laughing, Stacee joined him. It didn't matter if the helicopter was too far away, calling to it felt good. "Come take us away," she yelled.

The helicopter drew closer, the speck growing larger, steadily taking shape. Hope throbbed in Stacee's heart. They had come at last.

Then it turned and flew off in another direction. Stacee and the others watched it go in silence. Slowly, she lowered her hands. Her heart slowed in disappointment.

All three of them stared after it until it vanished, and the sound faded to nothing.

"They're not looking for us here," Helene reminded them after a handful of despairing heartbeats.

They stood in silence for a long time, staring aimlessly at the ground or into the sky.

At last, Marcos grunted and turned back toward the spire. "The sooner we get the radio working, the sooner we can get out of here," he growled.

Fighting the urge to sit down and give up, Stacee turned back to their path, forcing herself to focus on the task at hand. She flinched as a gust of hot wind kicked up around them, whistling across the silent desert, stinging her eyes with dust.

Over the dune behind them came the distinctive rattle of insect-like clicks. Panic shot through her as she spun back toward it.

"They're following us," Helene shrieked, backing away from the dune. "They're following us!"

"We have to get out of here," Marcos said. "Now."

He turned and moved toward the spire with a speed beyond their exhaustion and fatigue. Stacee, Helene, and the Burro followed.

Behind them, the rocks chattered again as they picked up their pursuit.

———

THRUM. THRUM. THRUM. THE PULSING SOUND PENETRATED Vivek's nightmares. The black rocks pressing in on him in the dreamscape scattered before thrumming, clicking and chattering as they retreated into the dark recesses of his unconscious mind.

The thrumming grew louder, calling him back to the pain-filled waking world. With an effort, he forced open his dusty eyes.

The canyon, lit by the desert sun, stretched out before him. He closed his eyes against the glare. Drawing a deep breath, he tried again, and the view of the banded cliffs on the opposite side came into blurry focus.

He took another breath, the hot air burning his lungs. He coughed, sending pain through his entire body, feeling every ache from his stiffened, battered muscles. His fingers, caked with dried blood and red dirt, throbbed.

Vivek leaned back against the rock wall behind him and closed his eyes, trying to persuade the world to stop spinning.

The thrumming sound was growing louder as its source drew closer. Vivek struggled to place it in his muddy thoughts. It struck him in a flash. *Helicopter! Rescuers!*

He looked up, half expecting to see it in the sky above the canyon, but it was out of sight. Furrowing his brow, forcing his thoughts to crystalize, he realized that the helicopter must be headed to the place where the others had crossed—where everything had gone wrong. He shuddered as he wondered what they would find there.

"Have to get out of here," he said, his voice little more than a croak. "Have to get to them."

Placing his trembling hands on the ground to either side of him and positioning his aching feet, Vivek tried to stand. Something sharp caught on his back. Searing electric pain shot out from between his shoulder blades. He screamed and fell back, slamming his head against the wall, as the agony coursed through him. Stars and dark spots danced before his eyes.

His whole body felt like it was on fire. Muscles spasmed, and his fingers twitched uncontrollably. He gasped for breath, coughing again as he inhaled dust, deepening the ache from before.

He tried again, pushing himself up more slowly this time. Again, something caught on his back. Pain radiated through him. He slumped against the wall, his heart pounding and his brain struggling to understand what was happening.

The thrumming of the helicopter had grown even louder. Vivek could imagine it settling on the canyon's edge just a few hundred yards away.

Trembling, he reached behind him, squeezing his fingers between the rough sandstone and the back of his dust-coated shirt.

Horror filled him as his fingers connected with a hard, glassy surface that protruded from the wall and cut into his back.

"Shit!" He jerked his hand away and saw blood on his fingertips.

Reaching back again, Vivek could feel the sticky wetness surrounding the point of contact. Tearing at his shirt, he found hard lines beneath his skin, radiating out from where he was connected to the wall. Memories of the rocks attached to Pato's body flashed into his mind. The sickening tearing sound as he'd torn them free and the open wounds they'd left behind lingered in his thoughts.

Terror and panic burst out of him in a desperate, horrified scream that echoed through the canyon. The rock in his back flinched. Agonizing electric pain shot through him, turning his scream into a gasp. He gritted his teeth and squeezed his eyes shut as convulsions shook him. The tremors passed, and he collapsed back against the wall, his whole body shuddering.

Knowing rescue was so close yet unable to reach it, he lay still for several minutes, listening to the slowing thrum of the helicopter somewhere above. Sobs burst out of him in loud barks, and the black rock inside him twitched in protest at the sound.

He thought of Sven and the others, wondering where they were and what horrors they were facing. He thought of his wife and son. They would never know what happened to him.

Everything was a waste.

"No!" he shouted, suddenly angry. "No! No! No!"

He would not die out here. Not without a fight.

Clenching his fists and gritting his teeth, he braced himself against the wall.

"Three," he yelled, ignoring the twitch of the rocks responding to his voice. "Two... One."

He screamed as he threw himself forward, straining with all

his might. Intense agony shot through him. He screamed louder and pulled harder.

Dark spots danced before his eyes. His whole body spasmed from the searing pain shooting through him. It felt like he was tearing off a limb. He kept pulling.

Something in his back tore away with a wet ripping sound. A new, almost-crippling pain shot through him as he gained a millimeter.

With a final yell, Vivek jerked forward, straining again against the rocks that bound him. His back tore away from the wall as his savage scream of defiance echoed through the canyon. He fell forward, landing on the hard ledge, almost falling over the cliff.

Vivek lay there for a long time as the world tilted around him. Every inch of him burned. His muscles spasmed and twitched as electric currents crackled through his body. The gaping wound on his back stung in the open air. Blood trickled down his sides, soaking his shirt and dripping onto the parched ground.

From the wall behind him, the rocks chattered angrily. He looked back to discover that veins of the black glassy rock criss-crossed the wall, converging in a single fist-sized point that protruded from the rock and dripped with his blood. The veins rippled and clicked hungrily for him.

In terror, Vivek backed away, remembering too late the canyon behind him as his hands landed on nothing but air. He scrambled for a handhold as his body tipped over the edge. There was nothing to grab but sand and rock.

The black veins rattled in satisfaction as he slid over the edge and fell. He hit the bottom of the canyon with a sickening crunch of snapping bone. His vision flashed red with pain. The thrumming of the helicopter and the chatter of the black rocks grew hazy and distant. Everything faded into the black of unconsciousness.

THIRTY

Two-thirds of the way up the side of the spire, the Burro came to a sudden stop. Clinging to the wall ten feet below it, Marcos looked up. He studied the mass of dented chrome and moving parts, searching for any obvious reason why it had ceased moving. None presented itself.

"What happened?" Stacee called up from below him.

He looked down at her. Like him, she hung on the side of the spire, using cracks and fissures as handholds and footholds. A rope connected her to him, and a second tethered him to the Burro. That was all the safety they could afford with their meager supplies.

Marcos thought of Sven and Helene. He and Stacee had laid the unconscious project leader out on a long, flat rock in the shadow of the spire. Helene had stayed with him, seated on a rock by his side, holding his hand. Marcos wasn't even sure she knew they'd gone.

They had been climbing for half an hour and were making good time, but the sun was quickly sinking toward the horizon.

The last thing Marcos wanted was to be caught up there after dark, but the logical side of him pointed out that he might not have much choice in the matter—especially if the damned robot kept stopping.

"What happened?" Stacee asked again, forcing his wandering mind back to the moment.

Marcos blinked, trying to focus. It didn't help much. "It stopped."

He wasn't trying to be funny or dumb. His mind was just so worn and his body so fatigued that he couldn't think of anything better.

Stacee grunted. She was exhausted, too.

"I'm going to find out why," he said, turning back to the cliff.

Moving as quickly as safety and his aching muscles would allow, he climbed up to the Burro. Its five remaining clawed feet clung to the side of the cliff as its chrome-plated legs, now covered in dust, dents, and scratches, flashed in the last rays of sunlight.

Maneuvering himself alongside the machine, he checked it for obvious damage. Nothing. He reached for the remaining monitor on the side of its head, mentally figuring the commands he would have to enter to pull up its sensor logs, but paused when a refracted gleam of light caught his eye from the cliff immediately above the immobile robot.

Furrowing his brow, he climbed a few feet higher and studied the cliff. At first, the wall appeared to be just more sandstone, but as he looked closer, he could make out glass-like black veins in the rock.

Fear lanced through him, and he scrambled back down a couple of feet, almost losing his grip. Holding there, Marcos stared up at the veins, his heart thundering against his rib cage.

"What is it?" Stacee called up to him. "What's wrong?"

Marcos didn't answer. Instead, he scanned the wall above

them. Now that he knew what he was looking for, he could see dozens—even hundreds—of black veins coursing through the rock. The farther ones were thicker than the capillary-sized ones inches above the Burro. Marcos could make out a few that were at least a half inch thick, maybe wider. He wondered how much bigger they got even farther up and shuddered.

"Marcos, what is it?" Stacee demanded, sounding irritated.

"Veins," he called down.

"What?"

"There are veins of black rock in the wall."

She was silent for several long seconds as she processed what he'd just told her. He could imagine her fear and despair mounting as high as his own.

"Are you sure they're the same thing?" Stacee asked at last.

"I'm not going to ask them," Marcos called back, shuddering at the memory of his stupidity in the valley the night before and what it had cost them. "The Burro thinks they're bad. That's good enough for me."

"What are we going to do?"

Marcos looked at the robot then back at the cliff again. He tried to think, tried to come up with something—anything. He was an engineer—a damn fine one at that. Solving problems was what he did day in and day out. But exhaustion, dehydration, and shock from the last few days made thinking impossible. He could feel the ideas at the edge of his consciousness, but they refused to materialize.

With a sigh of defeat, he leaned his forehead against the wall. The aches in his muscles, the pain from his still-wounded hands, and the loss of his friend throbbed through him. He wished he could just let go and fall, but Stacee was counting on him. They all were counting on him.

He felt Stacee moving below and heard the scrape of her feet against the rock and her grunts of effort as she climbed. A moment later, she was clinging to the wall next to him.

He thought she was going to say something, but she remained silent. When he glanced at her, he saw her staring at the Burro and the wall above, her brow furrowed in concentration.

"Any ideas?" he asked.

She ignored him.

Marcos grunted and turned away to gaze into the valley, seeing it stretch out before them. The sun was almost to the horizon, and sunset already cast the world in a harsh red glow. Long shadows cut across the land below them. He wondered about the helicopter they had seen earlier and the rescuers it had carried. *If we turn on the radio now, will they hear it?*

Stacee drew a sudden intake of breath, the sound causing him to flinch. He turned back to find her looking from the Burro to the top of the spire and back again. She closed her eyes, visibly running calculations in her head.

"What?" he asked.

"How much cable do we have in the winch?" she asked.

Marcos furrowed his brow. "The winch?"

"How much?"

He looked back at the winch housing on the back of the Burro. He and Pato had swapped out the longer cable they'd used for the initial drop that first day for a shorter one to lighten the load. "A hundred feet."

She looked up and bobbed her head back and forth as she did some quick calculations. Even covered in dust and blood and with ratted, tangled hair, she was still the most beautiful woman he'd ever seen. His heart ached at the thought, remembering how close she had been standing to Pato the night before, how their fingers were intertwined, and how he didn't dare violate that memory with his own petty jealousy.

"Okay," Stacee said, pulling his wandering mind back.

He shook his head to clear away the thoughts that crowded in on every side. They didn't have time for him to be somewhere else, mentally or otherwise. He focused back on her.

"What if we use the harpoon?" she asked.

"The harpoon?"

"Yeah, we attach the cable to the winch. The Burro fires the harpoon to the top, then we ride it all the way up."

Marcos's heart beat a little faster, adrenaline trickling through him, as he glanced up. He made a few quick mental calculations. It was going to be tight, but it just might work.

"Let's try it," he said, grinning at her the best he could in his exhausted state.

———

It took ten minutes to turn the robot around and get the harpoon set in the right direction. In that ten minutes, the sun began lowering itself beneath the horizon, deepening the shadows around them. Stars were starting to sparkle in the eastern sky. Marcos barely noticed, though.

The Burro's targeting system was offline, so he made his best guess and crossed his fingers that it was even close. As he keyed in the final sequence and set the timer for the harpoon, he felt the lack of his friend. Pato was so much better at those kinds of things. Marcos swiped at his eyes and kept working. The sun was almost gone.

"Here we go," he said, hitting the execute button and clambering away from the Burro as it started the countdown.

Ten seconds had never felt so long.

As the last beep echoed from the robot, the harpoon fired with a resounding crack. Marcos watched the sound ripple through the veins of rock, the stone clicking in protest as the steel rod sailed upward. It thudded home with a satisfying *thunk* that dissipated across the landscape and agitated the rocks even further.

Marcos looked up, squinting in the fading light. The harpoon was lodged just a few feet below the top of the spire.

First try! He whooped and punched the air. Beside him, Stacee laughed, the sound coming out of her in uncontrollable, nervous bursts.

As the last vestiges of sunset faded into twilight, they climbed onto the Burro's back, securing both their ropes to it. When they were ready, Marcos reached down and tapped in the final command on the monitor.

With a screech of metal and a whine, the winch turned. The first movement shook the Burro. Marcos and Stacee tightened their grips. The winch continued turning. The Burro inched toward the top of the cliff, its feet holding the cliff face just tightly enough to keep its balance.

Marcos whooped again. Stacee smiled.

They cleared the edge of the veins and kept moving, rising steadily upward, the Burro walking backward up the cliff as the winch pulled them forward.

Five feet.

Ten.

Twenty.

The wind picked up, moaning around the spire. The veins of black rock reacted to the sound, twisting and writhing under the robot's feet. They slashed out from the cliff with knife-like slivers of rock. The slivers shattered against the metal robot, showering the ground below with broken fragments that sparkled in the fading light.

Marcos and Stacee laughed, the sound gleeful and manic,

overriding the bleak, somber mood that had fallen over them since the canyon.

It's working!

Marcos was so caught up in the moment that he didn't notice that the wind's high whistling sound had turned into a deep moan until the Burro's seismic alarm went off. That was when he heard the cracking sounds joining the clatter of clicks above them.

THIRTY-ONE

HELENE TREMBLED AS SHE LOOKED DOWN AT THE PHONE clutched in her hands. It was, she thought, such a small and insignificant thing to have so much power over her. The burning need for what it could give her coursed through her entire body, consuming her. She resisted, her breath coming in short gasps as she struggled in a fight that she knew she would eventually lose.

She had thought her phone was lost the night before. Its loss had filled her with anguish, but it also filled her with relief. *At last,* she'd thought, *it is over.* But just before leaving her and Sven at the base of the spire, Marcos had slipped it into her hands, met her eyes, and walked away without a word.

The phone had called to her ever since, taunting her, repulsing her, pulling at her, and pushing her away. The world around her, and even Sven, had blurred as she struggled against the undeniable urge to just turn it on and give in.

With a shuddering sigh, she looked at her husband. He lay stretched out a couple feet from Helene's knees. His white-blond hair stood in sharp contrast to his burned and peeling skin and dirt-covered bandages. He moaned and shifted his head from one side to the other.

A lump formed in her throat. She could do nothing to help her husband. She was certain he was going to die.

Just like Pato.

Just like Emily.

Just like Kyle.

She looked down at her reflection in the phone's shiny black screen, taking in her disordered, tangled hair. Dust, blood, and sweat streaked her blistered skin, and her lips were chapped. Her hollow eyes were circled with dark bruises, and her cheeks had grown gaunt. She looked like an alien creature from one of the movies Kyle used to watch late at night.

Her chest constricted at the thought of her son. The need intensified, crashing into her with overpowering, all-consuming waves. She closed her eyes and tightened her grip on the phone, feeling its sharp edges cut into her palm.

Desperately, she pressed the power button. The phone sprang to life, her background image of Kyle and Emily stealing her breath away.

She swiped across the screen but hesitated at the PIN. Shaking, she glanced over at Sven. His blond hair rustled in a light breeze, and his chest rose and fell. Helene sighed and looked up at the dimming sky, wishing she still believed in a god who cared about her or her family.

Helene turned back to the phone, the piece of metal and plastic and glass that had become her whole world. Her hands trembled as she touched the screen. Its cold smoothness felt foreign in this place of rough stone and scorching heat.

Emotions welled up in her, emotions she had long kept at bay. The exhaustion, the terror, the dehydration, and the sense of impending doom flooded into her. Dry tears pricked at the edges of her aching eyes, and her heart beat out a mournful requiem. Darkness that had nothing to do with the encroaching night closed in on her. She welcomed it. She shrank from it.

Helene lowered her head and focused on nothing but breathing.

In. Out. In. Out.

Bit by bit, the need ebbed, leaving her alone with Sven, the phone, and an eternity of pain and self-recrimination.

She looked at her husband, wishing for his strong, caring, loving caress, wishing he could somehow make everything right, but he couldn't. All that was wrong could not be righted.

Kyle...

"I'm so sorry," she whispered, staring at Sven's face.

She'd lost count of the number of times she had whispered those same words to her husband while he slept or was just out of earshot. If he knew everything, he would never forgive her. She would never forgive herself.

Brushing at her eyes, she reached up and took Sven's hand again. It was so cold, so lifeless, but there was still a pulse. He hadn't left her. Not yet.

"I have to tell you something," Helene croaked, her voice dry and rasping. "It's something I should have told you a long time ago."

She sighed and looked into the distance, watching as the last vestiges of sunset faded, trapping the world in shadow.

"I killed our son," she whispered. "I killed him."

She looked back at Sven, a single tear—all her dried-out body could manage—trickling down her cheek.

"You know I didn't like Emily," she said. "I thought Kyle deserved better. Her UFO fascination... I didn't understand, didn't think that she was worthy of him." Her face burned with shame. The knot in her throat grew more painful.

"The night before they left for Williams, while you were at the office, Kyle and I had a fight. He told me he was going to propose. Showed me the ring. I was so angry. I told him..." She broke down, sobs convulsing her whole body. Her tears were all used up, but still she sobbed, choking on the dust and coughing through her sorrow.

At last, the sobs subsided. She cleared her throat and pushed on. "I told him that if he married her, he was no longer welcome in our home. I said that she would never be my daughter. That I could never accept her."

That terrible night was recreated perfectly in her memory. She saw the shocked, hurt look on Kyle's face the moment the hateful words had left her mouth, but her pride and anger had prevented her from taking them back.

Helene tightened her grip on her phone, turning her knuckles white. She sighed. "The next day, Kyle sent me a video. He'd made it that night. I don't think he slept at all."

She held up the phone and thumbed the power button again, bringing the device to life. Running on muscle memory, she tapped out K-Y-L-E and found the video app. She opened it and, without hesitation, started the video. She watched in silence as it came to life.

Her son stared directly at the camera. His eyes were red, his shoulders slumped in defeat, but there was a terrible determination about him.

"Hi, Mom," Kyle said after a long moment, his voice soft and distant. He hesitated, as if struggling with the words.

Helene had watched the video so many times, she knew every movement, every crease of the brow, every frown, every tear, and every heart-stabbing word by heart. She swallowed with her son and shuddered as he looked straight into the camera, peering at her with accusing eyes.

"Mom, I know you don't like Emily. I don't know why. I don't think any girl will ever be good enough for you. But, Mom, I love her. I love Emily more than anything in the whole world. She makes me feel alive the same way Dad does for you. When I'm with her, it's like anything is possible." He wiped at his eyes and continued. "I always thought that someday you'd see that. I guess not."

Even after so many repeat viewings, the words struck Helene like a whip. She closed her eyes, her whole body trembling.

"I'm going to do as you wish," Kyle continued. "We won't come into your home again. Not until you invite us. Not until..." He shook his head as his voice broke. "I don't know."

Helene's chest was so tight it was hard to breathe. She wanted to reach out, to take her little boy in her arms and tell him how sorry she was, how she hadn't meant what she'd said, how she loved him. But it was too late. Far too late.

"I'm going to propose to Emily tomorrow," Kyle said. "When we get home, we're going to take you and Dad out to breakfast. And then..." He paused, clearing his throat. Without opening her eyes, Helene could see him look down, brush the tears away, and look up with the stubborn determination he'd inherited from her. "And then we'll say goodbye.

"I love you, Mom. I love you, but the truth is that I love Emily more. After tomorrow, I don't think I want to see you for a while. Maybe... maybe at the wedding. I..." He shook his head, words failing him again. After a moment, he reached for the camera. "Goodbye."

The screen went black.

Helene thumbed the power button, sending the video into oblivion.

"I should have told you," she whispered to Sven, barely able to speak. Tentatively, she reached out and took his hand, holding it gently, supplicating. "I should have told you. I just couldn't. And then... He'd been up for over forty-eight hours when they started driving home. It was my fault. My fault. I killed him. I killed our son."

The tiniest flicker of pressure on her fingers brought her head up. She stared at Sven. He stared back.

THIRTY-TWO

Panic shot through Stacee as the Burro's seismic alarm blasted into the night. She tightened her grip and held her breath, waiting for the attack. Nothing happened. The winch continued to pull them up the cliff at a steady pace, and the wall continued to slide by as the top grew closer. Then, beneath the combined roar of the alarm, the wind, and the chattering rocks, something cracked.

Marcos yelled, and Stacee looked up the same moment that a softball-sized chunk of sandstone shot past her head. She flinched back as it flew by. The rock vanished into the growing darkness below. A second and a third followed. They struck the robot, shaking it with resounding clangs before disappearing into the night.

More rocks fell. Stacee dodged left and right in the limited space allowed on her side of the Burro's back, sometimes knocking into Marcos, who was doing the same on his side. A stone landed a glancing blow to her shoulder. She gritted her teeth and held on even tighter.

Above them, the wall rippled, the solid stone moving like a wave toward them. It hit the Burro with a jolt, almost dislodging it from the side of the cliff. Stacee and Marcos screamed as they were thrown back. Their screams were cut short as they slammed back into the robot, the impact almost driving the air from Stacee's lungs. She felt her hands slip on her handgrip and tightened her hold, clinging with all her strength.

The wall exploded into a cacophony of furious chatter from the veins of black stone. They twisted and writhed under the feet of the Burro. Stacee watched, wide-eyed, as the black veins grew, burrowing through the rock and expanding in girth. Black lines that could have been no more than pencil marks on the red sandstone were now an inch thick and growing. The wall cracked and split, dropping chunks of rock into the dark abyss as the black veins expanded.

Falling stones continued to crash into the Burro from above. The robot shook beneath the onslaught. Another rock glanced off Stacee's forehead, leaving a sharp, stinging pain and a trickle of blood in its wake. A second smacked into her forearm, almost causing her to let go, but she somehow held on.

"What do we do?" she shouted to Marcos, stealing a glance at him.

A line of blood from a small wound above his right eye trickled down his face.

"Just hold on," he shouted. "We'll reach the top—"

A stone the size of a volleyball smashed into the Burro with a thundering clang of rock on steel. The robot bucked with the impact. Stacee's feet broke free of their perch, and for an eternal, terrible moment, she dangled over open space. She screamed, instinctively tightening her grip.

Her legs swung back and connected violently with the Burro's hard casing. She gritted her teeth and pulled herself back into place. Pain radiated from her knee.

"Are you okay?" Marcos shouted.

"I'm good," she shouted back, ignoring the throbbing from her leg.

"Watch out!"

Another large rock struck the Burro. The foreleg above Marcos's head crumpled beneath it. Gears and servos whined and snapped as they broke. The large rock kept going, shooting past the engineer's head but striking his leg. Marcos screamed.

The Burro lurched, almost jolting Stacee from her place. Her hands were slipping even more.

The robot's damaged leg stuck out into the air. It twitched as the shattered inner workings struggled to continue functioning. Then something snapped and the limb went slack. It swung down, slamming into Marcos and knocking him across the robot's back into Stacee. Miraculously, they both maintained their grip.

With a yell of pain, Marcos pulled himself back to his side. He clung so tightly to his handhold that Stacee could see his knuckles turn white. His eyes were squeezed shut against the pain.

More rocks broke from the cliff above, striking the Burro again and again. The robot jerked and bucked with each impact. Chrome plating shattered, and sharp pieces of metal flashed as they flew away into the void. The machine's exoskeleton bent. Cracks appeared along the casing, exposing internal workings and circuitry. The winch whined as it struggled to keep pulling them up the cliff.

"How much more can she take?" Stacee shouted to Marcos as another rock struck the robot, widening a six-inch crack in the housing just below the winch casing.

Marcos still clung to his handhold, his head lowered and his eyes squeezed shut. He didn't answer her.

The barrage stopped. One moment, the world was trying to kill them, then the next, they were steadily moving up the cliff, disturbed by nothing more than the whir of the winch.

Stacee clung to her handhold, gasping as she looked around, trying to make sense of what had happened. Her skin crawled, and the hairs on her neck and arms prickled. Anticipation crackled in the air, louder than the chatter of writhing stones and the Burro's continuous alarm.

She looked up, gauging the distance to the top. Maybe forty feet left. They just had to hold on.

"What the hell happened?" Marcos asked, lifting his head and looking around. His voice was tense with pain.

Before Stacee could answer, the wall heaved outward. It slammed into the Burro with a screech of rending metal and the snap of gears. Stacee felt the robot's legs crumple as the wall crashed into them.

The wall heaved again, hitting them with a resounding crash. The last remnants of the Burro's legs shattered. Free from the wall, the robot swung at the end of the cable. Stacee's heart lurched as they flew over the dark abyss.

They crashed back into the wall. Rocks and metal debris filled the air. Pain shot through Stacee as she connected with the Burro's broken casing and jagged pieces of metal sliced into her. She screamed, her grip so tight that her hands ached.

She met Marcos's eyes. He clung to his own handhold as blood ran freely down his face. His eyes were filled with horror.

The wall bucked again, knocking the crippled Burro away from the cliff. They crashed back, only to be hit a second and a third time. Stacee yelled in pain as falling debris cut her skin and stones rained down on them like bullets.

The wall slammed into them again. Stacee's fingers slipped. She screamed as she fell into the night.

THIRTY-THREE

HELENE STARED AT SVEN. HIS EYES FLASHED IN THE moonlight as he stared back. Her heart pounded at the thought of what she had just said and how much he had heard. She'd wanted to tell him everything for so long, but the thought of what he would think of her was almost too much to bear.

"Hi," Sven whispered. His voice was so weak she could barely hear it, even though she was inches away.

"How much...?" She couldn't bring herself to finish the question.

Sven coughed, the rough, wet sound wracking his feeble-looking frame. Helene grasped his hand and leaned forward. The coughing subsided, and her husband looked up at her again. He attempted a smile, the corners of his lips twitching upward, but ultimately failed. He coughed a second time.

"It wasn't your fault," he whispered.

A shiver went through Helene, her heart both breaking and lifting free with the knowledge that now he knew the truth.

"Kyle..." Sven said. "It wasn't your fault. He loved you."

Helene dropped her eyes. "If I hadn't fought with him... If I had just..."

"Not your fault," Sven repeated, his voice sounding stronger. "It... It was mine."

Helene stared at him, unable to comprehend what he was saying or what he could possibly mean. "No," she protested. "No, it wasn't."

Sven coughed again and leaned his head back, staring up at the sky. He blinked as if trying to hold back tears. "Williams... The star-gazing event. The whole thing was my idea," he said at last. "I found out about it from Marcos. I got Kyle the tickets. I even helped him buy the ring. If I hadn't... If I had just..." He swallowed and closed his eyes. "Not your fault," he finished with the slightest shake of his head.

Helene stared at him, her mind whirling. Guilt collided with denial, brewing a storm inside her. There was no way Sven could have known, no way he could have—

"No," she said, cutting off her own thoughts and squeezing his hand. "It was me. It was what I said. You didn't see the look in his eyes. I don't... I can't..."

"He loved you," Sven whispered.

"But—"

"He. Loved. You." Another coughing fit overtook her husband. He groaned and lay back against the rock, panting.

Helene leaned forward, wishing she could do more than hold his hand and hope.

After a strained moment, Sven said, "You didn't mean what you told him. Kyle didn't, either."

"You don't know that." Helene sobbed. "You weren't there."

"I still know."

Helene stared at him, the man she loved, the man she had mistreated, ignored, and even hated for so long. In spite of everything, he still loved her. That, for her, had been the unforgivable sin. How could he love her when she hated herself for what she had done?

Another coughing fit struck Sven, and each hacking breath caused him to shake and tremble from pain and effort. Helene gripped his hand as tightly as she could. When the coughs subsided, he lay back, gasping for breath, his eyes squeezed shut.

They sat in silence for a time. Helene clutched his hand as if it were the only lifeline holding him to earth. Perhaps it was.

Sven breathed with ragged, dry breaths that came in painful spurts. At last, he broke the silence. "He was my son, too."

He closed his eyes again and swallowed, his whole body shuddering from the exertion. Helene brushed at her eyes and the painful lump in her throat almost choking her.

She studied her husband, her eyes tracing the outlines of his face in the darkness. Even after all those years, he was so handsome. She knew every detail of his face, every curve and line. Every blemish. Every scar.

Hesitantly, she leaned over and kissed his forehead. "I'm sorry."

"I'm sorry too." He squeezed her hand ever so slightly.

She squeezed back as gently as she could. She laid her head on his shoulder, listening to his labored breathing, hearing an ominous click in his chest. They sat that way for a long time, the seconds ticking away into darkness as the night deepened. The moments felt like an eternity as the weight of a lifetime and the echoes of years of sorrow disappeared into the gloom.

Above them, the wind whistled past the spire. Helene wondered whether Marcos and Stacee had reached the top and if they'd been able to get the signal working. She wondered what had happened to Vivek and the helicopter they'd seen earlier that day. All those people and things seemed so far away from her and Sven.

They were like a memory from another lifetime, as if here and now, only the two of them existed in the whole universe.

Inside, she could still feel the burning fires of guilt and anger that had ruled her life from that terrible moment she'd answered the door to the policeman and had known instantly what he was going to say. She didn't think those fires would ever go out, but in this moment, clinging to her husband, with the words "He loved you" ringing in her ears, their heat had abated. In that moment, the fury had calmed. In that moment, she was at peace.

Sven broke the silence, whispering in a voice sadder than she'd ever heard, "I should have never brought us here."

Helene opened her eyes and lifted her head. She peered at him through the darkness. He was staring up at the stars, his face stricken with grief.

"Pato..." he whispered, closing his eyes.

"You couldn't have known," she said, but he shook his head.

"I just... When Marcos came to me with the idea, I thought about all the times Kyle and I talked about doing something like this. I just wanted to feel close to him again. And then... And then you said you'd come, and I thought, maybe... maybe this would fix things, make them like they were before." He looked at her, his eyes staring deep into her own. "I should have known better."

Helene shook her head, her heart aching for his pain as much as her own.

"I came because I couldn't lose you," she whispered. "Not like Kyle. I don't think I'd survive."

Sven squeezed her hand, unexpectedly bringing a smile to her face. Suddenly, they were the perfect pair: they were both broken.

Something moved at the corner of Helene's vision, a shadow passing through the night. Slowly, moving as if she were in a haze, Helene turned toward it. She squinted into the darkness, trying to make out what she had seen.

"What?" Sven asked.

She shook her head, uncertain. Staring into the gloom, she searched for the shadow that had moved. Her heart pounded, the feeling of anticipation growing with each second.

It moved again. The shadow was a good twenty yards off and difficult to make out in the darkness, but as her eyes adjusted, its outline became clear.

It was a man.

THIRTY-FOUR

THE HUNGRY DARKNESS REACHED UP AS STACEE FELL AWAY
from the Burro. She screamed, the sound rippling through the
black veins in the wall. They chattered back in triumph.

Then Marcos was there. One bandaged hand shot out and
closed around her harness. Stacee slammed hard into the straps.
Pain jolted through her.

With a guttural, animal cry, Marcos strained, lifting her back
to her handhold. She scrambled for it, her fingers and feet
fumbling against the smooth metal of the Burro's back. The engineer heaved. Stacee's fingers closed around the grip.

The wall smashed into them again, bashing into the underside
of the crippled machine. Stacee tightened her precarious hold as
they swung into space and fell back with a bone-jarring crunch
against the side of the cliff. She pulled herself into a better position, clinging to the handgrip with everything she had left.

"The winch!" Marcos yelled.

Ice shot through Stacee as she looked up at the dented winch
casing a couple feet above her head. She could still hear the motor

grinding, but they weren't moving anymore. The top of the spire was still at least twenty feet away.

"It's probably caught on the housing," she yelled back, her mind spinning.

If the winch motor was caught on something, it could burn out, and they would be stranded.

Before Marcos could reply, the wall slammed into them again, catching the robot on the right side. They tilted as they flew into the night, the darkness blurring around them. Stacee closed her eyes and gritted her teeth as they crashed back into the wall.

She opened her eyes to Marcos reaching for the toolbox beside the winch. It was just out of his reach. He tried to pull himself up, yelled in pain, and fell back into his harness, his face pinched in agony.

The wall slammed into them again, almost flipping them over. Stacee pulled herself tight to the machine as the cliff loomed up behind her. She could hear the veins in the wall click angrily as she drew close.

The Burro spun back the other way. Rocks and debris rained down on them as it impacted with the stone.

"Can you reach the toolbox?" Marcos shouted to Stacee.

Her heart pounded in her ears as she looked up at the red toolbox nestled beside the winch casing. She reached for it, her fingers curling around the edge as she strained for the latch to the metal band holding it in place. Her shoulder burned as she stretched her arm as far as she could. She just needed a few more inches.

Gritting her teeth, she heaved herself up, using the remains of the Burro's shattered legs as handholds. The toolbox came within reach. With a triumphant whoop, she undid the latch.

The wall bucked again.

Stacee grabbed the Burro just in time but watched in horror as the toolbox jostled free and tumbled away. With a scream, she lunged for it. Her fingers closed around the handle just before it fell out of reach. The weight of the heavy box jolted her, pulling her from her grip, but before she could tumble away, Marcos grabbed her around the waist, holding her in place. Then the Burro slammed back into the wall with a jarring crash.

Marcos yelled. His face contorted in pain as he held her. Stacee grabbed onto the robot and pulled the box up to her level.

"You'll have to fix it," Marcos shouted. His left arm dangled uselessly next to him, his shoulder clearly dislocated. "Just remove the casing and find out what's jamming it."

Stacee nodded and turned back to the winch. Jagged pieces of metal bit into her hands as she climbed to a better position. Her fingers and palms grew wet and sticky with blood.

The wall heaved again, slamming them back into open air. Before they crashed back, Stacee saw something growing from the side of the wall—thick tendrils of black rock with razor-sharp tips. As the Burro struck the wall, one of the tendrils slashed at her, cutting deep into her leg. Blood trickled down her calf. The Burro rolled, shattering the tendril under its weight, but in her peripheral vision, she could see at least three more forming all around them.

Forcing the pain and the tendrils from her mind, Stacee balanced the toolbox on top of the Burro and flipped it open. She grabbed a handful of tools then tucked them into her belt.

Wielding a screwdriver, she attacked the screws holding the dented casing in place. They were tight and fought her. The Burro rocked and shook as the wind and tendrils of rock assaulted it. The maddening clicks of the black rocks and the constant blasting of the seismic alarm penetrated her skull, echoing in her mind. She worked faster. Thirty seconds later, she had two of the four screws free and was working at the third.

The wall heaved again. Stacee barely had time to grab hold as they spun away from the cliff. The unsecured toolbox clattered from its perch, flinging tools into the darkness as it fell toward the ground, barely missing the engineer below. Stacee screamed as they slammed back into the wall. A jagged piece of metal sliced deep into her thigh. Another tendril slashed at her, barely missing before shattering on the Burro's metal plating.

Without even taking time to gasp, Stacee lunged for the remaining screws. A moment later, she had them all out.

She grabbed the casing and pulled. It resisted. She jerked harder, yanking at the warped metal, feeling its rough edges cut into her fingers. It came free with a snap, almost causing Stacee to lose her balance. Marcos yelled as the useless casing flew past him.

After sharing a quick glance with Marcos to ensure he was all right, Stacee turned back to the winch. It only took a second to find the problem: a thick shard of black rock was jammed into the gears. The motor growled, fighting the block. It was only a matter of time before it gave out entirely. Using the screwdriver, she forced the rock out and knocked it away.

She whooped, but her elation was dimmed as the winch motor died.

Yelling in anger, she pulled herself higher and stared into the winch's inner workings, her mind spinning. *The gears aren't jammed anymore, so something must be wrong with the motor.*

She tore at the secondary housing that protected the motor, wrenching it free. The engine underneath was small but powerful. It was also a mess. Wires had been severed, and gears had been pulled from their places.

Stacee reached for the gears but jumped back as a sharp black spike shot out from a shadow, barely missing her fingers. She watched in horror as a fist-sized rock twisted into view, its sharp edges flashing menacingly in the darkness.

Anger boiling out of her, Stacee screamed at the rock. She

lunged for it, hammering into it with the handle of the screw-driver. It shattered, the shards tumbling away into the void below.

She grasped for the wires and gears, refastening and snapping them into place as fast as she could. The moment she reconnected the last part, the motor whirred back to life. The Burro started moving again.

With a triumphant yell, she looked down at Marcos. He gave her an agony-filled thumbs-up. Then the wall slammed into them again.

Stacee was caught unprepared. The impact threw her back. Her hand slid along the cracked and broken pieces of the robot. Rough metal sliced deep into her fingers. She scrambled for a more secure grip as the Burro crashed back into the wall. Jagged shards of metal cut into her arm.

Without pause, the wall bucked again and again, smashing into them, shoving them back. She screamed as she saw her blood splatter over the shattered plating around her. Her grip slipped even more. Below her, Marcos was yelling.

A fifth impact knocked her from her perch. She scrabbled for a better hold but felt herself slide down the machine. She caught herself just before tumbling into the darkness, clinging to one of the handgrips by the machine's head with a single hand as the world spun around her.

The Burro reached the end of its arc and swung back toward the cliff. Stacee screamed as she flew toward it. Sharp black tendrils reached for her.

"Stacee!" Marcos shouted.

They slammed into the wall with a resounding crash. Pain shot through her as black tendrils of stone cut straight through her shoulder and abdomen. Blood dripped into the darkness as they exited the other side. She tasted blood as it bubbled up in her mouth.

Above her, she felt the Burro slide away, continuing its steady climb up the slope. Marcos was yelling, but his words were lost in the sudden silence around her.

She turned and stared into the night-shrouded valley below them. Her eyes looked to the stars above. They were so bright.

She thought of the internship Marcos had promised her and of a dreamed-about future she would never have. She thought of Pato, his face looming before her in the darkness. She thought of her mother, the memory of their last argument echoing in her mind.

The tendrils slid away from her, coming out as cleanly as sharpened swords. Stacee fell. She felt the snap of the rope still attached to the Burro as she reached its end. With a painful jolt, she slammed into her harness, feeling her neck crack as she swung back toward the cliff.

She felt no pain or regret as her world went black.

THIRTY-FIVE

Helene bolted to her feet, staring after the shadow of the man. She watched, eyes wide, as he rounded the base of the spire and vanished.

"What is it?" Sven asked.

"A person," Helene gasped, fighting against the hope that surged through her. "A man."

"Vivek?"

Helene shook her head, uncertain. It was too dark to make out any details, but the man had seemed taller and his gait stiffer than Vivek's.

"Go," Sven whispered.

She hesitated, looking down at him, hope for a chance of rescue battling against her need to stay with her husband.

"Go," he urged again.

Helene began to move. Her legs were sluggish and stiff. Every part of her body ached. She pushed through it, forcing herself into a painful jog.

"Wait!" she called after the shadow. "Wait!"

She made it to the place where the man had disappeared. Even in the darkness, she could make out footprints in the sand as they rounded the corner and walked along the curving base of the spire. Helene ran after them, ignoring the wind that whistled around her, tossing her hair into her face.

The prints continued thirty paces then turned another corner. As she rounded it, she caught a flicker of movement as the shadow turned around another bend farther down the base of the cliff.

"Wait," she called again, rushing forward.

Her thoughts jumbled as she ran, filling her with questions: *Is he one of the rescuers? If he is, how did they find us? If not, who is he and what is he doing way out here?*

She pushed the questions aside and focused on the corner ahead of her. An unexpected gust of wind caught her full in the face as she rounded it, kicking dust into her eyes.

Helene flinched back, raising her hand and turning away. When she looked again, the man was standing twenty yards away, hands on his hips as if waiting for her to come closer. His features were still lost in the darkness, but something made Helene hesitate. There was something about the way the figure stood, the stiffness of his posture, the sharpness of his build, or the angle of his head that bothered her.

"Hello?" she called, suddenly uncertain.

Another gust of wind blasted into her. She turned away from it, protecting her eyes. When she turned back, the man was gone.

For a long moment, Helene stared at the space where he had been, blinking in stunned disbelief. Her heart pounded, and chills ran down her arm. She took a step backward as she scanned the world around her, looking for any sign of where he had gone. Her stomach twisted, and she swallowed, feeling something off about the whole situation but unable to say exactly what it was.

She thought of Sven, of his injuries and his diminishing

strength. Her need to be with him and the strange behavior of the man battled with the possibility that whoever the shadow was could be their salvation. Gritting her teeth, she forced herself forward. If there was a chance they could escape this desert alive, she had to take it for Sven's sake. She moved forward again.

The man's footprints led her to where he had stood moments earlier then abruptly vanished. Helene looked around, searching for any indications of where he had gone or how. There were no signs, no marks on the ground or the wall. Nothing.

Helene's stomach twisted again as the uneasy feeling grew stronger than before. The night seemed to advance on her, closing in, blocking her escape. Her hope from minutes earlier evaporated in the hot desert air.

Above her head, something let out a series of sharp, insect-like clicks. Flinching back from the sound, Helene looked up, squinting into the darkness. Ten feet above her head, standing straight out from the side of the cliff, was the man.

Helene backed away, staring in shock at the shadow. It regarded her, its eyes lost in the darkness. Closer up, she could see what had bothered her before: the shadow's edges were too sharp, its lines too straight and precise. Its outline suggested the shape of a human being without having replicated it perfectly.

The wind gusted around them, whistling and moaning around the spire and through nearby rocks and sagebrush. The silhouette quivered as the sound rippled through it. The resulting clatter became mocking laughter.

Helene's heart thundered as she backed away even farther. The knot in her stomach twisted as a lump formed in her throat.

The shadow watched her, studying her with its cold, black eyes, its face emotionless, as if it were carved from stone. Then, as Helene watched in horror, the man-thing shrank, collapsing into itself, melting into the rock. A moment later, it was gone.

Helene stood for several seconds, staring at where the figure had been, her mind spinning, trying to process what she had seen. It was all so impossible.

Sven!

The image of her husband lying alone at the base of the cliff, unprotected, flashed into her mind as a jolt of panic shot through her. Above, she heard the mocking laughter of the rocks. Her blood ran cold.

Helene turned and ran.

———

SVEN LAY ON THE ROCK, STARING UP INTO THE STARS littered across the sky. So many hundreds of miles from the city lights, he could see into forever. He wondered if somewhere up there, Kyle was looking back at him.

He coughed. The sound was wet and sticky, bringing with it the taste of blood. His chest rattled as he breathed, echoing the pain that continually coursed through him.

The half-moon was cresting over the horizon, bathing the red spire that rose above him in pale-blue light. In his drifting thoughts, Sven wondered about Marcos and Stacee. *Did they get the radio repaired? Is help on its way? Does it matter?*

He closed his eyes and thought about Helene. The words of her confession floated through him, carrying away the guilt and anger of the last horrible year. Perhaps, Sven mused, the trip had been worth something after all.

The wind moaned around him. Something chattered to his left. Beyond pain or fear, Sven turned his head and looked in the direction of the sound. Standing a couple yards from his head was a foot-high, pyramid-shaped pile of black stone.

It stood there, a silent sentinel watching over him. As he

watched, the pile moved closer, the individual rocks clicking as they twitched and writhed to create the motion. The faceted sides of the stones flashed in the moonlight.

With the detachment of the dying, Sven watched it come. He was vaguely interested to discover a second pyramid at his feet and a third approaching his head. He lay back and sighed.

He had been expecting them.

The piles paused a few inches from him. They sat for a long moment, churning and twisting, filling the air with their chatter. Then, as one, they advanced.

Sven closed his eyes and let them come.

———

"Sven!" Helene screamed as she raced along the base of the spire, heading back the way she had come.

The wind chased her as she ran. It howled at her, chiding her for being so stupid.

"Sven!" she yelled as she rounded the second corner, pushing through the aching burn in her chest. "Sven!"

Behind her, the chatter and mocking laughter of the rocks faded into the darkness. She ran faster.

She rounded the last corner and came to a sudden, horrified stop. For a long moment, she stared at the place where she had left her husband, her eyes wide in disbelief and her heart pounding with despair.

The flat rock was there.

The footprints she'd left behind were there.

Sven was gone.

THIRTY-SIX

MARCOS SCREAMED AS STACEE'S BODY HIT THE END OF THE rope and impacted with the cliff. The jolt caused what was left of the Burro to rock violently, but Marcos barely noticed. All he could see was her limp body dangling below him like a broken doll. Her face was covered in blood.

The whole thing had been so sudden and so unexpected that there had been nothing he could do. By the time he was able to react, she was already gone.

He rested his head against the back of the robot, his eyes struggling to form tears his dehydrated body couldn't support.

"Dammit!" he yelled, the curse rippling out through the wall as the veins of rocks chittered in response.

A large tendril growing from the wall struck the robot again, spinning it out over the darkness. Instinctively, Marcos tightened his grip. They slammed back into the wall. Fragments of sandstone and shards of black rock showered onto him. He barely noticed.

Below, Stacee's body crumpled as it hit the wall. Marcos was glad she couldn't feel it.

The winch stopped. Expecting some new horror, Marcos looked up. He was surprised to see the top of the cliff just a handful of feet above the battered remains of the Burro. They had made it. *He* had made it.

Now what?

He shifted, trying to gain leverage to climb up, but pain shot through him, radiating from his dislocated shoulder through his entire body. Stars danced before his eyes, and black spots flitted at the edge of his vision. He gritted his teeth and groaned. The moment and the pain passed, leaving him breathless.

Gasping, he looked down at his shoulder. It hung two inches lower than it should have. He shuddered, knowing he had to push it back into place—and that it was going to hurt.

Gritting his teeth against the coming agony, he looped his arm around a piece of shattered robot leg, wedging it as best he could. He braced himself, trying not to think about what he was about to do. After three quick breaths, he jerked back.

He screamed as his arm pulled out and snapped back into place. The pain was so intense he almost blacked out. He leaned his head against the Burro's back and closed his eyes, letting the waves of pain wash through him.

Eventually, the intensity subsided. Marcos flexed his hand. Fire shot through his arm, but it was operational. That would have to do.

For a moment, he hung on the back of the Burro, gathering his strength for what he had to do next. Slowly, he became aware of how quiet things had become. He looked around, startled to find that both the rocks and the alarm had fallen silent in the last few moments.

"The wind," he muttered to himself, noting that it had died to a gentle breeze.

He briefly wondered how long he had before it started up

again, before all hell broke loose. Minutes? Seconds? Either way, he needed to work fast.

Climbing around the side of the robot, wincing and groaning as he used his injured arm, he found the radio compartment. The protective cover had been hammered by the assault. It was dented and scraped, but it was still intact.

He grabbed for it. His trembling fingers gripped one of the bent edges, and he pulled, trying to pry it open. The metal plate wouldn't give. He tried again. Nothing.

He thought of the toolbox tumbling into the darkness and closed his eyes in frustration. He furrowed his brow, forcing himself to think, trying to come up with an alternative. He fought the urge to abandon the robot and climb the last few feet to safety. Helene and Sven needed him. By God, he would not let them down.

Marcos glanced down at Stacee again, wishing she were able to help. Her limp, broken body spun at the end of the rope. Guilt washed over him, joining the constant, overwhelming shame he felt over Pato's death. Marcos shuddered and started to look away when something glinted from her waist.

Marcos gasped. Tucked into Stacee's belt, flashing dully in the moonlight, was a set of tools—a screwdriver, a pair of pliers, and a wrench.

Without bothering to wonder how the tools had gotten there, Marcos grabbed her rope and heaved, trying to pull her upward. Pain shot through his arm, and dark spots flashed at the edge of his vision. He let go of the rope and leaned against the robot, panting. Obviously, if he wanted the tools, he was going to have to go down there and get them.

He looked at the wall, a shudder going through him. The moonlight glinted on the veins of black rock, but nothing moved.

The wind around him was still and silent. *But how long will that last?*

Marcos looked down at Stacee again, the fear building inside him, battling with his resolve. He forced himself to remember the look on Pato's face just before the surging rocks had driven him over the cliff, forced himself to remember the last words his friend had said to him: "Help Stacee." He thought of Helene and Sven and remembered the project leader's broken body. They were all counting on him.

"Help Stacee," Marcos whispered, turning it into a rallying cry. "Help Stacee."

Gripping her rope, he eased himself to the edge of the Burro and reached for the side of the cliff. The earlier assault had left countless fissures and cracks on the wall, so finding handholds and footholds was not difficult. He tested his weight on them, and they held.

Drawing a deep breath, he slid away from the Burro and clung to the rock. His heart pounded as he began to climb down. In spite of the panic that surged through him, urging him to greater speed, he took his time, deliberately testing each handhold and foothold. His labored breathing was loud and harsh in his ears as he inched his way past motionless veins of black rock. He expected the wind to pick up at any moment and for the wall to attack again, but he forced himself to keep moving.

Stacee's body hung a few inches from the cliff. It rotated gently at the bottom of the rope still attached to her harness. The girl's limbs were tangled in awkward and unnatural ways. A deep gash ran down her face, and three wide holes pierced her abdomen. She was covered in blood. Marcos shuddered and fought the urge to look away.

Hands trembling, he reached out and touched an unmarred part of her cheek. It was cold and lifeless.

"I'm sorry," he whispered. "I'm so sorry." He closed her eyes and mourned what would never be.

A breeze whistled past. Marcos stiffened, his heart leaping into his throat. Quickly, he grabbed the tools from Stacee's belt and tucked them into his own. He took one last look at her then started to climb.

Around him, the wind grew stronger, its whistle climbing to a higher register. A rock clicked to his right. Another to his left answered.

The veins in the cliff began to move, undulating slowly with tiny ripples as they woke, their sharp edges scratching at his fingertips.

Faster!

Four feet to go.

Three feet.

Two.

The wind's wail deepened as it gusted more powerfully, hammering into him. Clicks broke out all around him as the veins twisted and writhed in the rocks. The Burro's seismic alarm blared into the night.

With a powerful heave, Marcos grasped the bottom of the Burro and pulled himself up. His hands closed around a handhold just as a vein of rock where he'd been a moment before sliced through the air with a knife-like blade that shot six inches out of the cliff.

Panting, he leaned against the machine as the world around him returned to chaos.

THIRTY-SEVEN

HELENE STEPPED TOWARD THE EMPTY ROCK WHERE SHE'D
left Sven, her eyes wide and her mind spinning. Her breath came
in short, panicked gasps, and her heart pounded. The wind blew
around her, moaning its accusation.

In the pale light of the moon, she could make out the outline of
her husband in the dust that covered the rock, but otherwise, there
was no sign he had been there at all.

Something clicked behind her, and Helene spun around,
searching the dark landscape. She saw nothing but could sense the
black rocks out there. She could feel them watching her, drawing
closer. She backed away from the desert until she met the solid
wall of the spire. Her chest constricting, she stared into the darkness, searching for the monsters that lurked in the gloom.

The wind gusted around her again, its moan followed by a
distant chattering of rocks.

Anger flared inside Helene, burning away her fear and panic.
She screamed into the darkness, "What did you do with him?"

As if in answer, the wind blew harder. Sand stung her face and eyes. She withstood it, taking a furious step forward. "Where is he?"

A distant shadow shifted to her right. Helene turned toward it, squinting into the darkness. She found a small, pyramid-shaped pile of rock a half dozen yards away.

Her anger burned white hot. She charged toward the pile, screaming in fury. The rocks shuddered under the onslaught of sound as she approached.

Something else moved to her left. Helene spun, her heart sinking as she spotted another pile of stones, even closer than the first. Its individual pieces twisted and writhed, filling the air with clicks, but the pile kept its distance.

When she looked back to the first, it had drawn a few feet closer. It sat, less than six feet from her, clicking and chattering menacingly.

Helene hesitated, suddenly realizing how exposed and vulnerable she was. The night pressed in on her, the air growing thick.

The second pile shifted, followed by the first. She looked from one to the other, backing away from both.

A burst of snapping clicks sounded just behind her. Helene spun around and gasped at a third pile of stones barely three feet from her legs. They were boxing her in.

Her heart pounded as she looked one direction then the other. The piles advanced, drawing closer and closer. Then they stopped, each less than two feet from her, chattering angrily when she tried to push past them.

The rocks of the first pile were shifting, piling on top of one another, forming a thin column that rose into the darkness, coming level with Helene's shoulders. It looked like a black snake rising from a basket. As she watched in horrified fascination, the tip of the column split, dividing into five tendrils. The shape continued to shift and change, at last forming a human-like hand that reached for the sky.

Helene stared, her eyes wide, her breath caught in her throat. Her mind continued to spin, trying to understand what she was seeing.

The hand remained perfectly still, its rough, uneven surfaces reflecting the moonlight. It looked like an unfinished sculpture of black marble.

With a furious chatter, it lunged for her. Helene screamed and leapt back. One of the other piles struck at her leg, cutting a shallow gash in the skin. The others clicked with laughter.

With another scream, Helene kicked the closest pile. Her shoe connected with it. Stones cracked and shattered as she slammed into them. Black shards littered the ground.

The other piles flinched back. Helene turned and ran, racing into the desert. The rocks remained behind, chittering angrily after her.

She came to a stop in a wide moonlit area some fifty yards away. The wind had calmed, but the silence hung over her, heavy and oppressive.

Helene leaned forward and gasped. Her thoughts spun, trying to make sense of what she had seen and to reason through a plan of what to do next. Thoughts came and went, overlapping each other and filling her head with noise. They resolved on Sven. She had to find him. The need to be with him was more powerful than anything she had ever felt before.

But where could he be?

She looked back toward the spire, realizing that she had run in the same direction she'd gone to follow the shadow. Her brow furrowed at the thought of the encounter, her mind shifting to the moment the man-thing had melted into the cliff, vanishing into the sheer rock. She wondered if it had just blended into the rock, or had it disappeared into some kind of opening? She struggled to remember, but the memory was too hazy to recall with certainty.

Shaking her head, she decided to find out. She turned and walked toward the spire, listening for the telltale clicks of approaching stone.

The wind returned as she passed the first corner, little more than a breeze whistling idly through the air, but quickly gaining strength. As she rounded the second corner, Helene could hear the distant chatter of rocks behind her.

She ran. Her body ached and her lungs burned as she rounded another corner. The wind whipped around her, tugging at her hair and clothes, singing a high melody as it blew past the cliff.

She reached the place where the shadow had vanished. She paused, leaning against the wall, gasping for breath. In the darkness behind her, just over the wind, she could hear the rocks approaching.

Backing a few steps away from the cliff, she looked up. It took only a moment to find what she was looking for. Ten feet above the ground, a hole just big enough for a person to pass through had been bored directly into the spire. Without understanding how or why, she knew her husband was up there.

Helene rushed to the spire. She grabbed a long crack in the side of the cliff, testing her weight against it. The crack held. A moment later, she found a foothold, then another.

The climb was short but difficult. She struggled to find handholds and footholds, settling for cracks with barely enough room for her fingers or the toes of her worn hiking boots. Exhaustion and fear weighed her down, making each reach and pull more difficult than the last. Her muscles trembled with exertion. A stitch formed in her side, filling each breath with sharp pain. When she finally reached the mouth of the hole, she crawled into it and lay on the stony ground, breathing hard and letting the ache fade from her limbs.

At last, she rose to her feet and peered around her. The hole was larger than it had seemed from below, giving her just enough room to stand if she ducked her head. It extended directly into the rock, disappearing into darkness about five feet beyond the opening.

Helene hesitated and glanced back down the cliff. In the pale glow of the moon, she saw three of the piles of rock move to the base of the cliff directly under her and come to a stop. They stayed there, twitching and chattering rhythmically as the wind moaned past them. They were, she realized, sentinels placed there in case she should return.

"They're herding me," she whispered, ice running through her at the words.

She took an involuntary step back, her head brushing the top of the cave. She shuddered for a moment as the nightmare they were caught in seemed to loom around her. At last, she pushed the thoughts away and focused on Sven. He was her mission. He was the only reason she didn't just give up. Placing him firmly in her thoughts, she turned and looked into the black hole behind her.

The wind blew across the cave's opening, creating a sustained note that moaned through the tunnel. Resounding clicks echoed back from the depths of the rock, confirming that there was something down there.

Helene swallowed and drew a deep breath. Turning her back on the world and focusing on her husband, she stepped into the cave and let the darkness swallow her.

THIRTY-EIGHT

THE WALL HEAVED, SLAMMING INTO THE SHATTERED REMAINS of the Burro. Marcos tightened his hold on the handgrip. The lack of cable meant that the machine's trip away from the wall and back was very short. It crashed into the rock with minimal damage. Angry clicks expressed the rocks' displeasure.

Taking advantage of the momentary lull between attacks, Marcos grabbed the screwdriver from his belt and wedged it under the radio compartment panel. The wall attacked again before he had time to twist or leverage the panel open. He scrambled for a handhold as the machine flew away from the cliff and swung back.

Not even pausing for breath, he grasped the screwdriver, which was thankfully still wedged under the panel, and pushed with all his strength, leveraging it open. Slowly, painfully, the panel began to bend. The metal groaned as it gave way. Marcos threw his weight into it. With a resounding snap, the metal cover came free and tumbled into the darkness, clanging loudly as it bounced off the wall on its way down. It was so sudden that Marcos almost lost his balance. He cried out and flailed with his arms, struggling to steady himself. He barely managed to keep his grip on the screwdriver.

He hung for a moment, panting for breath, his heart pounding. At last, he turned back to the radio, heaving himself up for a closer look, wondering every second when the wall would attack again. For several seconds, he peered into the compartment opening, his trained eyes dancing over the circuit boards, wires, and other components with studied precision. He was stunned by the lack of damage inside the compartment itself. Maybe, just maybe, he could still make the radio work.

Swapping the screwdriver for a pair of needle-nose pliers at his belt, he set himself to work scavenging components from surrounding systems and cobbling them together to boost the power of the radio signal. He and Stacee had already done all the work they could back on the ground, but some of the power supplies and other parts had been needed for the climb. *Now,* Marcos thought ruefully, *we won't be needing them ever again.*

The wall remained blessedly and suspiciously still as he worked. Marcos's fingers danced through the wires, disconnecting and reattaching parts as if they were an extension of himself. He tamped down the anticipation of the next assault as he thought ahead, trying to piece together the commands he would have to enter into the console to get the signal out—assuming the console still worked. He wished Pato were with him. Give Marcos a random set of electronics and wires, and he could make it dance. *But,* he thought bitterly, *code is Pato's job.*

Was Pato's job, he reminded himself, wincing as the pain of that statement lanced through his battered heart.

He focused back on his work, untangling and rewiring as quickly as he could. Around him, the black rocks chittered angrily, snapping into the howling wind, building to something he didn't dare think about. He could sense a storm brewing, one that he was sure would be somehow worse than what they'd seen before, but he pushed aside the thought, forcing all his attention to the radio—on something he could fix.

Five excruciating minutes later, the components were reassembled. Marcos quickly converted the Burro's housing into a makeshift antenna to replace the one that had been damaged in the earthquakes. He could only guess at the radio's range with all the modifications, but it was the best he could do. It would have to be enough.

Satisfied, he lowered himself to what remained of the Burro's head. The left side had been smashed in, the outer casing completely cratered by what must have been an incredible impact. The console there was shattered beyond recognition. However, the console on the right side, while cracked, still appeared to be workable. Marcos leveraged himself over to it and tapped at the power button.

Nothing happened. Swearing, he worked at the edges of the console, snapping it from its mount and pulling it away from the machine. He flipped it over and studied the connections on the back. The complex wiring was a tangled mess—almost as bad as if Pato had been the one to install it. Marcos's friend had never been one for hardware.

Instantly regretting the guilt-inducing disparaging thought, Marcos threw himself at the repair. His trembling fingers snaked through the wires, sorting, checking, and reconnecting them as quickly as they could.

Around him, the wind's moaning swelled, becoming loud and angry. It battered at him, as if it were trying to tear him from the cliff. The chatter of the veins of rock matched it in volume and intensity. Marcos worked faster.

At last, he secured the final connection and tapped the console's power button. Nothing.

His eyes wide with disbelief and mounting terror, he tapped the button again, pressing harder, though he knew that wouldn't make any difference. Still nothing. Growling, he flipped the screen back over.

The rocks struck. A black tendril as thick as Marcos's wrist grew from the wall and slammed into his side before he could react. The sharp edges sliced through his shirt and skin, connecting with his ribs and knocking the wind from him. Marcos screamed and scrambled for a better grip to keep from being thrown from the back of the Burro.

The tendril drew back, dripping with blood, preparing for another attack. Ignoring it, Marcos concentrated on the console, his fingers quickly tugging at each of the connecting wires, searching for one that must be disconnected somehow.

The tendril struck again. He saw it move out of the corner of his eye and flinched away at the last second. Its tip shattered as it struck the Burro's metal casing. Reacting quickly, Marcos grabbed the pliers from his belt and slammed them down on the rock arm. The glass-like stone cracked under the blow, and the tendril jerked away from him. Marcos turned back to the wires.

A second later, he found the problem: a single wire in the middle of the tangle was disconnected. He quickly reattached it and flipped the console over again. With a silent prayer, he thumbed the power button. The screen sprang to life.

Another tendril slashed at him from his left. He saw it at the last second and ducked away just before it struck him. Like the last one, it slammed into the machine's housing, shards of broken rock falling around Marcos and scattering to the darkness. He barely noticed, concentrating all his efforts on the console.

Tapping as fast as he could, he entered the commands, setting the frequency, encoding the message with their coordinates, and setting it to repeat every five seconds. His fingers were sluggish and clumsy. He kept having to correct typos. His heart ached for Pato.

He finished the last command and hit *Execute* at the same time another tendril struck him, catching him on his other side and cutting deep into his shoulder. He screamed as the impact slammed into the side of the robot, splattering blood across the console screen.

As the tendril drew back to attack again, Marcos grabbed the wrench from his belt and drove it down onto the black arm. It cracked. Marcos struck it again and again, throwing his anger into every strike. The tendril shattered.

Marcos turned back to the console and watched as it completed the lengthy startup procedure. Lines of status codes flew across the screen. He prayed like he never had before, hoping that perhaps Pato would take his prayer straight to the ears of the Big Man himself. The startup finished, and the call command flashed across the console. A second later, it beeped. Marcos's message flashed on the screen next to the most wonderful word the engineer had ever seen: TRANSMITTED.

Five seconds later, it did it again.

Marcos leaned back and whooped, pumping his fist into the air. *It's working! The radio is working.*

Behind him, three tendrils of black stone snaked out from the cliff and struck his back, slamming him into the Burro. The tendrils twisted, their sharp ends digging into him. He screamed as pain became his entire world.

THIRTY-NINE

Helene moved steadily deeper into the cave, feeling her way along the walls, taking slow, measured steps. A breath of dry, cool air rose from the cavern's depths, swirling around her and causing the hair along her arms and neck to rise. Behind her, the wind moaned across the cave's opening. The sound echoed deep into the darkness before her. Chattering clicks responded.

Helene paused and shuddered. She closed her eyes and focused on her breathing, steadying her erratic, panicked gasps into long, controlled breaths. The absolute darkness of the cave and the looming threat of the unseen rocks pressed in on her, threatening to smother her. She shuddered again.

Leaning against a wall to steady herself, she reached into her pocket and pulled out her phone. She bypassed the video app this time without a second thought, flicking on the flashlight instead. The tiny light filtered through the darkness, causing shadows to dance around her on the stone walls. She swung the phone this way and that, getting her feel for the cramped quarters.

206 JEFFERY A. MOULTON

Something in the wall flashed back at her. Helene leaned toward it for a better look. It was a vein of black rock nearly a half-inch thick embedded in the sandstone. Another moan of the wind caused it to ripple and chatter softly.

Helene flinched back, hitting her head on the roof of the cave. Shaking away the pain, she searched the walls, finding dozens of other veins of black rock leading down the passage. Their angled sides flashed in her light, but otherwise they remained still.

Helene stood for a long moment, her heart and mind racing. Sven was ahead of her—she could feel it. She had to get to him, and the cave appeared to be the only way.

She looked at the rocks again. They still hadn't moved. They seemed to be encouraging her to move forward, to let them swallow her.

As much as she knew Sven was ahead of her, Helene was certain neither of them would be coming back. That was the price of being by his side. It was a price she was willing to pay.

Steeling herself, she moved forward. The cave's ceiling dipped toward the ground after only ten feet. Helene lowered her head and was at last forced to crawl, holding her phone in front of her to light the way. The rough walls pushed in on her, tearing at her clothes and scratching her exposed skin. The veins of rock rippled at the sound of her grunts and panting breaths.

The ceiling dropped further. Helene lowered herself to her belly and moved forward on her elbows. She felt the weight of the mountain and the rough stone pressing down on her from above.

Her mind spun. There was no way Sven could have been carried this way, and he couldn't have moved on his own. Still, the certain knowledge he was ahead of her compelled her to keep moving.

Behind her, the wind moaned across the cave's opening again. The doleful melody echoed deep into the darkness around her.

The veins in the walls chittered softly as it passed. Another, louder flurry of clicks from deep within the cave answered. They called to her, welcoming her, urging her forward.

Helene continued crawling into the darkness. The tunnel widened into a small chamber tall enough to stand. Helene pulled herself out of the tight crawlspace with a gasp of relief. She paused and stretched her cramped muscles before pressing onward.

She found a long crack wide enough to squeeze through on the far side of the chamber. The veins of rock continued through it, like indicators pointing the way. Helene drew a deep breath and swallowed her fear. Holding her phone ahead of her like a talisman warding off the darkness, she eased herself into the crack.

As she pushed through the tight space, her mind conjured images of the walls suddenly collapsing in on her, crushing the life from her one inch at a time. She closed her eyes and tried to banish the thoughts, but they would not fade.

Her foot slipped, catching in a tight crack. Helene grunted, pulling at her leg, trying to free it, but her boot was trapped. She pulled harder, groaning from the effort. The veins of rock around her chittered noisily, filling the space with ominous echoes. Ahead of her, a flurry of impatient clicks beckoned her onward.

Helene gritted her teeth. She reached for her boot, but the passage was too narrow to bend over, and she couldn't reach it. She tried backing out the way she had come, but the effort twisted her ankle even more, shooting pain through her entire leg.

For a moment, she panicked. The walls seemed to press in on her, crushing her. She closed her eyes and trembled as the full realization of what she was doing settled on her. The memory of hanging over the canyon as the line swayed and shook flashed into her mind. Then, she had felt the darkness reaching for her. Now, it seemed to have swallowed her.

She swallowed and shook the thoughts away. *Have to keep moving*, she told herself. *Sven needs me.*

Gulping air, she opened her eyes and pulled on her leg as hard as she could. With a sudden jerk, her foot came free of the boot and settled on the cool ground of the cave. It throbbed in the darkness. Helene gasped in relief.

She hesitated, wondering if she should retrieve her boot. Shaking her head, she decided to leave it behind. There was no easy way for her to reach it, and she didn't think she would need it where she was going.

Another impatient flurry of clicks sounded in front of her.

"Coming," Helene whispered, drawing a deep breath and pushing on through the cavern.

She emerged into another chamber. It was smaller than the first but still big enough to stand. She leaned against the wall and breathed in ragged, shuddering breaths, grateful for the space to expand her chest.

The veins of rock were growing thicker the farther into the cave she went. They coursed through the walls, flashing in her light like tendrils of black slime. They seemed to ooze along the walls of the chamber, bypassing a second entrance to her left but continuing down a third to her right.

Helene stared at the third entrance, imagining it as a throat about to swallow her. Ahead, she could hear the chatter of more black rocks. They sounded expectant.

"Better not keep them waiting," she muttered, pushing away from the wall and moving forward once again.

As she squeezed into the tight space, Helene idly wondered how far she had gone. It felt like a long way, but in the suffocating darkness, distance was impossible to judge. It may have been a handful of yards. It may have been hundreds. It may have been miles. She shook the thought aside and concentrated on putting one foot in front of the other and what she would find once she reached wherever she was going.

In just a handful of feet, the passage began to widen. Two minutes later, she stepped from the tight quarters into a chamber so large that the light of her phone was lost in the darkness without illuminating the other side.

Helene stepped through the opening and drew a deep breath of the cool, stale air. She held up the light, studying the chamber.

The veins of black rock spread out from the chamber entrance, wrapping around the bowl-shaped room and vanishing into the far gloom. Scattered across the floor in front of Helene were a dozen pyramid-shaped piles of black rock. They clicked in greeting.

Helene stared down at them, her heart pounding. The rocks did not move toward her, nor did they shift out of her way. They held their position, watching her.

Swallowing nervously, she looked away from them and back into the chamber, trying to decide what to do next. She lifted her light, trying to see farther into the darkness, but it's glow was tiny against a room so large. Even the ceiling was lost to her. For all she knew, this chamber went all the way to the top of the spire.

Her mind spun, trying to figure out what to do next. She watched the piles of rock, waiting for them to move, strike, or do something. They twitched as the wind moaned through the cave and seemed to fill the chamber, but otherwise they remained still.

Hesitantly, she moved forward, stepping carefully between two of the pyramids. They clicked at her but still did not strike out or make any move toward her. She took another step then another, holding her light ahead of her while straining to see in the darkness. The rocks let her pass.

A shape grew from the shadows ahead of her, indistinct at first but steadily coming into focus. It was a pile of sandstone roughly three feet high and seven feet long, shaped like an altar. A body lay on top of it.

Helene's breath caught in her throat, and ice shot through her veins. The body was Sven.

FORTY

HELENE RUSHED FORWARD, IGNORING THE PILES OF ROCKS that chittered on either side of her as she passed. She reached for Sven's face, running her fingers along his cheeks. They were so cold.

For a moment, her heart froze as fear lanced through her.

"Sven?" she whispered, leaning down until her forehead was millimeters from his. "Sven, you can't do this to me. You can't leave me here like this."

Her husband didn't respond or move.

Behind Helene, the rocks chattered more loudly than before. The sound filled the chamber, echoing through it with all of her sorrow and pain.

"You can't do this!" she shouted at her husband, the familiar anger bubbling up inside her. "You can't."

She collapsed on top of him. Her grief burst out of her in dry, heaving sobs that joined the cacophony of the black rocks.

"Still... here..." The words were barely a whisper, nearly impossible to hear over the chattering of the stones.

Helene looked up and stared at her husband's face, not daring to breathe. "Sven?"

He remained motionless and cold.

Furiously wiping non-existent tears from her eyes, Helene lifted Sven's wrist and searched for a pulse. Instead, she found a black stone the size of a fist attached to her husband's skin. Furrowing her brow, she tugged at it, but the stone refused to give. With a grunt of frustration, she pulled harder and harder.

The rock came away with a wet tearing sound, leaving behind a raw wound that dripped with her husband's blood. Disgusted, Helene slammed the stone onto the altar. It shattered, black shards scattering around the room and dark, viscous fluid splattering across the altar and onto Helene's hand.

Wiping the black fluid on the tattered remains of her shorts, she turned back to Sven. A quick search turned up more rocks attached to his chest and thighs. Helene tore at them, ripping them away and smashing them against the sandstone or throwing them into the surrounding darkness.

The rock piles chittered loudly as she worked. She could feel them shifting around her, but she ignored them. She was already resigned to death. What more could they do?

"Sven?" she called again, barely hearing her own voice in the surrounding noise. "Sven?"

"Here..."

Relief flooded through Helene. She wrapped her arms around him and lowered her head to his chest.

For a long time, she just held him, listening to his shallow, erratic breathing grow steadily fainter with each passing moment. Every inch of her urged her to action, to do *something*. Every part of her knew it was hopeless.

The piles shifted about the chamber, moving in the space

behind her. She could feel the air drifting as they moved, but none seemed to come any closer.

"Please," she whispered, looking into the darkness above them, momentarily forgetting her hatred of the God who had taken her son. "Please," she said again. "I can't... Not him, too. Please. Please."

The only response was the passionless clatter of rock and the distant moan of the wind beyond the cave.

Helene lowered her eyes and studied Sven's face. Her fingers traced the contours, lines, and imperfections she knew so well. She rested her palm against his cheek, feeling the coldness spread as his life faded.

He groaned, the sound deep and filled with pain.

Helene lowered her head and swallowed, her own sorrow overwhelming every other thought or feeling. *Just like Kyle.*

The chatter of the rocks grew in volume, demanding her attention. Slowly, resentfully, Helene turned toward them. The details of the room were impervious to the tiny light of her phone, but she could still make out a column of black stone that rose almost six feet into the air just beyond the head of the altar.

Helene stared at it, uncertain what she was seeing at first. The column was almost two feet wide. Its polished outer layer was so smooth that it reflected the altar and Sven's head back at her in the dim light of her phone, yet Helene could see the hairline fractures that separated the individual stones that made up the column from each other. Moving together, they twisted around the exterior of the black mass, making the column appear to spin. It flashed in her phone's light but remained in its place.

Helene expected anger, terror, or some other emotion to well up in her at the strange sight, urging her to attack or flee, but she felt only vague curiosity. For her exhausted, worn body, the column was somehow detached from her and Sven, a nonentity with little impact on their lives. Helene was too beaten to feel anything but despair.

Still, she stared at the column for a long time, expecting something to happen—a swarm, a wave, or an attack—but nothing did. It just stood there, churning, flashing, and clicking.

"Well?" she demanded of it. Her voice echoed through the shadows, rippling through the smooth surface of the column.

The black rocks chattered more loudly at her, but otherwise, the column didn't respond.

Helene scoffed and looked away.

Almost immediately, the clicking of the rocks surged in volume, growing deafening, demanding her attention like a petulant child.

With an impatient sight, Helene turned back to them.

"What?" she snapped, watching as the sound broke the surface of the stone once again.

For a moment, nothing happened. Then, with another flurry of clicks, the top of the column cocked itself to one side and paused, as if regarding her.

The movement was so human, so normal, that it forced a laugh from Helene. The sound was raw and inappropriate as it echoed in the stillness. The column rippled again but otherwise held still. It continued to regard her as she stared back.

Helene didn't know how long they held that position. It could have been minutes or hours. It could have been seconds. Her arms, still cradling Sven's head, began to ache.

Just when she was about to demand something else, the column straightened. It trembled and shivered, ripples coursing through its smooth surface. As Helene watched, it swelled and shrank rhythmically, beating like a heart.

The clicks and chatter from the column surrounded her,

pounding through the room. Helene covered her ears with her hands and backed away from the thing.

It continued to beat for several long seconds, and then it began to change. Waves and angles appeared in the stone, emerging from the smooth black sides as if they were being shaped out of water. Pieces lengthened and stretched, forming limbs and features. Soon, Helene was staring at a rudimentary face roughed in stone, though the eyes, nose, and mouth remained unfinished. The rocks in the column kept moving and shaping. The face grew steadily more refined with every passing second.

Helene took a step back. She lowered her hands from her ears and reached for Sven again, her fingers slipping down her husband's chest and gripping his cold, lifeless hand. Her heart pounded as she stared at the changes taking place before her.

The face in the column continued to sharpen, the contours becoming richer, the chin less pointed, the cheeks fuller. Details around the eyes and mouth grew more distinct, and the nose became less angular. Marble-like hair formed on top of what had become the head.

Helene gasped, her eyes growing wide with shock. The stone column had become Pato.

FORTY-ONE

MARCOS'S SCREAM ROSE OVER THE ROARING WIND AS THE three tendrils of black stone twisted into his back, cutting deep. Stinging, electric pain shot through him, radiating from each entry wound. The tendrils cut deeper.

Desperate, he grabbed the heavy wrench from his belt and swung it behind him. The tendrils twisted, causing him to flinch. He missed all of them and almost dropped the wrench. Drawing a sharp breath, he tried again, but this time the angle was wrong. The wrench clattered uselessly against one of the arms of black rock. It chattered angrily and dug harder into his back, slamming him into the Burro. His world flashed red, and he screamed. He wasn't sure how he managed to hold onto the wrench.

Pushing himself away from the Burro, he pulled himself to the left side and swung at the base of the nearest tendril where it connected to the wall. He connected, and cracks formed along the glassy black surface. The tendrils flinched, and the others drove harder into his back. Marcos screamed. Letting the pain feed him, he hammered at the tendril's base again. The black arm shattered, shards scattering through the air.

The tendril had bored so far into his back that it now hung there, its dead weight pulling him down. Marcos arched his back and tried to reach it, but it remained inches away from his fingers. He shrieked and shook his back as hard as he could. With a tearing sound and a searing jolt of agony, the tendril ripped free and fell into the darkness below. Marcos felt the sting of air on the open wound and blood trickling down his back, but he was free of that one.

The other two tendrils shuddered in fury. Pain shot through him. He screamed, but as the agony passed, he grinned, knowing exactly how he could hurt them.

Leaning toward the wall, he struck at the base of a second one. It was thinner than the first and shattered with a single blow. Tucking the wrench under an arm, Marcos reached up and yanked the remaining piece from his flesh, ignoring the pain as the stone came free. He dropped it, barely aware of the deep gashes its sharp edges left in his hand.

One more left.

The last one was on the other side of the Burro. Marcos gritted his teeth and pushed through the pain as he worked his way to that side. The tendril flinched away as he neared it.

Good, he thought. *It's scared of me.*

He grabbed the wrench and, gathering all his remaining strength, he swung at the final arm of black rock. The wrench connected with a satisfying crack that rippled through the black stones. With a yell, Marcos hit the tendril again. It shattered on the second blow, and he felt the bulk of it pull him down, attempting to tear him away from the Burro.

Marcos reached back, straining for the arm of stone that was still attached to his back. It danced out of his reach. He swung himself left and right. The tendril began to sway, tugging at him like a giant pendulum. On the third swing, he caught it.

The sharp edges of stone cut into his hand as he pulled at the tendril. It clung to his back, shooting fiery pain to every inch of his body. He screamed and pulled harder. He felt the rock crack under the strain.

With a snap, the bulk of the tendril came loose. Marcos dropped it, watching it fall away. It struck Stacee's body and shattered against the wall several yards down. He smiled in satisfaction, until he felt something twist in his back.

With a gasp, he reached back, feeling for whatever it was. His fingers grew slick with blood as they touched the raw wounds. He strained, at last feeling the place where the last tendril had been attached to him. Rather than a raw wound, he felt a stump of rock, still embedded in his back. Its sharp edges snapped at him as he touched it. He jerked away.

He tried to reach for it again, but it was too far back. He couldn't grip it well enough.

At the corners of his eyes, he saw other tendrils forming to take the place of those he'd destroyed. They bobbed and weaved just out of his reach, searching for an opening to strike. He screamed and waved the wrench at them. They withdrew, chattering angrily.

Still feeling the stone embedded in his back, Marcos turned toward the Burro and scrambled toward the top of the cliff. The stone twisted in his back, shooting lines of pain through his entire body. He did his best to ignore it as he reached for the harpoon embedded in the cliff just above the robot.

He grasped the metal at the same time the wall heaved again, slamming into the robot. The Burro swung out and crashed back to the cliff. The rocks clicked angrily that it didn't do more.

Still clinging to the harpoon, Marcos hesitated, tilting his head and listening for the beep of the radio. *One second. Two seconds. Three. There!* He breathed a sigh of relief. It was still transmitting.

Grinning despite his pain, he pulled himself up the harpoon, reaching for the ledge above. The wall heaved again, slamming the broken machine into Marcos's legs. A jagged piece of metal from one of the robot's leg's cut deep into him, and he screamed as his blood dripped down his shin onto the machine.

The harpoon bent under his fingers as the Burro crashed back into the cliff. Marcos stared at it, his eyes growing wide as he saw the place where the metal was weakening. It was already starting to crack. It was a miracle it had lasted this long.

Panicked, Marcos looked down, staring in horror at the harness around his waist and thighs. It was still attached to the back of the robot. He grabbed for the buckles, tearing at them. The piece of rock in his back twisted harder than before. White-hot pain seared through him. Spots flashed before his eyes.

The wall slammed into the Burro again, knocking it back. The harpoon screeched as it bent again under the assault. Marcos fumbled with the buckles. One came free, then another. *One more to go.*

The Burro crashed back into the wall. The rod bent more, the crack in the metal grew wider, stretching out as the robot's weight pulled on it. Marcos scrambled for the last buckle. His fingers grasped it just as the metal rod snapped, and the Burro dropped away under him.

He lunged for the cliff, grasping onto the stone he could hold. The full weight of the falling machine slammed into his body as the rope still attached to his harness pulled taut. He screamed as it dragged him toward the abyss. Just before he went over the edge and plummeted into the night, his harness snapped as the last buckle finally broke free. The buckle cut a deep gash down his leg as it flew past. The robot, with Stacee's broken body still attached to it, crashed to the canyon floor below.

For a long moment, Marcos clung to the side of the cliff, panting and feeling his energy drip away with his blood. The sadness of losing the Burro, which had been his whole life since he and Pato had first dreamed it up so many years ago, joined the agony of losing Stacee and Pato. Part of him wanted to just let go and join them. He almost did.

The veins of rock in the wall around him clicked at him in laughing approval. The sound brought him back, filling him with anger and the will to go on, to spite the rocks if nothing else.

With a scream, he pulled himself up and over the cliff's edge. He collapsed onto the flat, hard surface of the spire's summit and lay there, panting. He closed his eyes as the pain and terror of the last several minutes flowed into him.

When he opened his eyes, he froze. Scattered across the top of the spire were a handful of foot-high pyramids of black stones. They were already flowing and twisting together, forming a column like the night before. They chattered and shook menacingly as they joined.

For the briefest moment, Marcos was frozen with fear, but then the hatred and agony and fear of the last forty-eight hours seared through him. With a scream, he lunged for the column of stone. His leg that was injured by the harness buckle gave way under his weight, and he crumpled to his knees on the hard ground. Stars danced before his eyes, and his inevitable blackout marched closer. Pushing aside the pain, he lurched forward on his good leg.

He swung the wrench that he had, at some time, stuffed back into his belt. He struck the column dead center. It shattered, sending broken pieces skidding over the edge of the cliff. Marcos struck again and again, yelling incoherently. Shards littered the ground around him. Black viscous fluid splattered across his arms and face.

The rocks tried to strike back. Tendrils grew from the shattered pieces, striking at him. He knocked them away, focusing the force of his attack on the rest of the column.

"This is for Pato," he screamed, "and this is for Stacee!"

He had pushed the bulk of the stones to the edge of the cliff. He didn't let up, hammering into them again and again, pulverizing them. He screamed the names of his friends with each swing and each shattered stone.

"Pato! Stacee! Pato! Stacee!"

Then the column was gone. The last pieces of it shattered or tumbled over the edge of the cliff.

Marcos collapsed, heaving from the effort, the pain, and the overwhelming sorrow. The piece of rock in his back writhed, but he had become numb to it. He curled up, pulling himself into a fetal position on the ground, and wept.

Images of his best friend—who was more like his brother—and the girl he had loved from afar passed through his mind again and again. The Burro was gone, and with it went the chance anyone had received the radio signal. He had failed. He had failed Sven and Stacee. He had failed them all.

He felt his life leaking from him, dripping onto the rock of the spire. He did nothing to stop it. *What's the point?*

As he gave in to the despair, Pato's face loomed up in Marcos's mind, looking at him with that disapproving expression he'd always used to tell Marcos he was being an ass.

"You aren't dead yet," Imaginary Pato said.

Guilt surged through Marcos. Struggling, almost every ounce of strength gone, he pushed himself into a sitting position. Every movement brought more pain. His hands and muscles shook from exhaustion. Blood leaked from a dozen wounds and countless scratches. The rock in his back squirmed.

Marcos looked down at his leg, taking in the depth of the wound, seeing bone through the shredded muscle and tendons. His head swam, and he wondered how much blood he had lost.

He reached for his belt and pulled it from his waist. He looped it around his leg and cinched it tight. He screamed at the new pain and almost collapsed again, but he managed to keep himself upright.

He reached for the piece of rock in his back again, and his fingers brushed over the hard, glassy stone protruding from his skin. He tried to grasp it, but his fingers couldn't reach the edges. At last, he gave up. He had done all he could.

He sat still for a long time, his thoughts wandering aimlessly as the wind howled around him. He wondered what was happening with Sven, Helene, and Vivek. His heart ached at not being able to save them. He thought of his family, the ones he had avoided for so long. He wished he could tell them goodbye. He thought of Pato, Stacee, and the Burro.

Something rattled to his left. Feeling sluggish and lightheaded, he turned toward the sound. Through blurry vision, he saw a dark silhouette standing there, looking down on him with a familiar, skeptical expression. As the image crystalized, he recognized it.

"Pato?" Marcos whispered, shock shuddering through him as the rock in his back twisted a little more.

FORTY-TWO

Vivek woke slowly, reluctantly fading into consciousness. His whole body throbbed with pain. Every movement, even breathing, ached. His left arm lay under him, twisted back at an unnatural angle. His left leg, which had struck a basketball-sized rock when he fell, was snapped just below the knee. He was certain some of his ribs were also broken. It was amazing he was still alive.

He opened his eyes and saw the night sky above the canyon. The stars twinkled down on him, cold and lifeless, like they were mocking him. Breathing in short, rasping gasps, he raised his head. Pain lanced through it, and he lowered it almost as quickly, but not before he saw the horrifying world around him.

Surrounding him, inches from his body, stood half a dozen pyramids of chittering black stones. The rocks in the piles clicked at him as if in greeting.

Vivek looked away. He closed his eyes, trying to pretend that he was only imagining the stones.

A tickling feeling, like that of an insect crawling across his chest, caused him to look down again. His shirt had almost been torn away, exposing most of his chest. Vivek's eyes widened as he watched one of the rocks move across his bare skin. It reached his shoulder and hesitated, quivering in the moonlight. Suddenly, it attached itself to him, sinking into his flesh with a hundred needle-points. Vivek flinched, and then groaned as pain rolled through him.

Gasping, he looked down, becoming aware of other rocks spread over his broken body. They were attached to his arms and legs. One was attached to his inner thigh and another on his neck. He reached for the one on his shoulder, grasping at it, but his strength was all but gone, and he soon collapsed back to the earth.

He stared up at the sky, struggling to think. He wondered how long he had been at the bottom of the canyon. Night had fallen, so hours must have passed since his fall from the ledge. Questions about how long the helicopter's occupants had searched and where they had gone flitted through his mind, only to vanish into the murk.

He shook his head, trying to clear it, but it remained an impenetrable fog. Haritima and Rajesh, his wife and son, floated through the fog like ghostly images of a past that felt too distant to be real. The others of the group floated there, too: Sven, Helene, Stacee, the engineers. Vivek's failure to protect them weighed heavily on his mind, but then they, too, drifted away into the darkness.

The wind blew over the top of the canyon, sending a deep, rhythmic moan down the walls and along the ground. Around him, the piles of rocks clicked and danced, their individual stones shivering in ecstasy as the sound passed through them.

Vivek looked down at the stone attached to his shoulder. The black color seemed to deepen as it drained him of his life. *Where*, he wondered, *did they come from?* A vague memory of Marcos saying something about aliens drifted through his thoughts. It was, Vivek decided, as good an explanation as any.

One of the stones dropped from his side, landing on the dirt next to him with a soft thud. It was so sudden and unexpected that Vivek stared down at it for several seconds, uncomprehending. Another fell from his leg, then another and another.

Vivek looked back at the first one, struggling through the fog to think of a reason for what was happening. He found none.

As he watched, the first rock stirred, squirming and twitching almost as if it were in pain. Cracks spread across its glossy exterior. They oozed dark, viscous fluid that dripped onto the ground. With a snap, the rock broke open, splattering the dark liquid in a two-foot radius. The stone fell still.

Vivek stared, the fog preventing any kind of understanding, but his curiosity still burned bright. The other rocks that had fallen were twitching and cracking open like the first. He felt the black liquid splatter across his leg and neck. Everything fell into silence.

Breathing hard, he stared at the remains of the first stone, sensing something about to happen. Ignoring the pain, he leaned closer. Within the shattered pieces, he saw a flicker of movement. Vivek held his breath and lifted his head a little more for a better look.

A tiny worm-like tendril with a bulbous head twitched and stretched from within the remains of the rock. Slowly, it peeked up at the world and hesitated. At last, it stretched to its full height, almost two inches tall. It paused and shivered, as if cold in the desert night, and then somehow, it stretched higher, reaching almost six inches in a matter of seconds. The head trembled for a moment then split open, the outer layer peeling back as pale petals with black stripes blossomed into the night.

Minutes after the rock had fallen, a newly born flower danced in the wind. Around the flower, the ground that had been splattered with black liquid grew darker and swelled. Then it sprouted, each drop producing blades of grass that grew from whatever the black liquid had struck, even his own arm.

Vivek stared as the newly formed foliage quivered in the breeze. Suddenly, he understood: The rocks were drawing blood and probably other fluids and somehow turning it into plant life. They were terraforming the desert, transforming the harsh wilderness to one filled with life hospitable for new lifeforms.

What lifeforms? he wondered.

Shuddering at the implications, he closed his eyes and lay back, trying to will the thoughts away. In spite of the murk in his mind, these new thoughts remained persistent. As he felt the other rocks that had fallen sprout their own flowers and grass, he opened his eyes and stared up at the stars.

Where, he wondered again, *did the black rocks come from?*

As he lay, other rocks fell from him, thudding to the ground like the first until the only stone that remained was the one he'd seen attach itself to his shoulder. A minute later, it, too, detached and fell to the ground. Soon, Vivek lay in a field of grass and flowers. He drew in the smell of the foliage, sensing beneath it the coppery scent of blood.

A movement drew his attention to his left. With effort, he turned toward it. The pyramids, he noticed, had moved away from him, leaving a gap of three to four feet. He wondered when they had done that when he saw the large, soccer-ball-sized sandstone sitting between two of the black piles.

Before he could remember whether he had seen the rock earlier, he spotted another one just a few feet from his feet. A chill ran down his spine. That rock, he was certain, was new.

Other large sandstones moved at the periphery of his vision, inching toward him. Looking again at the nearest rock, he saw dozens of small black rocks beneath it. They were twisting in concert, moving the rock ominously closer to him an inch at a time.

Vivek's heart beat faster and his breathing increased. Pain from every movement radiated through him. He reached out and tried to pull himself away, but the pain was too great, the blood loss too much, and the stones blocked his path.

The closest sandstone reached him, stopping just a couple of inches from his arm. Vivek watched as the black stones under it twisted together, forming a column underneath it, raising it into the air. More black rocks joined the first, and the rock lifted over his head, coming to rest nearly a foot and a half above him.

Vivek stared at it, struggling to think of what it could mean and what the stones were doing. He tried to move, but his strength had been stolen away. He was little more than a shell. He could just stare up in mute horror, waiting to see what would happen next.

The black column tipped toward him. The rock fell, crashing down onto his arm. Even in his dulled state, he felt the shock of impact and the shattering of his bones. He screamed.

Another rock, near his good leg, tipped from its own column. His leg snapped under the blow. He screamed again.

Another stone then another and another. Vivek felt his bones shatter and break as more rocks were piled on top of him, burying him. The black stones chattered and clicked as they worked.

Vivek's screams filled the night.

FORTY-THREE

HELENE RAISED HER HAND TO HER LIPS IN SHOCK AND STARED at the recreation of Pato's face in the stone pillar before her. It stared back, observing her with impassive black eyes. The face was nearly perfect, recreating the young man down to the last physical detail, omitting only his spark of life and personality.

In spite of her terror, she leaned forward, studying the face more closely. She could still see the tiny, hairline fractures that separated the individual rocks forming the column and the impossible statue before her. Otherwise, the surface was as smooth as tempered glass. She wondered why the rocks would show her such a thing.

Another deep moan of wind from beyond the cave filled the chamber. The column and statue rippled in response. Pato's face undulated like water. The moan passed, but the face kept shifting and rolling. Clicks from the stones filled the air. Helene watched in horrified fascination as a deep gash formed across the young man's forehead and his jaw twisted unnaturally. His left eye swelled shut and marble-like blood ran down his smooth cheek.

Helene stepped back with a gasp. She grabbed Sven's hand, squeezing it tight, seeking comfort from his ice-cold skin. She found none. The twisted, damaged Pato stared back at her, unmoving, unfeeling. Its remaining eye was vacant and cold.

Breathing heavily, Helene stared at the stone creation. Instinctively, she understood that was how the young man looked when he had died, when the rocks had consumed him, but that did not explain why the stones were showing it to her. *What do they want?*

Helene cocked her head to one side, squinting in the darkness as impossibilities tumbled through her mind. Pato's damaged face also cocked to the side, mirroring her action.

Helene blinked.

Pato blinked.

Helene furrowed her brow and swallowed, remembering scenes from science-fiction movies Kyle watched. *Are the rocks trying to communicate?* she wondered.

The column shifted again. Pato's face melted away. The gashes and other wounds faded back into the smooth glassy surface like ice melting into water. In three heartbeats, the face was gone.

The column spun, the stones clicking and chattering as they moved in concert. They expanded and shrank before they split, divided, and blossomed. The column bulged, wavered, and straightened, looking as if it were birthing something from the inside.

An image began to take shape in the stone—another crude face with roughed-out features. Steadily, as the rocks snapped into place, the image grew more refined. Surfaces smoothed and sloped. Sharp angles flattened. Eyes, a mouth, and a nose formed. A moment later, Helene gasped as she recognized the new face.

Vivek.

Curiosity overriding her fear, Helene stepped closer. She leaned forward, studying the guide, examining its unblinking eyes.

The figure held perfectly still under her scrutiny, like a soldier standing for inspection.

Her fingers trembling, Helene reached up and felt its cheek. The surface was cool to the touch, but life thrummed and pulsed beneath.

Without looking away from the statue, Helene picked up her phone from where it lay next to Sven and shone the light onto the face. The glow dispersed through the murky translucent stone, filling it with an orange luminosity that accented the Indian guide's features. Helene studied the intricate network of veins that spiderwebbed through the column, noting how they joined from rock to rock, somehow making the statue a single entity made up of smaller ones.

She lowered the light and stepped back, her mind reeling. Nothing of what she had seen explained how the stones did what they did or what they wanted from her.

Another moan echoed through the cavern. The rocks shifted again. Vivek's face melted away, reforming into one with thinner, more feminine features that were almost too perfect for reality. A moment later, Helene was staring at Stacee.

Helene shuddered, suddenly wondering why these faces were the ones appearing. Pato, she knew, was dead. *Are the other two dead as well?*

A lump formed in Helene's throat. She tightened her grip on Sven's hand.

The column was already shifting again, Stacee's hair molding into neatly cropped strands over a higher forehead. The nose became more pronounced and the cheeks fuller. Helene's stomach lurched, and her breath caught as she realized what she would see next.

"No!" she hissed. Helene wanted to look away but couldn't.

The column ignored her, the rocks rippling and slotting into place. Lips, a nose, and eyes grew from stone, turning the rough sketch of a man into a perfect recreation of the face she loved more than any other.

Helene spun toward her husband's cold, lifeless body, wrapping her arms around him. Above her, Sven's face, etched in stone, watched with cold detachment.

"No," she hissed again. Then she screamed the word, her voice echoing through the chamber. "No!"

The column rippled as the sound passed through it, but it quickly returned to its previous shape.

Helene grabbed her husband's wrist, feeling for his pulse once again. She couldn't find it. She listened to his chest, straining to hear a heartbeat. It never came.

Shaking, she felt Sven's cheek. It was ice cold, almost like stone. For the briefest moment, she thought she felt the flutter of warmth, but it was gone as soon as it came, almost certainly her imagination.

Sven was dead.

"No. No. No." She said the word again and again.

Above her, the stone face stared down, heartless and impassive.

Seconds, minutes, or hours later, another moan traveled the length of the tunnel and filled the chamber. Without looking at it, Helene could hear the column shifting, creating some new horror that would wrench her heart away. She closed her eyes, refusing to look, refusing to acknowledge it.

The chatter of the shifting rocks died away. The last click echoed through the chamber, accenting Helene's pain. She squeezed her eyes shut and gripped her husband's body even more tightly. She wouldn't look—she refused to give the rocks the satisfaction.

A familiar need built within her, growing and throbbing through her entire being. Her resolve weakened. She had to know.

Giving in to the battle she knew she would eventually lose, Helene looked up at the face above her. At first, it seemed like the statue hadn't changed at all. It still looked like Sven staring down at her. But then Helene began to notice differences. The forehead was narrower, the hair was cut differently, the smile crooked slightly to the left, and the cheeks were thinner, but it was the eyes that caused her to gasp. The face was Sven's, the eyes were hers.

Kyle!

Helene shook as her son's dead face stared back at her. Her eyes took in every detail, noting that, while the other recreations had been perfect, Kyle's was less so. Some of the edges were hazy and blurred, others were too tight or too large, as if the angle were somehow wrong. It wasn't Kyle looking back at her—it was his face from the video, complete with the imperfections caused by the screen and the camera angle.

Helene glanced at the phone in her hand then back at the creature before her. She shuddered. She knew it wasn't her son standing there, but her heart ached too much to be reasonable.

"Kyle," she whispered. "I am so sorry. I am so sorry."

The statue rippled, the mouth moving in response, but the only sound was the clicking of the rocks. Helene filled in the words for it. She knew them by heart.

"I love you, Mom," she quoted. "I love you, but the truth is that I love Emily more. After tomorrow, I don't think I want to see you for a while. I... Goodbye."

Helene hung her head in defeat. All the fight, all the energy, and all her will to live drained out of her. She slumped to the ground and leaned against the altar where her husband lay.

She barely noticed the cold tickling sensation as black stones touched her fingers and moved up her arms, barely registered the sharp pricks on her skin as they settled onto her like cold, hard leeches. She just lay back and let them come.

"Kyle," she whispered again, "I am so sorry."

The face of her son stared back at her, unmoving and unfeeling. She lowered her eyes and wept as the darkness consumed her.

FORTY-FOUR

MARCOS STARED AT PATO'S SILHOUETTE STANDING AT THE
edge of the cliff through the haze of exhaustion and blood loss. His
mind spun, trying to make sense of what he was seeing, of how his
friend could be standing there in front of him. In the back of his
mind, Marcos heard a whisper of danger, but the sight of his friend
and the all-consuming guilt that filled Marcos overrode it.

"Pato," he whispered, his breath short and his heart pounding.
"Pato, I am so sorry."

The memory of all the terrible things he had done to his friend
over the years—the dangerous and stupid stunts, the embarrassing
and humiliating pranks—and everything else that culminated in
Pato's death passed through his mind. He swallowed against the
lump in his throat, which was growing so large that it was difficult
to breathe.

"I'm so, so sorry." Marcos lowered his head. "So sorry."

When he looked up, the silhouette had not moved. It just
stared down at him in cold silence. Then, with a distinctive clatter
of clicks, it cocked its head to one side, assuming the all-too-

familiar posture of Pato trying to understand one of Marcos's bad jokes.

"Pato?"

A shudder went through Marcos as he stared at the shadow. His skin crawled and his throat constricted as realization of the truth began to override his guilt. He squinted, trying to pierce the darkness, to see his friend's face. Slowly, details emerged from the gloom—a nose, a chin, and ears, all perfectly shaped but lacking the essence of his best friend.

He realized with a start that the figure wasn't his friend cast in shadow but a perfect recreation of the rocks. Rather than Pato, it was the thing that had taken Pato away.

The figure leaned over, bringing its face inches from Marcos. It cocked its head again, as if studying him. The closeness of such a perfect likeness to the friend he had failed caused the guilt to burn hotter than before. Marcos shuddered and retreated, pushing himself to the edge of the cliff, ignoring the pain that accompanied every movement and the trail of blood he left behind. The thing watched him go.

For a long moment, they regarded each other over the handful of feet that separated them. Neither spoke. Guilt and anger clashed with fear and revulsion inside Marcos. He glanced toward the wrench, lying where it had fallen, a few yards away. What would the Pato-thing do if he reached for it? It didn't give him a chance to find out.

With an angry chatter of clicks, the living statue lunged forward. It cleared the distance between them in less than a second. Before Marcos could react, it slammed a stone fist into his shoulder.

Marcos gasped as the impact knocked him to the hard surface of the spire. His head cracked against the ground. New pain shot through him, and spots flashed before his eyes.

He tried to rise, but the statue hit him again, knocking him back. One of Marcos's arms dangled over the edge of the cliff. He rolled, trying to escape as the Pato-thing kicked him. It connected with his injured leg. Marcos felt bones snap. He screamed as he dropped back to the ground, almost tumbling over the cliff.

The thing kicked again and then again, hammering into Marcos's side. He felt ribs crack. His breathing became wet and sticky. Darkness flickered at the edge of his vision.

Curling into a ball, Marcos held his head as the statue kicked again and again. The razor-sharp stones shredded through his clothes then his skin. His arm shattered. Darkness almost overwhelmed him. The edge of the cliff drew closer.

Marcos howled, the sound bursting from him in a sustained note that pierced the air. It tore into the creature, rippling through it and pushing it back. It retreated a step, then another.

Before the statue could recover, Marcos lunged for the wrench with his good hand and swung it at the creature's leg with every ounce of strength he could muster. It connected with a satisfying crack. The leg splintered and broke. Marcos hammered it again, finally breaking all the way through.

The statue teetered and fell, slamming into the hard ground. Stones cracked on impact, scattering shards and splattering black fluid across the top of the spire.

What remained of the statue quickly formed a tendril and lashed out at Marcos. It struck his face, leaving a deep gash in his cheek. Marcos swung back but without much strength. He missed.

The rocks struck again, connecting with his hand. Marcos screamed as his wrist snapped. The wrench clattered to the ground, tipped over the edge of the cliff, and disappeared.

The monster was regrouping. The scattered stones rejoined, creating something that was part Pato, part something else.

"What are you?" Marcos screamed at it.

The rock creature shuddered at the sound and swung at his face with another tendril of stone. Marcos raised his arm and the tendril slammed into his broken hand, piercing through it into his shoulder. Marcos screamed.

The creature yanked the tendril back and swung again. Marcos flinched away, and it landed a glancing blow to his thigh.

He pulled back his good leg and kicked. A few of the stones shattered beneath the blow. The creature shuddered and jerked back.

As Marcos raised his leg to kick again, another tendril, this one flat like a blade, slammed into it. The rocky blade sliced into his flesh, pulverizing his bones. It connected with the ground under him as everything just above his knee separated from the rest of his body.

He screamed. The world blurred and swam before him. His eyelids fluttered, and he fell back. He barely felt his head strike the hard surface of the spire.

In the haze of agony, Marcos could sense the creature coming nearer, could feel it prepare to strike him again, but there wasn't enough of him left to feel fear or attempt escape. All he wanted was for it to end.

Time seemed to slow. He turned and looked off the edge of the cliff to the moonlit world beyond. It stretched out before him, beckoning to him. His eyes lifted to the shadowy mountains in the distance then to the stars. He wondered if that was where Pato—the real Pato—and Stacee had gone. Would he join them there? Would the others be there too?

His eyes caught on one of the stars. It glowed brighter than the rest, standing out in the sky just above the horizon. As he watched, it grew bigger and brighter. *Is this the light people talk about after near-death experiences?*

He lifted his pierced, broken hand and reached toward the

light, welcoming it. A new sound filled his ears as it approached—a powerful thrumming that echoed above the roaring wind and the furious clicking of the rocks.

Behind him, Marcos felt the stone creature shudder as the thrumming sound struck it. He turned and looked, watching in detached silence as the thing staggered back, its many malformed limbs flailing. Pieces of the monster started to fall away, cracking and bursting as they hit the ground.

Deep beneath the pain, the engineer in Marcos wondered what was happening. The rest of him floated on a sea of shock and indifference.

What was left of the creature retreated, staggering back to the edge of the cliff. It stopped there, shaking. Pieces of it fell away, clattering over the side of the cliff. It staggered, righted itself, staggered again, and tumbled over the edge. The angry clicking of the rocks faded as it fell into the abyss.

Marcos turned back to the approaching light and thrumming sound. It was so close, hovering right over him. He could feel the wind as it rushed down on him, pushing the shards of shattered rock away into the night.

His vision grew hazy, and his mind floated into distant mists, only half aware of what was happening around him. He barely registered the presence of the man who dropped from the sky. *An angel?*

The man was so big and somehow familiar. Marcos barely felt the arms that wrapped around him, barely felt the air swirl as he was lifted up. He closed his eyes and drifted away into unconsciousness.

His last thought was of Pato and Stacee. Marcos pictured them standing close together at the edge of a dancing valley, their hands intertwined. He smiled.

FORTY-FIVE

HELENE DRIFTED IN DARKNESS. THE WORDS KYLE HAD SAID in the video repeated through the void again and again: "The truth is that I love Emily more. I don't think I want to see you for a while."

In the darkness, Helene could sense her son standing in the distance, an inky shadow in the black. "Kyle!"

Helene struggled to reach him, to grasp him, to beg his forgiveness, but the darkness held her back. She strained against it, screaming for her son.

The darkness laughed at her. The laughter sounded like the clatter of rocks.

Kyle's shadow turned its back to her and began to fade away, melting into the void. His footsteps echoed through the dream, loud and intense as they beat out a steady cadence. *Thump. Thump. Thump.*

Around her, the darkness became agitated. The clicking laughter dissolved into a flurry of furious, uncontrolled clatter. The echo of Kyle's steps continued, growing louder and more insistent. They tugged at the edge of Helene's consciousness, pulling her back from the abyss, back into the world of pain, struggle, and death.

Kyle's shadow hesitated on the edge of Helene's perception, looking back at her, watching her. He didn't move, but the thrumming footsteps grew louder, turning into her pulse. Her heart beat against the despair, the anger, and the guilt. She tried to scream for her son, to call him back, but the void swallowed the words as they left her throat.

A new voice—deeper, kinder, and wiser—floated through the black. Quiet at first, the voice grew stronger, repeating three words. "He. Loved. You."

A chill coursed through her, filling her with strength. She struggled against the undulating darkness, forcing her will against it, fighting to reach her son. It fought back, binding her with strong black tendrils that snaked around her body. They pulled at her, their hard, cold edges digging into her and slicing into her skin.

The silhouette turned away.

Helene screamed and threw herself against the darkness, holding nothing back. A tendril snapped, flying away into the void. Then another and another.

She heaved one more time. The last tendrils gave way, and she soared through the void toward her son. The echo of his footsteps —her heartbeat—grew louder and louder. She screamed his name. "Kyle!"

Helene came awake with a start, the world slamming into her, pain coursing through her exhausted body, and a deafening noise overwhelmed her senses. The sound beat at her, its constant, unyielding rhythm becoming her entire world. Next to her, something moved, jerking this way and that as the rhythm pounded into it.

At first, she couldn't remember where she was. The dim

outlines of rocks casting shadows on stone walls from her still-lit phone were too indistinct. Then her eyes fell on the black stones.

The column had returned to the pyramid-shaped piles—a dozen or so were scattered about the chamber floor. They quivered in the pounding, relentless sound that reverberated through the chamber, as if they were shaking apart. Some of the black stones had already fallen to the ground. Their clicks were lost in the roar around them.

The sound...

Helene knew she should recognize it. The word for its source was on the tip of her tongue, but when she tried to find it, her mind was too slow. Her thoughts skittered away from her.

Another sound cut through the noise, carrying over the first. It was a voice, but the words were lost in her muddled mind.

Helene thought of her dream, thought of Sven's voice calling to her through the darkness, giving her the strength to break free.

Sven!

She was leaning against the altar-like pile of stones, and the rough surfaces dug into her back. In her mind, she could still picture Sven's lifeless body stretched out above her.

The new voice spoke again. The words bounced through the chamber, the echo blurring them beyond Helene's ability to understand. The rocks spasmed at the sound. More of the individual stones tumbled from their place to writhe on the ground.

The sound... The voice...

Helene shook her head, trying to clear through the mud. *Why is it so hard to think?*

She pushed down on the ground and tried to stand, but a sharp electric pain shot through her. She screamed and fell back. Her head slammed into the rock altar, and white flashed through her vision.

Shutting her eyes and gripping her fists in front of her, Helene waited for the pain to subside. She panted, her gasps short and ragged, as her heart raced.

She looked down at her body, trying to figure out what had happened. The details were vague in the dim light, but she could still make out five solid lumps under her shorts and T-shirt. Like the stones scattered across the floor, they also squirmed in the relentless sound, twisting back and forth, but they still gripped at her skin. She could feel the stinging, prickling sensation where they made contact, as if they had each pierced her with a hundred needles.

She pulled up her shirt and grabbed one of the stones attached just below her bra. She pulled at it. Agony shot through her as the rock fought to maintain its grip. Helene screamed and pulled harder, tearing it away from her skin. It ripped away, leaving an open wound. Blood trickled down her stomach.

Helene threw the rock away from her. The clatter of its landing was lost in the darkness and pounding rhythm.

The voice spoke again, the words more familiar this time but still just beyond her comprehension.

Helene shook her head and grabbed one of the rocks on her leg. Screaming, she tore it loose and threw it away from her. The cool air stung the raw open wound, and the pain made her gasp, bringing her focus. She grabbed another and another, tearing at them, yelling through the agony.

As the last one vanished into the far shadows of the chamber, Helene leaned back, breathing heavily. She closed her eyes against the pain that coursed through her. For a moment, it was her whole world. As it faded, her head cleared, as if a thick fog had been lifted.

With a start, she recognized the continuing, merciless sound. *A helicopter!*

The voice spoke again. It was distorted by the echoing of the room and whatever was being used to magnify it, but this time, she understood.

"Sven? Pato? Can anyone hear me?"

The voice was familiar. Helene furrowed her brow and concentrated. The image of an acne-prone young man with thick glasses sprang into her mind. *Ryan?*

A chill went through her. It was the rescuers. They had come at last.

Drawing a deep breath, anticipating more pain, Helene tried to stand. The piercing electric shocks did not come. However, her body was stiff, and every movement ached. She fell back and had to try again before finally managing to rise to her feet.

The black rocks around her chattered angrily. Some twitched toward her, fighting their convulsions as they threatened her. She kicked the nearest away, sending it skittering into the altar, where it shattered, splattering dark, viscous fluid across the sandstone. The others held back, still writhing from the incessant beat of the helicopter.

Helene stepped toward the chamber's entrance but hesitated. Her eyes fell on her husband's body one last time. A knot formed in her throat, and she reached out to feel along his cold cheek.

New rocks had replaced the ones she'd torn away from him earlier. With an angry shout, she ripped them free and smashed them against the flat rock.

Breathing heavily, she looked down at her husband again. The urge to flee and the urge to lie next to him and give up warred within her.

"I love you," she whispered then swallowed hard. She gripped his hand, intertwining their fingers, ignoring the stiffness of his joints. She bent over him, kissing his lips and laying her head on his chest. The blood from her wounds stained the tattered remains of his shirt.

In her mind, the urge to run, to flee to the rescuers, pressed on her. She knew Sven would want her to go, and she could feel the black rocks behind her, regrouping and marshaling their strength for a new assault. But she couldn't leave her husband. *Not like this. Not yet.*

She lay there for seconds and forever as the pounding rhythm of the helicopter's blades settled over them like a comforting blanket.

"I'm sorry." She closed her eyes, swallowing the lump again. "I'm sorry for everything. I love you." She hunted for more words, but she had used them all.

Drawing a deep breath, she steeled herself. She squeezed his hand and kissed it before laying it across his chest. She leaned over, holding him one last time, her cheek brushing against his.

"Still... here..." Sven whispered.

FORTY-SIX

Helene jumped, her heart pounding. She pulled back and stared at Sven's face. He didn't move or give any sign that he was still among the living.

Did I just imagine it? She wondered, her mind racing.

She laid a trembling hand on his chest, feeling for a heartbeat. She waited. There was nothing. She held her breath. His heart fluttered softly against her fingers.

Helene gasped and jerked back as if she had been burned. *He's alive!*

At her feet, she could feel the piles of black rock starting to stabilize against the thrumming of the helicopter, the small stones clicking back into place. Their chatter was a constant, pounding cacophony, but she ignored them.

Sven is still alive!

Moving through the shock, Helene tried to decide what she should do next. Leaving him with the rocks was not an option. Somehow, she had to take him with her.

Without thinking through the logistics of how she would get

him through the cavern to the world outside, she reached for her husband, pulling him into a sitting position and shifting him toward her. His body slumped onto her shoulders, and she lowered him to the ground.

"Sven? Pato? Helene? Anyone there?" Ryan's distorted, amplified voice echoed around her, rippling through the rocks.

"Here!" she screamed back. "We're here!"

She grabbed her still-lit phone and shoved it into her breast pocket. The material filtered the light, dimming the room.

The rocks chattered angrily as she dragged Sven toward the chamber entrance by his arms, but they were unable to muster enough strength to attack with the pulsating beat of the helicopter still hammering into them. Helene kicked at any that came too close, scattering them across the sandy ground, shattering a few.

By the time she reached the narrow chamber entrance, her shoulders already ached from pulling her husband's dead weight. Drawing a deep breath and steeling herself, she backed into the narrow tunnel, dragging him behind her. The rough stone walls scraped at her shoulders and tore at her shirt, but she kept moving.

The black rocks in the chamber had regrouped and were lurching forward, staggering as if they were drunk. Finger-like tendrils reached for Sven's legs, leaving long scratches on his skin.

Helene screamed, the sound leaping up from deep inside her, carrying all her anger and pain. The rocks flinched back as the scream tore through them.

Panting, Helene grasped Sven's shoulders and pulled. The chamber and the chatter of the black rocks faded into the darkness as she dragged him deeper into the tunnel. She moved as fast as she could, knowing that the rocks would be coming back for them.

The black veins writhed in the walls. They lanced out with short spikes, jabbing into her, drawing blood. It trickled down her face and along her arms and legs. Her body ached. She kept pulling.

"Sven? Pato? Can anyone hear me?" Ryan called again.

Helene pulled faster, her strength almost gone. A moment later, she stumbled into the next chamber. Sven tumbled after her.

Gasping for breath, she stood and searched for the exit. There were two. *Which way?*

"Sven? Pato?" Ryan's voice came from the tunnel on the left, the one that was mercifully free of the black veins.

Helene grabbed Sven's shoulders and pulled him down it. The walls closed in on them once again, growing tighter than before.

The chatter and click of rocks echoed down the tunnel, alerting Helene that the rocks had recovered and were coming after them. With a scream of defiance, she strained harder, dragging her husband faster. The cave narrowed even more, the ceiling forcing her to her knees. She kept moving.

Through the tunnel, she could hear the rocks draw closer and feel the ground shaking with their approach. She strained against her husband's shoulders, pulling with all her might. Her mind spun with grim possibilities of what would happen if the rocks reached them. She pulled harder.

A gust of warm desert air tickled her back. She glanced behind her and saw the stars beyond the cave opening. Hope flooded into her. She almost laughed.

The rocks attacked, surging down the tunnel in a black wave, faceted sides flashing in the dim glow of the moon filtering into the tunnel. Tendrils slashed at the air, reaching for Sven.

Helene grabbed her husband and yanked him forward, just as one of the tendrils sliced the air where his foot had been. It slammed into the rock wall, breaking into a thousand shards. Three others took its place.

She reached the end of the cave. Her toes slipped over the

edge of the cliff beyond, curling over open space. She glanced down. They were ten feet above the flat rock where Sven had been taken. She could see the helicopter two dozen yards away, the blades still spinning. Two men were beside it: Ryan and Tybet.

"Here," Helene yelled to them. "We're here!"

Miraculously, Tybet heard her and began sprinting toward the cave. Ryan followed.

The rocks reached them again, like a tidal wave bearing down on them. Helene screamed and threw herself over her husband, protecting him. The rocks crashed into her, knocking the wind from her lungs and slicing through her clothes and into her back. Streaks of fire burned through her. Her blood splattered the cave walls.

With a scream of pain and anger that momentarily caused the rocks to flinch back, Helene grabbed Sven and pushed him toward the entrance. The black stones grabbed for him. Helene smacked them away with her fists, driving him forward. His body tipped over the edge but caught on a protruding rock before tumbling over.

The black stones slammed into Helene, digging inter her flesh. She screamed as black spots flickered at the edge of her vision.

Focusing, she pushed at her husband's body. For a breathless moment, he hung suspended on the edge, his blond hair catching the moonlight and being tossed by the breeze. Then he tipped over and fell into the night.

Helene leapt for the edge of the cliff in time to see Tybet catch Sven in his large arms. She closed her eyes and let out the breath she had been holding. Her husband was safe—that was all that mattered.

The rocks chittered as they crashed into her again. The white-hot anger she had lived with since that terrible moment she first heard of Kyle's death surged through her. She welcomed it, stoking the fires until they blazed beyond her control.

With a scream of fury, she spun back to the rocks, hammering them into the walls with her fists and feet. Shards and drops of black, viscous fluid filled the air.

"Go to hell!" she screamed, kicking and punching them again and again. Her shoeless foot and her hands bled from contact with the sharp edges. She continued smashing at them, throwing all her anger and hate into their destruction. Bit by bit, they gave way before her.

With a final furious kick that left a large splatter of black ooze on the wall, Helene pushed herself from the cave and fell into the night.

The wind caught her. For a breathless moment, she was weightless, floating in the moonlight. The howl of the wind, the beat of the helicopter, and the angry clicking of the rocks above faded into silence. In that moment, Helene was free.

She slammed into the ground with a force that drove the air from her lungs. Bones cracked, and red pain shot through her.

She could see Sven laid out on the same rock where he'd lain earlier. Using all her remaining strength, she pulled her broken body toward him.

She could feel the two men rushing to her then lifting her. They peppered her with questions, but in her mind, they were inconsequential, ethereal ghosts. For her, there was only Sven.

The men laid her next to him. Ignoring the pain, she reached for her husband, pulling his limp body close. She kissed his lips, feeling how cold they had become but sensing the warmth of life deep within them.

"Still here," he whispered again. They were the only words Helene needed to hear.

Holding him in her arms, she lay back and cried. Above her,

Tybet and Ryan moved quickly, working to get them away from that godforsaken place. Beyond them, she could hear the furious clicking of black rocks in the cave. She ignored them all as she slipped into blissful unconsciousness.

She woke in the helicopter, lying on a gurney. Turning her head, she found Sven next to her. Beyond him lay an unconscious Marcos, half covered by a blood-soaked blanket, an IV dripping blood into his veins. Matching ones fed life to herself and her husband. From the cockpit, she could hear Tybet preparing for takeoff while Ryan frantically loaded supplies through the open doorway next to her.

Looking down, she saw her phone was still in her breast pocket, the light still filtering through fabric. Shaking, she managed to pull it out. She held it in a trembling hand, studying the cracked, blood-smeared screen.

A ghostly echo of the need that had once driven her drifted through her mind, but it was quickly muted in Sven's words: "He. Loved. You."

Helene held the phone out the open door of the helicopter and let it drop. She did not hear it hit the ground. She did not see the blowing dust bury it in the red dirt. She didn't need to.

Reaching for her husband and taking his hand, she drifted back into peaceful unconsciousness.

FORTY-SEVEN

THE BRIGHT LIGHTS OF THE FLAGSTAFF HOSPITAL HELD BACK the night. Within its walls, doctors, nurses, and orderlies rushed along illuminated hallways, studying charts and pushing carts of medical supplies and equipment. They ignored the two strange men sitting in silence in the waiting room.

Jonathan Tybet, the larger of the two, leaned forward with his elbows on his knees, staring at nothing over his fingers steepled in front of him. Occasionally, his index fingers tapped together, but otherwise, he was perfectly still. Ryan, on the other hand, fidgeted, his legs bouncing nervously and his fingers tapping on his knees in perpetual motion.

The two had barely spoken since arriving at the hospital in the helicopter more than five hours ago. They just sat in silence, each lost in his own thoughts and memories of the horrors they had seen that day and how close they had come to losing Sven, Helene, and Marcos as well as the others.

The doors leading from the room to the emergency room itself swung open, and a doctor paused there, checking a chart. Tybet and Ryan looked up in anticipation, but the doctor moved on, striding purposefully down another corridor toward the depths of the hospital. The two returned to their previous positions.

With a sigh of exasperation, Ryan leapt to his feet and began pacing. He muttered to himself as he walked. Tybet tapped his fingers together but gave no other sign of having noticed.

The young man made three full circuits of the waiting room before returning to his chair. He leaned back, resting an ankle on the opposite knee, only to drop his foot a second later. He stared at the ceiling for several minutes. At last, he grunted in frustration and looked toward Tybet.

"What's taking so long?"

The larger man met Ryan's eyes over his steepled fingers without giving an answer. The young man squirmed under the gaze but asked no further questions. Tybet tapped his fingers together and returned his gaze to where it had been before.

Ryan sat for a moment longer, staring at his hands. The blood from lifting Marcos, Sven, and Helene and bandaging their wounds had been cleaned away, but he looked at his fingers as if it were still there.

With another grunt, he stood and resumed pacing. Half a lap later, he paused, facing the door where the doctor had appeared moments earlier.

"Do you think they'll survive?" His words were tentative and scared.

Tybet looked up again, his thoughts and emotions inscrutable.

"I don't know," he said at last, his voice a deep rumble.

The two of them had almost given up their search when they picked up the Burro's transmission. They had arrived at the top of the spire just in time to save what was left of Marcos. Helene and Sven's miraculous appearance at the mouth of the cave a few minutes later had given them hope, but a moment later, they had discovered Stacee's mangled body under the wreckage of what once had been the Burro. They couldn't spare any more minutes searching for Pato and Vivek. A brief conversation during the frantic flight had revealed that both assumed they were dead. The three survivors were barely alive when the helicopter touched down. Neither wanted to think about what would have happened if they'd arrived a minute later.

"I'm going to find a vending machine," Ryan declared suddenly, looking relieved to have thought of something to occupy his time. "You want anything?"

Tybet shook his head, and the young man disappeared down a corridor with a sign indicating the way to the cafeteria.

The older man stared after Ryan. He breathed once, twice, then unfolded his large body with surprising quickness.

He extracted a phone from his pocket and called the first contact on his list. It rang only once.

"Hello?" The voice was alert and anxious in spite of the hour.

"I'm alone," Tybet rumbled, glancing again after Ryan.

"Well?"

"It's another encounter."

"Are you certain?"

The large man shifted and pulled something else from a pocket. He held it up, watching the lights reflect off the black stone's faceted surface.

"I'm certain," he said. "It's Ceres."

"How bad?"

"Very bad. It's spreading. And there's something else."

"What?"

"It's adapting, getting more aggressive. And it's taking on other traits."

"Other traits?"

"Emulating humans. I think it might be trying to communicate."

"How is that possible?"

"I don't know."

There was a pause before the voice asked, "What about the others?"

Tybet glanced after Ryan again, but the corridor remained empty. "Three survivors. Sven, his wife, the robotics engineer. They're in surgery. I think they'll survive."

"We'll take care of them."

Tybet gave a curt, impassive nod without bothering to respond vocally. It wouldn't matter either way to the man on the other end.

"Does Sven know?" the voice asked.

"Maybe," Tybet replied. "There's a lot of notes on his home and work computers. But I'm not sure how much he's actually found, and I don't think he can prove anything either way."

"What about the woman? The one from before?"

"Elizabeth. She's still off the grid, but I think I finally have a lead."

"Good. We need to tighten this down."

"Agreed."

Tybet glanced toward the hallway again, trying to determine how long Ryan had been gone and how much time remained before he came back. "I have to go."

"Keep me informed."

Tybet hung up the phone and returned it to his pocket.

He sat for a long moment, staring at the rock lying on the flat of his palm. Drawing a breath, he leaned forward and began to sing in his deep, rumbling voice. "Hush little baby. Don't say a word. Papa's gonna buy you a mockingbird."

The rock began to twitch, its sides rippling and clicking in time with the melody.

"If that mockingbird don't sing, Papa's gonna buy you a diamond ring."

The rock skittered across his palm, dancing to the music, the sharp edges prickling his skin.

"If that diamond ring turns brass, Papa's gonna buy you a looking glass."

The song faded into the muffled sounds of the hospital, and the rock went still. Tybet sighed.

"We meet again," he whispered to it, his tone sad and filled with remorse.

Ryan came back through the double doors, carrying a bag of Cheddar and Sour Cream Ruffles and a sixteen-ounce bottle of Dr Pepper. Tybet palmed the rock and slipped it into his pocket before assuming his earlier position as if nothing had happened.

"How much longer, do you think?" Ryan asked as he settled in the chair across from the larger man. He crunched one of the potato chips, scattering crumbs on his shirt.

Tybet turned and looked at the doors leading toward the emergency room. He didn't give Ryan an answer.

Outside, one of the lights of the hospital flickered and failed. The darkness pressed a little closer, like a predator seeking a way in. In Tybet's pocket, the black rock twitched.

FROM THE AUTHOR

Thank you for reading, *Sorrow's Echo*! If you enjoyed this book, please leave an honest review on Amazon, Goodreads, or the book review platform of your choice and spread the word to all your friends.

I would also love to hear from you! You can write to me directly at jeff@jefferymoulton.com, reach me on my website (www.jefferymoulton.com), or find me on my Facebook page (facebook.com/jefferymoulton). You can also find me on Twitter or Instagram using the handle jefferymoulton, where I frequently post news, writing updates, and event details, as well as my thoughts on science fiction, horror, and superheroes.

Also, you can signup for my newsletter. I promise I won't flood your inbox, but I will include awesome bonuses like sneak peeks at upcoming projects, answers to frequently asked questions, and even free short stories. Sign up at newsletter.jefferymoulton.com.

Again, thank you for reading. See you in another book!

Jeffery A. Moulton

ACKNOWLEDGMENTS

I am so grateful to everyone who made this book a reality. First, I am indebted to Brandon Sanderson. He won't remember me, but without whom, this book wouldn't have happened. Also, a big thank you to The Scrawl Club — Tom Hansen, Deanna Browne, Brian McCain, and Dan Yocum — who gave frequent (and often painful) feedback and encouragement throughout. I am also eternally grateful to the most awesome group of beta readers, ever, especially: Brennan Platt, Crissy Healy, Jeff Hall, Jenna Moulton, Kevin Mitchell, Melissa Palacios, Miranda Moulton, and Sharon Malloque. A special callout goes to Crissy, Melissa, and Sharon, who doubled down as proofreaders.

I also couldn't have done it without the support and help I received from the team at Red Adept Editing. From editing (Stephanie Spangler Buswell), to proofreading (Kim Husband), to keeping everything moving and on track (Lynn McNamee), they were a pleasure to work with and provided timely and invaluable advice.

Most of all, thank you to my family, first to my parents for nurturing my passion for writing, even though I'm sure I was obnoxious about it. And finally, most important, thank you to my amazing wife, Jenna, and our five (yes, five!) incredible children. Their love and continuous support and encouragement kept me going, in spite of the late nights and blurry mornings. Also, a special thank you to Dexter, our blind dog, for spending hours at my feet and scaring the crap out of me after late night sessions writing creepy scenes in darkened rooms. I love you all!

ABOUT THE AUTHOR

Jeffery A. Moulton is an über fan of science fiction, horror, and superheroes. He loves reading, watching, speaking, and writing about them.

In addition to writing scary stories about aliens and monsters, he is also considered an expert on how 9/11 changed super-heroes. He once wrote a non-fiction book about the topic and even appeared in *Robert Kirkman's Secret History of Comics*.

By day, Jeff is a software engineering manager and architect for a video streaming company. By night, he writes creepy stories and spends time with his amazing wife, Jenna, their 5 children, and Dexter, their blind dog. He lives in Gilbert, Arizona.

Sorrow's Echo is his first novel.

facebook.com/jefferymoulton

twitter.com/jefferymoulton

instagram.com/jefferymoulton

www.ingramcontent.com/pod-product-compliance
Lightning Source LLC
Chambersburg PA
CBHW021957170626
46808CB00001B/192

* 9 780985 806149 *